AF260482

Not Such A Stranger
Copyright©2014 Dalia Craig
ISBN 978-1-909934-68-9
Cover art and design by Dalia

Published by
Lydian Press 2014
Find us on the World Wide Web at
www.lydianpress.com

Two women, a lovely old house, and an ancient family feud, come together in this lesbian romance set in and around the picturesque seaside town of Whitby, North Yorkshire.

NOT SUCH A STRANGER

Dalia Craig

Lydian Press

DEDICATION

Larkin... Without your support and encouragement this book would never have been possible. You are a true friend. I love you to bits. Muah!

CHAPTER ONE

"Who are you? And, more importantly, what the hell are you doing in my house?"

There was no mistaking the note of outrage in the stranger's voice. Jaime Fyre skidded to an abrupt halt on the lowest tread of the wide staircase and reached for the carved newel post to steady herself. The shock of this unexpected encounter robbed Jaime of the power to comprehend what was going on. She forced herself to take slow measured breaths whilst she attempted to get a grip of the situation.

The woman – at least she looked like a real live woman and not a ghost – had somehow walked into the hall through a locked door and to add to the confusion was now claiming ownership of the house.

Jaime's head whirled alarmingly.

Have I strayed into a nightmare?
Am I going mad?

No. Jaime quickly rejected both questions but doing so didn't begin to solve this new twist to an already surreal day. Every which way she looked at the day's events and the growing list of questions, the answers always centered on the house, although the word house hardly described this mansion. A museum, or a stately home, might be a more accurate description. Ordinary folks, like her, didn't aspire to such wealth and faded elegance. Yet from the outset, she'd experienced a weird sense of déjà vu as though the house knew her and was welcoming her home with a big cozy hug. Her puzzlement and sense of unreality mounted as she moved from room to room, finding familiarity at every turn, while knowing that she'd never set foot inside the place before. In fact, she hadn't even known the house existed until a couple of hours ago and in turn had spent little more than a brief half hour exploring the amazing rooms.

There was a lot to see and Jaime had been so intent on her quest that she'd initially dismissed the faint scrunching sound, like tires on gravel, as a figment of an over active imagination. Not until she heard the unmistakable solid clunk of a car door had she accepted it wasn't her mind playing tricks. Reluctantly abandoning her exploration to check out the unexpected caller she hurried along the upstairs hallway. After a couple of wrong turns she'd found her way back to the top of the main staircase.

A brief glance out the large arched window and her first sight of the visitor stopped Jaime dead. A frisson of excitement trickled down her spine. She knew this woman, intimately.

No, not literally, but she was the perfect embodiment of Granby. Jaime couldn't believe her fictitious hero was a real person, here, in the flesh, and looking so perfect.

Good enough to eat.

Jaime's heart missed several beats as she feasted her eyes on the tall stranger who was clearly in no hurry to announce her presence. Instead the woman leant casually against an expensive looking black SUV while she scrutinized the house giving Jaime ample time to study her. Every detail fitted Granby to a tee, exactly as Jaime had defined her lead character all those years ago. Early forties, short cropped hair, graying slightly, and naturally tanned skin that spoke of a life spent mainly outdoors. Stone washed denims, worn with a red plaid shirt over a white vest, completed the picture and emphasized her rugged good looks.

Strong, sexy, and unmistakably butch.

A tingling awareness radiated through Jaime's body and ignited a flame deep inside her core. She couldn't wait to discover if the woman matched the other qualities she'd bestowed upon her hero. Anticipation propelled her swiftly down the wide staircase to arrive at the bottom step breathless, and excited, just as the stranger burst through the inner doors into the hall. Whatever Jaime had expected, an ugly confrontation was the last thing on her mind.

"I asked you a question." The curt, authoritative, tone a clear indication that this woman was used to giving orders rather than taking them. "And I want a straight-forward answer. What are you doing in my house?" She advanced several paces toward Jaime, as she spoke, reinforcing her air of authority.

Slowly, small fragments of clarity began to emerge from the jumble of unintelligible white noise jamming Jaime's brain.

What the hell is going on?

Jaime swallowed hard, seeking to make sense of this increasingly bizarre situation. A host of conflicting emotions, disbelief, bewilderment, and curiosity raced, like express trains, through her head then disappeared into a distant fog. There was an overwhelming sense of sadness too. The stranger may be the perfect semblance of her hero in looks but there the similarity ended.

Bemused by the wealth of unanswered questions, Jaime attempted to find her own answers and a way to seize control of the situation.

Whoever this woman is, it's clear that she believes I'm an intruder or, at least, that I have no valid reason for being here alone.

Yet she didn't look or behave like a servant, or a caretaker, which might be the logical explanation, she was much too sure of herself and besides, the emphasis placed on 'my house' definitely implied ownership. Jaime pulled herself together, this was not the time for a lily-livered retreat, she needed to fight back, and fight hard. To establish her position, and right of ownership, without a shred of lingering doubt.

"I was about to ask you the same question, and how you got in?" Although her voice was steady, Jaime battled to keep hysteria at bay and the continued unswerving scrutiny of the stranger brought uncharacteristic warmth to her cheeks.

The woman's glare might easily have cut metal. "With my key, unlike you I presume."

She has a key!

That put a different slant on the situation. A key inferred some legality. Yet it didn't prove more than a passing connection. Jaime sucked in a sharp breath and tightened her grip on the wooden post. She must stifle the rising panic before it reached the surface and betrayed her vulnerability.

"Did you indeed! I would be very interested to hear how you obtained a key to my house."

The ensuing silence was palpable, like a thick film of gooey gel.

"Y…Your house?" The woman eventually spat out the words in denial of Jaime's claim. Her face a picture of disbelief combined with contempt.

In any other circumstances Jaime might have found it rather funny but this situation was no laughing matter. She began to wish that she'd taken the lawyer up on his offer to accompany her then she needn't have faced this person on her own.

"Dream on girlie. I'm the rightful owner this house. Or I will be when…" The woman stopped speaking abruptly, snapping her mouth shut like a trap.

Girlie?

Anger bubbled like a cauldron set upon the roaring fire in Jaime's gut. The snarky bitch had taken one glance at her blonde hair and immediately labeled her as an empty headed bimbo. Although, on the plus side, Jaime knew she'd trapped the stranger into making an inadvertent admission. This woman, whoever she was and whatever her motivation, appeared to believe that she owned the property or had a valid claim to ownership but Jaime was certain that couldn't be right.

Admittedly, she'd been in a state of shock at the time the lawyer explained the details. It's not every day one learns that a hitherto unknown relative has died and left you both a mansion and a small fortune. However, a misunderstanding of the magnitude that this woman's claim implied was impossible. Jaime was certain that, there'd been no mention of anyone else. Aside from a few small bequests to servants, and several more substantial donations to various charities, Colonel James Alexander Osbert Montagu-Fyre had left her his entire estate.

Jaime took a much needed breath. If this was a clumsy attempt to rip her off then the woman would find she'd met her match. "There's an easy way to settle this. Why don't you telephone Henry Carr – I presume you know him? He will quickly confirm my bona fides."

"Nice try." The woman's lips twisted in an ugly sneer. "The landline is disconnected, as I'm sure you're already aware."

The bitch had an answer for everything. Jaime clenched her jaw in frustration. "So use your cell phone. Or, better still, go to his office then you can ask him directly." Jaime had no interest in how this stranger solved her problem, providing she went away, preferably right now. There were many more rooms to explore but little enough time left to do so before she had to leave for her appointment back in town.

"There's no signal this far out, and I have no intention of leaving you here alone. No way…" The woman returned to the attack with devastating force. "You can't think I'm that gullible! Neither of us goes anywhere until I say so."

Jaime swallowed, trying to shift the sudden lump blocking her throat. It was bad enough that a complete stranger had invaded her house but now the invasion had turned into threats of kidnapping, or worse. Rising panic dried her mouth so her voice sounded distinctly unsteady when she protested. "You can't keep me here indefinitely, I've got an appointment and if I don't arrive on time then somebody will come here looking for me"

"I have no intention of keeping you here. I'm not into kidnapping. You are free to leave whenever you choose. But—"

"That's big of you!" Jaime said, employing sarcasm to hide her relief. If the woman didn't care what she did as long as she left then, presumably, she hadn't got too much to worry about, at least on that score. The remainder, however, was a real conundrum.

"But," the woman repeated, placing menacing emphasis on the single word. "I also have a duty to make sure you leave empty handed and if that means I'm forced to wait with you until you go, then so be it!"

"You think I'm a common thief?" The implication that she was up to no good was the final straw.

"No… Not exactly." A disdainful sneer accompanied the dismissive gesture. "Although I suppose anything is possible."

"Then what did you mean?"

The stranger's eyes narrowed as she surveyed Jaime from head to toe and back again. "I rather assumed that you must be one of the Colonel's little friends, here to collect what you consider he owed you. He had a penchant for a certain type of woman, particularly petite blondes." The accusation, heavily loaded with disgust, hung in the air between them like an invisible curtain. "Or maybe, you nursed him in the clinic and seized the opportunity to feather your own nest, by duping a sick man, a patient, into rewriting his will."

Ouch! Jaime flinched, feeling completely naked and vulnerable under such keen scrutiny. "How dare you!"

How can she say that, without knowing the slightest thing about me?

"Do I really look like either of those descriptions?"

"How should I know?" The accompanying shrug spoke volumes. "I don't really care what you are... but be warned, I will stop at nothing to protect myself and my interests. If necessary, I'll fight through every court in the land to ensure you don't get your hands on a penny. This house, and all the money that goes with it, is mine. Mine by right."

"I suppose everyone is entitled to dream." Jaime remarked sweetly, having come to the conclusion she wouldn't gain a thing by prolonging this exchange. Her best course of action was to consult the lawyer; maybe he could throw some light on the matter. Taking a firm grip on her nerves, she unstuck her feet then, head held high, swept past the woman into the library to retrieve her purse. When she emerged a couple of minutes later, Jaime ran right into another venomous attack.

"Going are we? Well I hope you have seen all you wanted because you won't get in again.

We'll see about that. Jaime tossed a defiant glare at her adversary. "I don't believe I caught your name…"

"Kim – Kimberly Marshall."

Jaime savored a moment of triumph that the change of tack had caught the bitch off guard. "Well Ms. Marshall. I can't honestly say it's been a pleasure, but I'm looking forward to trouncing you in court. If you've got the nerve to take me on." Jaime didn't wait around to see Kimberly's reaction, nor did she want to. Instead, she turned abruptly on her heels and stalked out of the house slamming the door hard behind her.

Forced to sit in the car for several long minutes, because she was shaking so violently that she couldn't risk driving, Jaime gave her mind over to reviewing the confrontation.

Why didn't I think to question her more carefully?

Jaime shook her head in dismay. Given the unexpected nature of their confrontation, she supposed it was understandable. The element of surprise had driven all rational thought from her head, but she doubted whether Ms. Marshall would have given her any answers anyway. She clearly wasn't a fool or someone likely to be caught out too often.

Jaime also wondered how Kimberley had known to come. Had she seen her arrive? Not very likely, there were no other properties close by and the house was invisible from the road.

Or maybe somebody had given her the information?

That posed the question. Who?

Jaime frowned. There was only one person in Whitby with prior knowledge of her movements and that person was Henry Carr, the lawyer. She always believed lawyers, like other noble professions, followed a code of conduct. Would he really risk compromising himself by betraying her?

Her meeting with Henry Carr earlier in the day had thrown up plenty of questions but the answers to most of them were conspicuous by their absence. When his letter had arrived just over a week ago, Jaime hadn't really grasped the formally couched legalese. It had come as something of a surprise to learn that she was the recipient of legacy. Even more so that she would need to present her credentials in person, but nothing had prepared her for the real shock. Learning she was heiress to a fortune and a stately mansion would take a lot more adjustment.

For the past ten years she'd believed herself to be alone in the world. Ever since a holiday sightseeing trip in a hot air balloon had turned into a moment of unbelievable horror killing all on board including her parents. Now, with this startling development, she wasn't so sure. Maybe she had lots of other relatives, ones that she knew nothing about, and what of Kimberly Marshall? Where did she fit into the picture? What was her relationship, if any, to James Montagu-Fyre?

Jaime frowned. The list of questions grew longer by the minute and the only person who could supply the answers was Henry Carr. Her frown deepened.

Can I really trust him?

Overnight her life had descended into the realms of fantasy. Maybe the whole thing had been a dream, from which she would wake up and find herself safely at home in London. No, Jaime focused her gaze on the house; it was real enough as was her car and the black Range Rover parked alongside it.

She hadn't been dreaming. She'd actually inherited a house and an absolute fortune from a hitherto unknown uncle. Plus, Jaime shivered convulsively, a serious problem in the shape of Kimberly Marshall.

Now, totally confused, she attempted to recapture a sense of normality. Her gaze wandered idly over the façade. Bright midday sunshine warmed the York stone, mellowed with age to creamy beige and highlighted the pretty creeper scrambling over the stonework. The lower windows were large, coming almost down to ground level, whilst those above were smaller and, in between them, above the imposing doorway, was a tall narrow window with a rounded top – the window through which she'd first seen Kimberly Marshall.

What is she doing in there?

Jaime toyed with the idea of going back inside, to establish her right of ownership and order Ms. Marshall to leave – she had a perfect right to make a stand, this was her property, after all. However that would almost certainly result in another unpleasant confrontation, something she was reluctant to face.

Anyway, she wavered, it might be much wiser to consult the lawyer first, get his expert opinion it would certainly be a lot safer than trying to tackle Kimberly Marshall. She might even discover why Ms. Marshall had made those outrageous claims.

CHAPTER TWO

Back in Whitby Jaime parked her car in the hotel parking lot, on the east side of the harbor, near the ruined abbey. She locked the car then leant against a wall and watched the fishing boats bobbing lazily at anchor. She needed to collect her thoughts before tackling Henry Carr. Somebody had given Kimberly Marshall the information that she was at the house and he was the obvious suspect, having both the knowledge and the opportunity.

Jaime hated the thought of him divulging details about her movements to all and sundry. It was scary, especially now, when she might be a target for those criminal elements who prey on the wealthy. Ideally, she would have preferred to engage another lawyer but, until probate came through, that was out of the question.

Although, thanks to Ms. Marshall's intervention, she was now on the alert for any suspicious activity on the part of Henry Carr. Until she was certain of his complete trustworthiness, she would resist any attempt to talk her into making hasty decisions.

He had, after all, already advised her to dispose of Rykesby and invest the funds in safe government bonds. It didn't take much imagination to conjure up a picture of him and Kimberly Marshall in cahoots, even if it was a farfetched idea.

Leaving her place by the harbor wall, she turned uphill rather than down, putting off the meeting with Henry Carr while she made sense of her chaotic thoughts. Jaime strode out briskly toward the grassy plateau making for the ruined Abbey, the eerie setting that had provided inspiration for Bram Stoker's Dracula. Jaime chose an empty seat, one that offered an excellent overview of the tiny harbor, nestled below at the mouth of a river. The harbor itself was overshadowed by the town, a cluster of unmatched buildings that clung precariously to the steep cliffs on either side of the estuary.

Jaime took a deep breath of the fragrant salt laden air and set her brain to work.

First, she must come to terms with the implications of her new position. It would take some while before the full impact sank in but, she'd already conceded, this legacy would change her life irrevocably. Hopefully, it wouldn't affect her work. She made a small moue of regret at the very idea of not being able to carry on. There was, of course, no reason to stop. She loved writing, and got immense satisfaction from developing the plots and characters.

The central character in all her books was Granby, a very special woman. Clever, honest, fearless in the face of danger and, above all, loyal. A private investigator by profession, she solved complex cases of blackmail, fraud, money laundering, and technological crimes with consummate ease. Jaime loved Granby, or to be quite truthful, the image she had created of her ideal woman. It had come as quite a shock to meet her double, and then to find Kimberly Marshall so totally devoid of the qualities that made Granby the special person she was.

Jaime smiled, recalling how she'd become an author by accident. She'd originally started writing fiction as form of relaxation, a pleasant hobby, to relieve the pressures of studying for a degree in computer science and, once finished, had sent the manuscript to a publisher more because she needed to do something special to celebrate its completion, than with any real hope of them actually accepting the story.

It had never occurred to her that she might take up full-time writing using her knowledge of modern technology to provide a basis for the story lines. She'd had to read the acceptance letter several times before the amazing news sunk into her brain.

The publisher liked her work and had offered her a contract.

That very morning she'd started work on the follow-up book and in thirteen years, she hadn't regretted the decision to turn her back on the chosen career path. Having discovered the joys of creativity, she'd taken to writing like a duck to water, finding the inspiration for her plots in the unlikeliest of places.

With a total of eleven books already published and more in the pipeline. Writing had been very good to her by providing a steady and growing income, especially now that there was talk of a television series. Somebody recently said, in her hearing, *"The world is crying out for a female rival to Morse and that Granby fitted the bill."* Jaime wouldn't have gone that far. In her view, Granby lacked the classical background of Colin Dexter's famous creation. Although, she would probably overtake Morse when it came to her understanding of technology and financial crime.

Nevertheless, her income from writing amounted to peanuts, when compared with the fortune she'd just inherited from her Uncle James. Such a vast sum was difficult for her to comprehend, even though most of it was tied up in a trust fund for the children she would never have, it didn't make it any less, or any easier to come to terms with.

Jaime sighed. Her thoughts returning to the thorny problem of Henry Carr and his possible link with Kimberly Marshall. There wasn't a single thing she could do without conclusive evidence and that might be difficult to find, but she could and would be on guard now which was something.

A clock somewhere down below chimed the hour.

Time to move!

With a new resolve, Jaime made her way back to the town still deep in thought, her positive pace only slowing as she neared the building where Henry Carr had his office. Taking a deep calming breath, she pushed the door, entered, and met the uninterested gaze of the receptionist, who now occupied the desk in the foyer which had been empty this morning. After she'd announced herself, Jaime selected a magazine from the central table then settled into one of the comfortable armchairs to wait until the lawyer was free to see her.

She didn't have to wait long, barely a couple of minutes elapsed before Henry Carr emerged wearing a broad smile of welcome.

"Ah! Miss Fyre… After an effusive greeting accompanied by a lengthy hand clasp, he ushered her into his office as if she was minor royalty. "What did you think of the house, a bit too large and gloomy for your liking, I suspect?"

"On the contrary." Jaime flashed him a smile. "I found it absolutely lovely." In carefully phrasing her response, she hoped he might reveal his hand.

"Really?" His eyebrows almost disappeared into his receding hairline. "Well, I suppose there is no accounting for taste." His faux pas hung in the air between them lengthening the hiatus.

"Oh dear!" He finally broke the tense silence. "What on earth must you think of me? I do sincerely hope you are not offended, but I did not expect a young lady, such as yourself, to appreciate the house for what it is." His obsequious apology did little to reassure her.

"No, I don't suppose you did." Jaime said, favoring him with another smile, to demonstrate forgiveness on her part. "I believe you mentioned some other business we needed to discuss?"

He nodded, clearly nonplussed. "Yes… So I did." His tone lacked the enthusiasm of earlier. "There are several urgent matters that need our attention but first, maybe some afternoon tea?" On her nod of agreement he pressed a button on the intercom and requested tea for two.

The minutes dragged in total silence, apart from a faint rustling sound as the lawyer shuffled through the pile of papers littering his desk. It occurred to Jaime that for some reason he was deliberately avoiding eye contact then she dismissed the idea as being too fanciful. He was just doing his job. What else did she expect? It wouldn't help if she allowed paranoia to raise its ugly head and cloud her perception. However, the protracted inactivity frustrated her until she wanted to scream. Then, without realizing that she'd actually put her thoughts into words, she heard a voice asking.

"Who is Kimberly Marshall?"

"Kimberly Marshall?" Henry Carr jerked upright and fixed her with troubled stare. "Are you saying that you met Kimberly?"

Jaime frowned, perplexed by his reaction. "She came to the house." Henry Carr appeared quite astounded and less than pleased at the information. Not, she reasoned, the behavior of somebody who'd betrayed a confidence and yet she couldn't think of anybody else who might have done so.

"I didn't know she was back–" The lawyer paused as the receptionist arrived with the tea. He thanked her then waited until she'd left the room before continuing. "Was she very…"

"Furious?" Jaime finished the sentence when he appeared unable to commit himself to a particular state of mind. "Yes, I believe that aptly describes her reaction. I think, perhaps, you owe me an explanation?"

"Oh dear!" Henry wrung his hands, distress evident on his face. "I can see that you are annoyed and rightly so. Had I believed that there was even a slim chance of you and she meeting then I would not have dreamed of letting you go to the house on your own, or certainly not without first putting you in the picture."

Does Kimberly Marshall pose a serious threat to me?

Certainly, it appeared so, from the limited information forthcoming. Jaime shivered. How much of a threat remained to be seen. It was time for Henry Carr to do the job of looking after her interests, for which she was no doubt paying him a small fortune. "What exactly is the picture?" Jaime directed her gaze to his face. "I think it's time we stopped pussyfooting around and got to the point."

Henry looked distinctly uneasy at being put on the spot.

"Um…I have to admit this is a rather complicated situation."

He removed his spectacles, polished them meticulously, then held them up to the light, before he put them on again and finally met her gaze.

"Kimberly is your distant cousin – very distant – several times removed on her mother's side. There has been a long running dispute between the two sides of the family for over two hundred and sixty years. Sadly, Kimberly's mother maintained the feud to her dying day, fanning the flames of hope in Kimberly's mind, encouraging her to believe the myth, that she would be the one to inherit everything and reunite the family. In fact, with only you and Kimberly left, that is a rather academic point." He paused to extract a folded sheet of paper from the pile in front of him then pushed it across the desk.

Jaime opened it up and found a lengthy family tree, handwritten in beautiful flowing calligraphy. She found her name and Kimberly's then followed both lines back seven full generations to their common ancestor before she turned her attention back to Henry Carr.

"As you can see, the Fyre's originally came to prominence in the late thirteenth century when Edward the First granted a parcel of land, in perpetuity, to Osbert Fyre – one must assume this was in return for a particular service rendered since it doesn't appear from the documents that Osbert Fyre was in any way part of the royal circle. Then in seventeen fifty three, James Fyre, the Colonel's great, great, great, great, great, grandfather, married Agnes Montagu and that is where all the trouble started. The Montagu's were not nobility so their estates were not entailed. They were merchants, with a substantial income derived from the wool trade. However, without a male heir to inherit, they wanted the man whom Agnes married to add Montagu to his name and so continue the line. She chose James who, as you can see, was the second Fyre son, so it was a good match for him, he would inherit the Montagu fortune, whilst his elder brother, Ralph, inherited Rykesby and the Fyre money. Unfortunately, due to a number of bad investments, the Fyre fortunes had dwindled to nothing by the time Ralph inherited and he was forced to sell the family estate in order to recoup his losses. There is one last twist to this tale. The new owner of Rykesby was none other than James Montagu-Fyre."

"Yes I see…" Jaime traced the lines of descent with her finger. "So now there are two quite separate branches, sharing a common ancestry in the parents of Ralph and James?"

The lawyer nodded. "That is correct. James had everything that Ralph coveted, a lovely wife, Rykesby, and a sizable fortune, whilst Ralph had almost nothing and, to make matters worse, Ralph's wife, Phoebe, had died in childbirth leaving him to raise his son alone. Sadly, his envy festered like a sore. In the end, Ralph's hatred destroyed him and he died a broken man, although I understand still vowing revenge to his last breath.

"How sad," Jaime murmured.

"Yes it is," Henry Carr agreed. "Hatred is a very destructive force, especially if one allows it to rule one's life but, even worse, Ralph passed the legacy on to his son, perpetuating the feud, then he in turn to his children and so on down through the generations to Kimberly.

On that point they were in full agreement, Jaime decided grimly. She'd experienced at first hand this very afternoon just how destructive hatred could be.

Ms. Marshall hadn't pulled any punches in making her claim to the property and now… Jaime found it difficult to imagine what she might to do next.

"There is still something I don't understand," Jaime frowned at the paper in her hand. "I can see, here, that Edward, my father, and James were cousins, their fathers were brothers. Why is my name plain Fyre without the Montagu?"

"That provides us with another intriguing twist to the story." Henry Carr paused to take a sip of tea. "In nineteen twenty nine, your grandfather Arthur split with his family. I believe, although I don't know all the details, it had something to do with the stock market crash that precipitated the great depression. Anyway, after the split, he joined the opposite side of the family and, presumably, chose to drop Montagu from his name at the same time."

"I see…" In fact, Jaime didn't see at all. However, given time and detailed search of the family records in the library, she would probably be able to sort the information into logical order. "So where does Kimberly fit into the scheme of things?"

"She doesn't. If you're referring to the Colonel's will." Henry Carr shook his head. "Your claim to the estate is irrefutable. She was never a contender. However, in the wider context she is a very distant relation."

Jaime frowned. Why did she get the impression there was something, probably quite a lot, he wasn't telling her. Then she posed the question that had been bothering her all afternoon. "How come Kimberly has a key to the house?"

Henry Carr reacted visibly and his eyes widened. "You say she has a key? Are you sure?"

Jaime nodded. "Yes. I'm very sure. I clearly recall relocking the door after me, and then I put the key into my purse, which I subsequently left on the desk in the library." She reached for her purse then felt around inside. "Yes. Here it is!" she brandished the ornate key with genuine relief. "So I was right. That means she definitely let herself in with her own key."

Henry Carr looked thoughtful. "Well, I do know she spent a lot of time up there as a teenager but I had no idea James had given her a key. I will call the locksmith;

we must get the locks replaced as a matter of urgency." He stretched out a hand to pick up the phone, but Jaime stopped him.

"Wait! Please, let me deal with this. I want to make sure we treat this situation, and particularly Kimberly, with respect. I need to talk to her first, before we leap off the cliff or do anything rash. It's important to me to, at least, try for a truce." She knew instinctively that this was the right thing to do. It would be far too late once the locks were changed. Kimberly wouldn't be prepared to listen if she discovered they'd gone behind her back.

"Do you think that wise?"

"Yes, I do. This feud has gone on far too long already and it's high time it was resolved, beyond any doubt, so I have no choice but to do or die."

"Please, do not joke about things like that!"

"Why ever not?" Jaime laughed at his serious tone. "It's just an expression. Surely you can't believe Kimberly is capable of actually harming me?" The idea was too farfetched to consider, not in this day and age, people just didn't behave like that over a stupid family dispute. Or did they?

"No…certainly not but, on the other hand, I do not like tempting fate."

The lawyer's remark forced her to consider both the wisdom and consequences of her proposed actions. After giving the matter careful thought, she arrived at the conclusion that she didn't have any choice if she wanted peace of mind. Sometimes, one has to take chances, even if the odds are stacked firmly against success. A shiver of something, maybe fear, crept slowly up her spine. Kimberly could prove to be a very difficult and potentially dangerous adversary and Jaime wasn't confident of a successful outcome but, she knew, it was important for her self-respect to try.

Recalling now, how this afternoon's encounter had turned her into a panic-stricken wreck, unable to start the car, gave her pause for thought. However, forewarned was forearmed, next time they met she would be much better prepared and consequently more able to cope with Ms. Marshall.

"What sort of woman is Kimberly?" Jaime sought any information that might be useful. "I wasn't able to form much of an opinion in so short a time. Where does she live? What does she do for a living?"

Henry Carr gave her a meditative look. "I do not know her that well myself. However, from what I have heard – this is a small town that thrives on gossip – she is well liked by everybody. She studied architecture at the university in York. After graduating, she spent several years with a local firm. Then about ten years ago, after her mother died, she left Whitby to pursue her career overseas – America, I believe. I thought she was still there but, and I can only guess at this, having heard news of the Colonel's death she probably came home with great expectations. Now, I imagine she must be a very angry and confused young woman."

Not that young, Jaime reasoned recalling Kimberley's graying hair, but she supposed forty may seem young to Henry Carr who must be close to seventy. "That's all the more reason to sort this out now. I couldn't settle easily into the Rykesby with the prospect of her turning up on my doorstep hell bent on revenge."

Henry Carr's cough turned into an unseemly splutter. "Surely you are not actually thinking of living there?" He wrung his hands and shook his head, clearly unhappy with the idea.

Until that moment, she hadn't known what she wanted but suddenly she was sure, very sure, this was the right thing to do. She was a Fyre, the last of a long line, so where else would she live but in the family home.

Granted Rykesby was an enormous mansion, compared to the modest townhouse in which she'd grown up and where she still lived. However, it also had compensations; one of the most important was peace and quiet to write. During the past couple of years, she had struggled to concentrate through a whole series of noisy disruptions right outside her window. First, it had been the gas company, then the water, and now, just last week, a fresh bout of noise and dust, with men laying fiber optic cables for HDTV and high speed internet.

"Why ever not?" Jaime winced. Irritation had pushed her voice up an octave so she sounded like a shrew. "Is there a sound reason, something you haven't told me, why I shouldn't?"

"No. Nothing as drastic as that but I… have you thought the whole thing through properly. You're a young woman; you would be living all alone in an isolated house. It might be different if you were married. Do I really need to spell out the dangers?"

She gave a dismissive shrug of her shoulders. "I live alone now, in London, I honestly can't see the difference." Jaime finally lost patience with Henry Carr. "We are in the twenty-first century." His insistence on treating her like a Victorian maiden, in need of protection from herself and the world at large, had become quite wearing.

He gave her a reflective look. "Well perhaps you know best. Things are rather different nowadays for young ladies. You are much more independent. Now what about Kimberly. Shall I arrange a meeting for the three of us here?"

She fixed him with determined stare. "No, I don't think that would solve anything. What I had in mind was a more subtle approach, on neutral ground, say at my hotel, with just Kimberly and myself. However, you can help me. I'd like you to set up the meeting, without mentioning my name, let Kimberly believe she'll be dealing with you."

"Are you sure?" Henry Carr shook his head in dismay. "I do not like this."

He obviously wasn't happy with the situation. Jaime realized that he would have loved to talk her out of going ahead but, in the face of her implacability, he couldn't. So he reached for the telephone, dialed a number and made an appointment for that evening, at eight o'clock.

As she listened to the exchange. Jaime tried to assess Kimberly's mood. It appeared, certainly from the little she did hear, to be a slightly tense and stilted conversation but, Henry Carr kept his nerve steady and achieved the desired result.

Now it's up to me, Jaime grimaced. I ought to be able to use the element of surprise to swing the odds in my favor.

For almost two hours after that, they worked their way steadily through a mountain of documents, until her brain was like a limp rag. Sign this, read that, the papers just kept coming.

Jaime hadn't really appreciated before, how much work was involved, granted it was all new to her but even so, she would need to get to grips with a whole range of subjects if she was to play her part in the running of the estate.

From that point of view, Henry Carr was proving an asset, she decided as she walked back to the hotel a while later. She could learn a lot from him. His knowledge of Rykesby and of the whole locality was very impressive. Although she still had reservations, concerning his ultimate trustworthiness, Jaime knew she couldn't have wished for a better teacher. He'd exhibited great patience in his dealings with her; always ready to explain anything she didn't understand, going over it point by point until she grasped the essentials. In the meantime, however, there was only one thing occupying her mind the meeting with Kimberly Marshall.

After this afternoon's fiasco, she hadn't any great hopes of success but she knew it was important to attempt to make peace with Kimberly or at the very least discover what she was up against and then try to come to some compromise.

Once in her hotel room, Jaime showered and changed in readiness for the encounter, opting for a plain black dress that expressed her present mood. She actually didn't have much choice. Not knowing what to expect or how to dress for this visit, she'd brought just two outfits, the little black dress and the gray pants suit she'd worn all day. She kept her make-up to the bare minimum too. A dab of blusher on her cheekbones, a smear of pink lipstick, plus a quick spray from the perfume bottle were sufficient to complete her toilet. Although she did unpin her hair. Once released from the confines of the neat pleat it cascaded about her shoulders in golden waves. Jaime surveyed her reflection in the mirror and winced, deciding the result was way over the top for the circumstances. No point in providing Kimberly with more ammunition to take her down. She searched her purse for a clip, found one, then caught up two strands of hair one from each side and fixed them in place. Jaime smiled with satisfaction. Now she had the right image and the confidence to face Kimberly Marshall.

It was nearly five minutes after eight when Jaime slipped into the cozy lounge bar through the doorway from the hotel reception. She spotted Kimberly at once, sitting well away from the dozen or so other patrons at a table in the far corner, nursing a bottle of some new designer beer between long tanned fingers.

Just as earlier, Kimberley's sexy persona hit Jaime forcibly in the gut. She felt more alive, her body tingling with anticipation. In other circumstances, she might have succumbed at the sight of such heady sexuality but this wasn't one of those situations. Wearing an emerald green shirt over dark trousers Kimberly really did look good enough to eat. Only somebody with her tanned complexion could possibly get away with wearing such flamboyance and still look butch – and so hot.

No, I'm not attracted to her.

Jaime dismissed the thought with a horrified shudder.

I can't be. I mustn't be.

She reminded herself firmly that Kimberly's close resemblance to Granby was only superficial. Nevertheless, she stayed where she was well hidden from view by a large potted palm, for a couple of minutes, whilst she got her libido in check and decided on her opening gambit.

"Good evening, Ms. Marshall." Jaime approached from behind banking everything on the element of surprise and hoping, that by catching her unawares she would gain the initiative. "I do hope I haven't kept you waiting?"

Kimberly jerked to her feet. "You!" Her gaze moved on, away from Jaime, as if scanning the lounge for the person whom she'd expected to meet. Returning to Jaime, she flicked a contemptuous gaze down the length of her body.

Heat instantly flooded Jaime's face. She felt as if Kimberly was mentally undressing her and her imagination had no trouble deciding what might be going through her mind. She wanted to tell her that she wasn't available but the words wouldn't come and besides, she doubted Kimberly would believe her anyway. Kimberly hadn't packed any punches this afternoon, leaving Jaime in no doubt of her opinion and judging by the way she was behaving now she obviously hadn't changed her mind in the interim.

So what had Jaime expected? Certainly not a miracle, that would have been too much to hope for, but maybe some slight softening in her open hostility. Jaime stood her ground, smothering the urge to run – if she did so then she could say farewell to any hope of reconciliation – and faced up to Kimberley with as much aplomb as she could muster.

Kimberly huffed loudly, having apparently satisfied herself that Jaime wasn't here for her sexual pleasure or to offer the house on a plate, she demanded. "Why are you here and where's Henry Carr?"

It was a moment or two before Jaime gathered her scattered wits enough to reply. "He isn't coming. So you'll just have to make do with me."

"You bitch!" Kimberly made as if to leave but Jaime stepped forward blocking her path. Determined to finish what she had come here to do, she gulped in a generous lungful of air and gave it her best shot.

"I don't believe I introduced myself earlier. I'm Jaime, Jaime Fyre…" She paused, to let this information sink in, before adding. "I understand from Henry Carr that we're related."

CHAPTER THREE

No!

Jaime's claim hit Kimberly with force, like a bolt of lightning. Her brain whirled out of control as she tried to assimilate the shockwave. She knew, for a fact, it couldn't be true. There weren't any relatives left now. Her last link with a family that stretched back untold generations had gone. Uncle James, the man who'd been her rock whilst she was growing up, had died almost six months ago and she hadn't even got to say goodbye because nobody bothered to inform her. She'd only learnt of his passing by chance and still hadn't come to terms with her loss.

If only I hadn't been so far away or so wrapped up in my own stupid affairs I might have known or guessed he was ill.

The room began to spin. Kimberly reached for the table to steady herself, then slipped quickly back into her seat. It wouldn't do her reputation any good to pass out in a bar, like some drunk. She blamed Henry Carr for plotting behind her back. He ought to be struck off for setting her up like this.

She was acutely aware when Jaime slid into the seat opposite and calmly ordered a glass of white wine from the lounge server as if this was a normal social evening. Kimberly couldn't believe her nerve. The cruel bitch was an impostor, a liar and a cheat. The sooner she got rid of her and her spurious claims the better.

Yet on another level, she'd be sorry to see her go. Jaime Fyre had dominated her thoughts ever since they'd met earlier in the day for a completely different reason and now, once again, the sexy beauty was doing unspeakable things to her body. Things that even a cold shower would not remedy. Kimberly wanted to throw up. An icy shiver snaked down her spine at the realization she actually fancied this bitch big time. Lack of sex must have addled her brain or driven her crazy. Seven months nine days and...six hours since she'd kicked Maxine's cheating ass out of the apartment that they'd shared for five years and in all that time, she hadn't glanced at another woman. Too bad the first woman who stirred her sexual pot turned out to be another consummate liar.

To think, when Henry Carr had proposed this meeting, she'd believed the tide had turned in her favor. Some hope of that now because the evil bitch was back, as bold as brass, with new and equally false claims. How had she managed to put one over Henry Carr? Kimberly knew he was a wily old bird. Little Ms. butter-doesn't-melt-in-my-mouth Fyre must be a very accomplished fraudster. Kimberly was amazed, at both her nerve and her ability to deceive.

However, she wasn't so easily fooled, especially by a little tart on the make. Ms. Fyre, or whatever her real identity, had met her nemesis and she'd enjoy the task of taking her down by exposing her for what she was – a fraudster.

She took a swig from her beer and fixed her gaze on the bitch. "You're a fraud. I know you are and I can prove it."

"No." Jaime met the challenge with a firm denial. "You can't know anything of the sort."

Kimberly watched fascinated as Jaime's eye color turned from dark amethyst to smoky charcoal in an instant, as if she'd flicked a light off. "I do, because my mother left me the proof."

"Then I'm afraid she was mistaken."

The bitch had a ready answer for everything but she still hadn't provided any hard evidence to back up her claim. Time to up the pressure and see how this cookie crumbled.

"So, what do you want with me?" Kimberley kept her gaze firmly fixed on Jaime's face. "I'm sure you're a very busy lady. What with counting your ill-gotten gains and, no doubt, researching your next target." Her harsh words got their reward. Jaime flinched visibly, as if she'd been slapped, then she sucked in a ragged breath.

"I don't want anything, except perhaps to hope we might reconcile our differences. I'm sure even you can see the logic of that, since we are the only two remaining members of the family. Although from studying the family tree, I'm willing to concede any blood relationship is tenuous to say the least. Jaime broke eye contact and lowered her gaze. A soft glow crept up her neck and colored her cheeks.

Holy cow!

Kimberly couldn't believe her ears. This sexy bitch had some balls, she'd give her that. Her immediate reaction was to tell Jaime to fuck off. Then she had a rethink and decided to string this out a bit. If her supposition was correct, Ms. Fyre would very quickly run out of answers and drop herself firmly into the mire.

"There is no relationship, tenuous or otherwise, other than in your imagination."

"My imagination?" Jaime's head shot back up.

"Exactly." Kimberly nodded, and allowed her gaze to lock with that gorgeous smoky glare.

"You're a fine one to talk when–" Jaime broke off to thank the waiter for her wine and sign the tab.

Kimberly lost patience when Jaime didn't continue speaking. "When what? I admire your persistence but not your ability to grasp facts or produce the evidence to back up these outrageous claims. You're trying to play me for a fool."

Jaime's eyes widened and she set her wine glass down untasted. "If you've got any intelligence, which I doubt, you'll realize I'm not the dumb blonde you've labeled me."

No, Kimberly was happy to concede that point, she wasn't. Granted Jaime was both blonde and petite, in common with most of the Colonel's women friends, but there the similarity ended. The tailored gray trouser suit and upswept hair of earlier, plus the little black dress she wore now – which if Kimberly wasn't mistaken bore a famous designer label – put Jaime in a different league from the succession of sultry sirens who'd graced Rykesby for as long as she could remember. This young woman had definite class, a measure of intelligence, and lesbian tendencies which Kimberly found incredibly distracting.

She drew in a sharp breath and reminded herself appearances were often very deceptive. Despite the strong signals from her gaydar and the way Jaime sometimes looked at her, as if she wanted to eat her up, there was still an element of doubt. Besides which, she would never allow herself to be seduced by a pretty face or a sexy body ever again, she'd learnt that lesson the hard way. Whatever nefarious scheme Ms. Fyre had devised to get her hands on Rykesby and the money she was about to discover she'd met her match.

"Very well, give me your version." Kimberly let a skeptical smile form on her lips. "However, I may as well warn you, in advance, I am far from convinced by your spurious claims. Come on, I'm listening."

Kimberly watched Jaime open her mouth then just as quickly close it again seemingly lost for words. Disappointment flooded over her. Was the battle won so soon? She sure hoped not, she always relished a good fight and Ms. Fyre promised plenty of sport. Kimberly dragged her gaze away from Jaime and glanced idly around the lounge. There wasn't a single familiar face amongst the couples and small groups settling in for a pleasant evening. How times changed. Before she went away she'd have known most of the out-of-season patrons of this hotel bar.

"What makes you so certain I'm not genuine?"

Jaime's question drew Kimberly back to the matter in hand. "Because my mother kept a detailed family tree and your name doesn't appear anywhere on that list. Nor, I may add, are there any unexplained gaps – everybody is accounted for."

"I've got a copy of the family tree too. Mr. Carr gave it to me this afternoon."

Did he really?

Kimberly frowned as Jaime delved into her purse and extracted a folded sheet of paper.

This should prove very interesting.

Jaime pushed the paper half way across the table but kept firm hold of it with her fingers, meeting Kim's gaze with a steady stare. "Perhaps we should compare notes?"

Refusing to be wrong-footed by this crafty move, Kimberly reached quickly for the document before Jaime could change her mind. "What's the point? I'm certain your copy will support your story but that doesn't prove a thing." As her hand replaced Jaime's their fingers brushed and Kim felt a spark of electricity pass between them.

She drew the paper quickly toward her, a brief smile of satisfaction playing on her lips. "Unfortunately I don't have my files to hand right now. I'm just back from working abroad and haven't had a chance to unpack any of my boxes yet."

And that's where the documents are staying.

She had no intention of sharing any more information than necessary with this bitch.

Kim unfolded the single sheet, glanced at the diagram fully prepared to dismiss it as irrelevant and then she did a double take.

"This is Uncle James' writing."

"Is it?"

Jesus, this bitch is cool.

Kimberly challenged Jaime's blank expression with a long, hard, stare but failed to find a chink in her armor. "Yes, it is and now I know there's something odd going on."

"Something odd?" Jaime's gaze remained steady although her brow creased in a frown. "I'm afraid you've lost me."

Kimberly shrugged, ignoring the question. "It's not important."

Her hands shook as she refolded the sheet of paper and laid it on the table between them. Uncle James' flowing script was unmistakable, yet its authenticity still bothered her because other documents in the family archive clearly contradicted this information.

Was it possible someone had concocted a very clever forgery?

"So, you claim that Uncle Edward was your father. How very interesting."

Jaime blinked, hopelessly confused by Kimberly's barbed sarcasm. She opted to remain silent and ignorant while she mulled over what she'd learnt from Ms. Marshall's reactions. Notwithstanding her already biased viewpoint, Kimberly had wasted little time on the family tree before rejecting the information therein. It was clear, from her expression, that Kimberly believed she had evidence which disproved Jaime's claim. Only she didn't appear willing to share it, and Jaime wasn't prepared to beg any favors. Why should she give Ms. Marshall the satisfaction of slapping her down? Besides which, if her smugness was anything to go by, it was only a matter of time before Kimberly would be falling over herself to spill the beans.

Until Kimberly voiced her surprise, Jaime hadn't thought about the origin of the document but, she supposed, it made sense. Who else but James or Kimberly's mother would bother to keep such records.

Why had recognizing the handwriting given Kimberly such a shock?

Jaime couldn't get her head around the conundrum. Even though Kimberly had proof of her bona fides, in James's own hand, she still wasn't satisfied.

What more did the woman want?

What made her so sure she'd discovered something amiss?

Answerless, her gaze drifted back to Kimberly whose hazel eyes had taken on a rich tortoiseshell hue. Jaime's stomach flipped, her likeness to Granby produced a cascading reaction that shot arrows of fire right to her core. She drew in a sharp breath and clenched her thighs to trap the throbbing heat before forcing herself to speak.

"Yes, Edward was most certainly my father. He was killed, along with my mother, in a hot air balloon crash ten years ago. Did you ever meet him?

Kimberly shook her head. "No, but my mother did. She knew Edward really well back in the mid seventies. He helped her fill in some of the blanks in the family history.

"Before my time I'm afraid." Jaime's dry humor hit stony ground. "Edward, and my mother, weren't married then."

Kimberly huffed. "I'm aware of that. They married in nineteen seventy nine."

"If you know that much I'm surprised you don't also have the details of my birth."

"Oh, you may well have been born when you say…but not to Edward."

Her emphatic statement sparked Jaime's curiosity. "Why not?"

Why is she so sure?

Since Kimberly had refused to accept the family tree as authentic, surely she couldn't argue with an indisputable piece of evidence like a birth certificate.

Want to bet!

Jaime drew her bottom lip between her teeth. It wouldn't take a minute to run upstairs for both that document and her passport but did she want to go down that route. She knew they must heal the wounds of the past if they were to have any chance of a future relationship. Without a truce, there could only be a continuation of the bitterness and hatred. Was it worth all the hassle involved in a vague hope of achieving the impossible? Especially when Kimberly had made her position perfectly clear. She didn't intend to make any concessions.

Perhaps Henry Carr had been right in condemning her idea. A slight nod of her head reinforced the though. Maybe she shouldn't have tried to tackle the problem head on but worked up to it gently. Her motives were genuine rather than deliberately cruel or vindictive. It wasn't fair to continue the misconception indefinitely, Kimberly deserved to hear the truth and now had seemed as good a time as any. However, there must come a point when the desire for fairness outweighed good intentions and forcing the shock truth on somebody became unfair.

This is absolutely useless I'll never get through to her.

Jaime decided to leave as soon as she finished her drink. She picked up the glass, resisting the urge to down the remaining wine in a single gulp, and sipped slowly. Kimberly was obviously too bound up in the chains of hatred, and her perceived rights, to listen to or accept any other point of view.

"I suppose you're going to sell Rykesby?"

What?

Where had that come from?

Jaime frowned and set her wineglass back on the table. The change of topic threw her thought process into disarray.

Henry Carr had also wanted her to sell, a fact that had worried her all afternoon and now Kimberly had posed the same question, and it left Jaime wondering. Maybe her initial thoughts about collusion weren't so far off beam. What if Kimberly and Henry Carr had a nice little deal lined up? They could buy Rykesby through a dummy company without her being any the wiser. It wasn't too difficult to imagine the scenario. After a suitable time they could sell it on to a developer and make a small fortune in the process. She recalled the recent newspaper report of a similar scam and wondered again, as she had at the time, why nobody spotted what was going on sooner.

Jaime took a deep breath, deciding on a vague response to test the water and draw Kimberly out. "Maybe... I know it's rather large and certainly needs extensive work to make it habitable but it has interesting possibilities." Kimberly immediately sat forward, her expression eager, her eyes shining. Encouraged by this reaction Jaime continued. "I'm not saying I will sell, but just supposing I did. What do you, as an architect, imagine might happen to it?"

"How do you know what I do? Have you been spying on me?"

Kimberly's accusative tone and suspicious glance implied what?

Jaime fixed Kimberly with an icy stare. "No. Why should I? What have you got to hide?"

"Nothing."

Unconvinced by this flat denial Jaime quirked her brow. "Really?"

Ms. Marshall was certainly a very touchy individual, although it wasn't yet clear why she so easily jumped to all the wrong conclusions. "For your information I didn't know you existed until this afternoon. Our encounter at Rykesby was as much a surprise to me as presumably it was to you. Even then your name meant nothing. I had no idea of our relationship, not until much later when Henry Carr gave me the information. So in a way we are both in shock here."

"I suppose… Oh, forget it… It doesn't matter!" Kimberly shrugged her shoulders. "You wanted my opinion about the house?"

"That was the general idea." Only by getting Kimberly to speak her mind, a task made easier by her raising the topic, could Jaime begin to satisfy her concerns and gain an insight to her ultimate intentions.

"Well, I did have some ideas. As you mentioned, I'm an architect. My particular area of interest is hotels, health clubs and other leisure based facilities. While I was in the States, I got involved in a project setting up a chain of exclusive club-style hotels. You must know the sort of thing I mean – luxury accommodation with attached conference suites and sports facilities – everything under one roof, so to speak. Golf, tennis, swimming, all with first class instruction, plus a health spa, sauna, and a fully fitted gym."

"Interesting concept." Jaime drew in a sharp breath. "Although I'm surprised that you planned to use Rykesby for such a scheme. Isn't it rather small for that?"

Kimberly leaned toward Jaime. Her enthusiasm for the idea evident in her expression and body language. "On the contrary. For what I have in mind I believe it's just the right size." She paused, fixing Jaime with a penetrating gaze, making certain of her full attention before continuing.

"There are ten double bedrooms – if you count the studio. Each with plenty of room to install en-suite facilities and then there are the old bathrooms, they'd convert into good sized singles. That would accommodate twenty four guests at a time and considerably more if one converted the stable block into an annex. Although I wouldn't necessarily do that right away. I'm looking at something different here. Small scale and very exclusive, a luxury experience with a price to match rather than the mass market – that's already covered by the various multi-national chains. Think here of diplomatic entertaining, corporate team building exercises and top executives in need of R and R. Or even celebrity guests in search of total privacy. The inclusion of a sound studio might also attract musicians seeking a relaxed environment in which to record a new album. Then, finally, there's the ever growing market for private wedding venues."

"*Really…* How fascinating." Jaime forced herself to remain calm to encourage further disclosure. "What about all the sporting facilities.? Where would you put them?"

Kimberly used her finger to outline the same areas of land that Henry Carr had earlier listed as leased to tenant farmers. Before she moved on to mention the various outbuildings, and the uses to which they might be put. Then she relaxed back in her chair her eyes gleaming and her lips parted in eager anticipation.

It was Kimberly's first genuine smile since they'd met and it gave Jaime quite a jolt. The breath caught in Jaime's throat emerging as a strangled gasp of raw emotion. No matter how hard she tried Jaime couldn't pull her gaze away from Kimberly's lips, they held her captive drawing her like a magnet. She wanted to taste those lips, seal them in a kiss, then part them and delve into the cavity beyond. A virtual image of their drugging kiss, tongues entwined, sent heat coursing through her body as she tasted Kimberly on her tongue sexy, sweet, and oh so addictive. Her imagination ran out of control to them naked, fresh from a shower, skin slick with moisture. Kimberly had her pinned to the wall, trapped, her hard body melding to Jaime's soft curves. Fingers exploring, caressing, every inch of aching, sensitive, flesh. Lips sucking, teeth biting, and then she felt Kimberly's hot breath on her clitoris. Jaime shuddered. She'd lived with these desires for years, vicariously through Granby, without ever experiencing them for real. Having Kimberly in front of her increased the sensation tenfold.

"What do you think?"

The sound of Kimberly's voice penetrated Jaime's consciousness and pulled her out of the erotic trance. She blinked and tried to focus her mind.

"Do you see it as a viable proposition?"

"See what?"

Oh!

Jaime shook her head as the details slowly filtered back into her addled brain.

"We were discussing my plans for Rykesby, once everything is settled. I asked if you thought them viable."

Kimberly's comments demonstrated clearly that she'd given the matter serious thought, maybe even done some market research and drawn up plans. In any event it proved the point, Kimberly was obviously very keen to get her hands on Rykesby, a situation Jaime was equally determined wouldn't arise.

Showdown time.

Jaime took a deep breath before she answered. "Frankly no. As I told you earlier, I have no plans to sell the house, in fact, if things go according to plan I'll probably move in and live there myself."

A dark scowl immediately blanketed Kimberly's face. "Why did you ask me to outline my ideas, when it's clear you never intended to take them seriously?"

"You brought the subject up first." Jaime kept her tone bland. "Besides which, I was curious to discover how keen you were to wrest the place from me. Now I know the answer, I can protect my interests properly."

"You bitch! I might have known I couldn't trust you. You're just like all the others, you couldn't resist the opportunity to string me along, then stab me in the back and twist a knife in the wound."

Jaime flinched from Kimberly's venomous attack. She appeared to have hit a raw nerve. It appeared that Kimberly had serious chip-on-the-shoulder issues. Did she hate all women? Men too? Not that the discovery offered any comfort. Jaime sought to present an outwardly impassive face to the world, and Kimberly in particular, determined not to give her the satisfaction of discovering how deeply those insults had penetrated. She took a deep calming breath, before lifting her head to meet the antagonistic gaze of the woman opposite.

Kimberly leant toward Jaime until her face was menacingly close. "You won't get away with this!"

Jaime glared back, unflinching. "We'll soon see."

"I…I'm taking legal advice so don't get too settled, because you'll find yourself out on your ear when I win!"

"I wouldn't be so sure, if I were you."

Jaime stood, preparing to leave. Kimberly followed suit, towering over her

"Bitch!" She pushed Jaime aside and strode away without looking back.

Jaime sighed, the die was cast there could be no going back now. The realization that she'd failed miserably left a sick feeling deep in the pit of her stomach. It would've been rather nice to have had someone, even Kimberly, whom she could call family but it wasn't to be.

The feud was still alive and flourishing, they may be from a new generation but nothing could prevent them perpetuating the legacy of hatred.

Kimberly was so sure of herself and her rights. What she must do now, Jaime decided, was to check her facts and make really sure her back was covered.

Henry Carr reassured her, when she consulted him first thing the following morning. "You have no cause for concern."

"I'm not so sure." Jaime settled into the seat she'd occupied the previous day. "Kimberly means to…I think she intends to challenge the validity of the will."

"Then she will need to move quickly, because probate will be through any day now, and she will have to put up a very good case."

"What do you mean?"

"It is quite simple. To challenge the will she must lodge a claim and prove that either, the Colonel was coerced into drawing up a will in your favor – which as most definitely not the case. Or produce concrete documentary evidence that he fully intended to change the will in her, Kimberly's, favor. Unless she can prove either case, then I am afraid she will be a very disappointed young woman."

Jaime frowned. "If she does. What then?" She pressed him for answers, wanting to know, in advance, what to expect.

"Well… She will have to prove her case in court but, on the basis of my knowledge, I doubt any legal advisor would encourage her to waste both time and money on such a hopeless cause."

"Perhaps we should offer her something. After all, I do have a great deal more than one person could possibly need." Jaime knew as soon as the words left her lips it was a non-starter. Kimberly wanted Rykesby plus sufficient funds to turn it into her dream, and that was out of the question. She wasn't prepared to consider giving up Rykesby, not even if Kimberly offered to buy it. She didn't want to see it turned into a luxury hotel or anything else. It was the family home and that is what it would stay as long as she had any say in the matter.

"No." Henry Carr shook his head. "Kimberly has done very well out of the Colonel over the years. I do not believe I am betraying a confidence when I tell you that he did everything he could to make sure she had a share of his wealth. He not only financed her through university and beyond by buying her a partnership in a well respected practice. He also set up a trust fund, similar to yours, from which she derives a substantial income and, as a final gesture of goodwill, he signed over the deeds of a house worth close on a million pounds at today's prices. Taking everything into consideration Kimberly has had her fair share of the estate."

Jaime agreed. What she'd just learned put a totally new slant on the situation. She gave him a smile. "Thank you for clarifying the situation. There's also something else I wanted to ask. Have you got a key to the desk in the library?"

Mr. Carr frowned, peering at her over the top of his spectacles. "Yes, I expect so. I have a lot of keys, but... Are you staying on here?"

Jaime sensed his intense disapproval then common sense prevailed. She smothered her irritation. His intention probably nothing more than concern in case she clashed with Kimberly again.

"No. I have to go back to London today but I plan to return next week and I'd like to have the key so that I can look through the desk then.

Henry Carr nodded, as if suddenly understanding her motives. He got up from the desk and fetched a substantial box from the safe together with a number of keys attached to a large key ring.

"Please take care of these," he cautioned as he handed the keys and box over. "The main keys, those you will need every day, are on the ring, I can vouch for them. I think you will find that the others are unique and only fit particular doors or pieces of furniture. Many are old, and irreplaceable, and if there are copies hidden somewhere in the house I didn't discover them."

"Thank you, I will and thank you for all you've done. It's been a great help, having your knowledge and expertise to smooth my path." Jaime stood then offered him her hand. "Good bye, I'll be in touch in a few days."

Half an hour later. She stepped out of the car onto the cobbled yard at the rear of Rykesby.

Assailed by a feeling of guilt, for her deception, she consoled herself with the knowledge that she had not deceived Henry Carr deliberately. She'd always fully intended going straight back to London but the hand of fate had struck. Somehow, she had found herself on the wrong road and within a stone's throw of Rykesby by the time she'd discovered her mistake. The temptation to stop off and spend a little time browsing had just been too great to resist. So here she was, alone this time and eager to discover the secrets of the library.

Jaime entered the house by the back door. Having decided that it would be imprudent to risk a repeat performance of yesterday's little fiasco, by parking out front in full view of anybody who might possibly be watching, she'd driven on around to the stable yard at the rear then parked close to the wall well out of sight.

After a short exploration of the outbuildings, she turned her attention back to the house proper. There must be a back door. Yes, she was in luck. Now all she had to do was find the right key to gain entry.

An examination of the bunch of keys taken from her bag proved inconclusive and it took several minutes to find the right one but, eventually, the door swung open revealing a long stone-flagged passage.

Locking the door behind her, Jaime followed the passage until she came to a flight of steps that took her to the central hall. No, it was much more than a mere hall, it was large enough to hold a grand ball. She moved to the middle then turned slowly, her eyes taking in every detail. From the dark oak paneling – richly decorated with beautiful carving, the intricate designs of fruit and acanthus leaves repeated in finer detail on both the staircase and the doors. To the vast open fireplace, complete with wrought iron grate and firedogs, that took up most of one wall then on to a suit of armor, standing in the corner, flanked by an assortment of swords and other militaria.

It felt like an age since she'd last stood in this very spot not, as in reality, less than twenty four hours. Such a lot had happened in the interim, much of it unpleasant, like the disaster with Kimberly, which she would have preferred to forget. If only the image of what she'd like to do to her didn't keep intruding into her subconscious.

Once again, just as yesterday, Jaime felt the house welcomed her presence. Bright morning sunshine filtered in through the windows, bathing everything in soft dappled light or, where it fell upon a sword, a bright shaft, as highly polished metal glinted with jewel like precision. Jaime spent several minutes examining the relics before reaching the conclusion that all these rather gruesome souvenirs from past military campaigns should, by rights, be in a museum. She'd need to consult an expert on these matters since they were probably quite valuable and collectable to the right people but not to her. She didn't want to own anything that had violence as its main objective, there was too much suffering in the world already and preserving things like this only served to glorify it. Not to mention the temptation of such hardware to any hooligan who might break in and, she didn't want to feel responsible for the outcome, if anybody got their hands on such lethal weapons.

Jaime found it incredible that all this was hers and hers alone. Inheriting a fortune and a mansion was, she supposed, most people's dream of heaven but, there was a sense of responsibility involved too. It was clear that this house, and the large estate that went with it, didn't run itself. Granted a large part of the land was leased out to two tenant farmers but that fact did not absolve her completely and there was still the house, with a housekeeper, two other staff and a part-time gardener. Henry Carr had explained the details yesterday; the staff was being paid a retainer and would return to work when she required their services.

Jaime still had not fully come to terms with the difference all this would make to her life but, with the knowledge that James had intended things to work out this way, presumably, on the assumption that she would be capable of managing things, she was equally determined to do her best to fulfill his wishes.

Pushing the negative thoughts firmly away, Jaime wandered into the drawing room now striated with shafts of shimmery yellow light, from the partially open shutters. Although cluttered with heavy Victorian furniture and ugly chairs covered in faded dark red fabric, Jaime saw real potential for this room. She imagined it refurnished and redecorated, using delicate shades of yellow and soft grays with maybe just a hint of rich peacock blue. Developing the idea, she conjured up an image of deep comfortable sofas – large ones – flanked by low tables, with lots of plants and a few good pictures.

Carrying this exciting picture in her head Jaime returned to the hall then made a beeline for the library. After all, that was why she had come. She wanted to discover for herself what secrets, if any, the desk held. She turned the ornate handle and got the door half open then halted abruptly, expelling a harsh gasp of anger mixed with surprise through parted lips.

CHAPTER FOUR

"So you came. I knew you wouldn't be able to stop yourself." In one fluid movement, Kimberly unwound her tall frame from the depths of the large armchair in which she'd been waiting.

Jaime fought for breath, thankful for the support of the door as the scene whirled before her eyes like a fairground carousel. Eventually she managed to subdue the palpitations enough to speak.

"What are you doing here?"

The shock of finding Kimberly ensconced in the library, especially after she'd taken such trouble to hide the car, was beyond belief. She hadn't thought Kimberly would have the gall to try the same stunt two days running. She'd obviously misjudged both Kimberly's steely determination and her motivation. Although, bearing in mind the firm assurances Henry Carr had given her this morning, Jaime found it difficult to imagine how Ms. Marshall expected to achieve her goal.

"To see you, of course." Kimberly smiled. "I rang your hotel but they said you'd checked out so I came here to wait."

For a fair time too, Jaime thought, surveying the debris of what had presumably been breakfast. While her attention strayed, Kimberly moved forward reducing the distance between them to a couple of yards before Jaime gathered her wits to react.

"Why?"

Jaime's anger bubbled to the surface belatedly but, nevertheless, effectively, the challenge stopped Kimberly in her tracks. She stood, almost as if poised for a fight, her brow creased in a deep frown.

What does Kimberly hope to gain by harassing me like this?

If she imagined this little charade would instigate a change of mind about parting with Rykesby then she was going to be sadly disappointed.

"I wanted to apologize. I behaved like a bitch."

So you did!

Jaime barely held onto her temper. "I don't want to hear apologies. We have nothing left to say to each other. I just want you out of my house and my life!"

Kimberly's laughter echoed around the quiet room. "You know that's not feasible." She fixed Jaime with a penetrating gaze and took a couple more steps forward. "You're the one who started this, you claimed our relationship. I'm just playing along. Although I think it's only fair to warn you, I'm very big on family togetherness. So, whether you like it or not, I aim to stick around and get to know the *little cousin* I didn't know I had."

The faintly mocking tone grated on Jaime's nerves. She didn't like it. Particularly the bit about their relationship. Kimberly's emphasis on the words 'little cousin' bordered on sarcasm and yet, she supposed the bitch did have a point. However distant their connection, there was no escaping the fact that they carried some of the same genes in their blood.

Jaime's sense of apprehension grew apace with each passing minute, She hadn't changed her view of the situation. Subsequent events had merely crystallized her thoughts. Unlike yesterday, when she'd wanted to tackle the problem of Kimberly by herself today, having had time review her approach, the idea didn't seem such a great one anymore. Being near Kimberly scared the pants off her. That she didn't trust Ms. Marshall or her motives was only a part of the problem. There was something else. An indefinable but nevertheless potent something that prompted her to strangely disturbing thoughts.

Thoughts, Jaime admitted tacitly, which were both wildly exciting and alarming at the same time.

Determined not to give an inch, Jaime responded with cool firmness. "We're hardly even cousins. I've studied the family tree myself, right back to the split between Ralph and James, our relationship, such as it is, is quite distant."

Kimberly shrugged. "Distant or not. I believe you had the right idea. It's time we buried the hatchet and stopped fighting. I can think of much better ways to spend our time."

Damnation!

Jaime moistened her dry lips with the tip of her tongue.

Why did I start this? If I'd left it to Henry Carr, then she wouldn't be on my back now.

She couldn't decide whether Kimberly was on the level or if this was just another way of breaking her down so that she could get her hands on Rykesby.

"You've certainly changed your tune! Last evening you were all set to fight me, even take me to court and now you're... Do you really expect me to believe that you've had a change of heart?"

Kimberly had the grace to look abashed. "Yes, I have."

"Don't make me laugh!"

"I'm serious. Honestly. When I thought about what you said last night it began to make a lot of sense. Why would I lie?"

Why indeed?

This astonishing volte-face threw Jaime for six. She found great difficulty believing a single word Kimberly said.

Does she really think I'm so naïve?

"Good question. I can think of several answers to that one." Jaime regarded her adversary with grim determination. This sudden switch to sincerity was laughable. Once Kimberly discovered that she didn't stand a chance of overturning the will, it was a foregone conclusion she would try a different approach to obtain her ultimate goal.

Studying Kimberly's face, whilst she struggled to find a response, gave Jaime no clue to her thoughts although it made her much more aware of the other woman in ways she didn't want to be aware of her. Kimberly's likeness to Granby continued to prove very distracting. No, more than distracting, extremely disturbing. A shiver ran down Jaime's spine. She couldn't understand how she'd got every detail so accurate – from Kimberly's hair, eye color, and height, to the clothes she favored, and even her choice of vehicle. Almost as if she'd studied a photo montage then used all the best bits to construct the image of her perfect woman. Alongside Kimberly, most other women would fall into the distinctly second-rate category.

Jaime felt like a fragile moth trapped in the orbit of a naked flame, unable to escape the fatal attraction certain to destroy her. The realization gave her pause for thought. Even supposing they were strangers, rather than locked into this unseemly dispute over property, she would be mad to get involved with Kimberly. The heady combination of sex appeal together with an inflated ego meant she'd be exposing herself to a dangerous trap. Kimberly would chew her up and spit out the pieces. Jaime tried to resist the overwhelming desire to move toward her, telling herself that what she felt wasn't real but just an emotional reaction to the sudden upheaval in her life.

No matter that common sense dictated otherwise, Jaime felt inexorably drawn to Kimberly. She positively hungered for that first touch. She imagined the strength of her arms, their passionate kisses, and hands stroking bare flesh. An unbelievably erotic frisson spread throughout her body until it reached the most sensitive core as she visualized Kimberly sending her spiraling out of control into a mind-blowing orgasm.

"I know I said some awful things but it was all rather a shock, I had no idea you even existed until we met."

Kimberly's conciliatory tone grated on Jaime's nerves. "Then last evening… Well, what I said was inexcusable, and I have apologized."

"So you have." Jaime sucked in a long breath in an effort to pull herself together. "However, I'm more interested in what prompted the apology. Did you by any chance consult your lawyer first?"

"What's that got to do with it?" Kimberly frowned.

"Everything, as far as I'm concerned. Well, Kimberly. Did you?"

Jaime waited for her answer, hardly daring to breathe. If Kimberly had consulted her lawyer and received unequivocal advice that any challenge to the will would fail, then she could draw the obvious conclusion that Kimberly's apology was no more than a ploy, an artful underhand attempt, to get her own way.

"Yes, as a matter of fact I did, but I fail to see what—"

"No you wouldn't." Jaime interrupted Kimberly mid-sentence. The bubble of hope burst with a loud pop in her head shattering her dreams and leaving behind a cold empty void. "I, on the other hand, see very clearly and I don't particularly like what I see or hear."

That was a gross understatement. Kimberly clearly regarded her as a soft touch, somebody she could manipulate to her advantage. Well, she was in for a rude awakening. Jaime stiffened her resolve. She might be a distant relative but soft she certainly wasn't when it came to protecting herself and her interests.

Kimberly sighed. "I'm afraid you've lost me. I haven't the faintest idea where you're coming from but I do think you're being totally unreasonable."

I'm sure you do.

Jaime flashed Kimberly a withering glance. "That's your prerogative. However, since you've now accepted this is my property, legally and indisputably, you must also accept that I have an undeniable right to decide who my visitors are."

A dark frown clouded Kimberly's expression then it morphed into a smile and she gave a soft laugh. "Well, at least you have a sense of humor. For a moment there I thought you were telling me to leave."

"I was." Jaime's tone dripped ice. "And whilst we're on the subject you can leave your key on the desk. I don't want to see you here again." She moved to the right, holding the door open to reinforce her point, whilst trying to maintain a cool impassive exterior. Not for one second was she prepared to concede Kimberly the ego boosting satisfaction of knowing the impact she'd made, nor did she want to. She just wanted the bitch out of her life. With Kimberly out of her life, Jaime reasoned, she would in time, be able put this episode and the feelings that she had stirred up firmly behind her.

Jaime sighed. Her poor mother must be spinning in her grave right now. She would never have understood Jaime entertaining such brazen and erotic ideas. Nor, for that matter, Jaime's overwhelming, and all consuming, attraction to another woman. That part would have invoked the most intense disapproval. Both her parents had subscribed to a strict religious dogma, one that held rigid homophobic views.

Kimberly took her time but eventually she appeared to realize the futility of further resistance. With due ceremony she placed the key precisely in the center of the blotter then moved, albeit slowly, toward the open door. What Jaime hadn't bargained for was that when she reached it they would be within touching distance and way too close for comfort in the circumstances. She held her breath and tried to keep her expression blank as Kimberly stopped in right front of her.

"Such a pity," Kimberly murmured softly. "I had hoped we might have reached an understanding." She reached out and stroked one finger down Jaime's cheekbone then leaned in and touched her lips to Jaime's.

The brief kiss sent pulses of heat and exquisite sensations spiraling to every zone of Jaime's body culminating in a wild frenzy of desire mixed with fear.

Stop! This is madness.

Common sense overcame desire. Jaime raised her hands, palms outward, and pushed away from Kimberly. The surge of adrenaline through Jaime's veins added weight to the action and carried such force that Kimberly crashed against the door frame with a resounding thump then, in slow motion, she slid downward until she was sitting on the floor.

"Ouch!" Kimberly clutched at her left shoulder, grimacing in pain, and then she held her left arm across her chest supporting it with her right hand.

Jaime was immediately aghast. She hated violence and had never before in her life raised a finger against anybody but Kimberly had asked for it, and if she was injured then she had no one but herself to blame. What else did she expect, Jaime fumed, instant capitulation? Well perhaps after this she'd learn to be more careful.

"I thought you were leaving?" Jaime stepped back out of reach. Let Kimberly think what she liked, she wasn't going to give in to a soft heart.

"I'm not sure I can, at least, not without some help." Kimberly winced as she tried to straighten up. "I think you'll have to drive me."

This was a total disaster. Jaime huffed, wondering if she would ever manage to free herself of Kimberly's presence. "Where did you leave your Range Rover?" She hadn't seen any vehicle on her way in, let alone one so distinctive and hard to miss.

Kimberly gave her a startled look then shook her head. "It's at home. I walked across the moor. It only takes ten minutes – less than by road actually – but I can't… I don't think I can make it back, because it feels as if I've broken my collar bone."

Is this another of her tricks?

A searching glance confirmed that Kimberly did actually look quite ill. Stunned by the realization that she might have caused her a serious injury Jaime resolved not to allow her preconceived ideas about Kimberley's motives get in the way of normal common sense courtesy. "I see." Jaime sucked in a long breath and assumed the calm response of a first-aider. "Then I suppose the least I can do is drive you to the local hospital for an X-ray."

Kimberly shook her head. "No thanks." Her voice sounded dull, fatigued, but it might just as easily have been pain. "I hate hospitals. I'd much rather just go home and rest. I'll call my doctor out later, if the pain doesn't improve."

The logic behind Kimberley's reasoning baffled Jaime. If she had indeed broken her collar bone then the sooner she got a diagnosis and proper support the better but, Jaime admitted, Kimberly's decision suited her too because she wouldn't have to waste yet more time driving her to the hospital and back.

"It's your choice. However, it would be a good idea to support your arm in a sling first. Excuse me a moment, I'll just see if I can find something suitable." The obvious place to find what she wanted was in the linen cupboard, but she had no idea where that was.

Pausing uncertainly in the hall, she debated where to try first – upstairs or down? Then she remembered the dining room, perhaps she could use a tablecloth? However, all she found there were a few napkins, which were far too small

With a sigh of impatience, she cast them aside and made for the kitchen, perhaps she'd have better luck there. This business with Kimberly was a hindrance, it was eating away the time and, if she wasn't careful, she would have no chance to look through the desk. She raced along the passage and into the kitchen but that too proved fruitless. Then as she was about to leave empty handed she spotted the very thing, a large white apron, hanging on the back of the door. Grabbing it off the hook, she ran back toward the library and Kimberly.

CHAPTER FIVE

The apron made an ideal sling, after several false starts and some clever folds Jaime tied the ends around Kimberley's neck, and then stepped back with a satisfied nod.

"There, that should be more comfortable." Jaime attempted a matter of fact tone but didn't quite pull it off.

Kimberly moved carefully testing how far she could go. "Yes, it is. Thanks." She managed to stand unaided and leant against the wall her breathing ragged.

"Shall we go then?" Jaime offered her arm for support. It was the last thing she'd have chosen to do but given the circumstances. She took a calming breath and told herself to ignore Kimberly's close proximity.

Despite her resolve, Jaime was acutely conscious of Kimberly's body, close, almost touching, as they settled comfortably into a pattern of movement. She felt the heat burning into her skin. Burning, like a branding iron, even through two layers of clothing.

By forcing herself to concentrate on the difficult task ahead, they made slow but steady progress out to the car. Jaime supported Kimberly as best she could although she had misgivings about the wisdom of their actions. What if all this movement made things worse? Perhaps she should have insisted they contact the local doctor or call for an ambulance rather than struggle like this but without a landline and with no cell phone signal, it meant driving into town or to Kimberly's cottage anyway.

After carefully negotiating the long driveway, she'd stopped the car at the road, unsure which way to turn. "Which way now?" Jaime risked a brief glance at Kimberly.

"Right, then first right, by the big tree." Kimberly winced in pain as Jaime accelerated from a standstill. "My cottage is on the left, about half a mile down the lane."

She followed the directions in silence and, pulled up close to the Range Rover outside a substantial detached house. Henry Carr certainly hadn't exaggerated its probable value. Constructed from the same material as Rykesby, the double fronted property was on a much grander scale than, Aspen Cottage, the name engraved in the stone lintel over the door, suggested.

"I'll help you inside but then I must go." Jaime didn't want Kimberly to get the idea she was available to nursemaid her. It crossed her mind that Kimberly wouldn't be short of admirers. She could probably call upon a bevy of women who'd be only too happy to play Florence Nightingale. Jaime, however, wasn't one of them. Massaging inflated egos wasn't her bag.

"Oh… How lovely!" The large airy room with comfortable sofas and a beautifully restored inglenook fireplace took Jaime by surprise.

"It's great isn't it?" Kimberly said. "I must admit that this room is probably my favorite. Although if you'd seen it before…" She lowered herself into an armchair then waved her hand in dismissal. "I mustn't keep you."

Glad to escape, Jaime took her leave.

Back at Rykesby, she began the task that had drawn her there in the first place. Although her task was important, her attention frequently strayed away from the papers in front of her. Annoyingly, she couldn't get Kimberly out of her mind.

Damn the bitch! Jaime dumped the contents from one of the drawers onto the desk with a thump.

Why can't I forget about her? I…

Oh!

The pile of papers swayed then cascaded in an unstoppable avalanche from the desk top to the floor.

Amid the jumbled mess, Jaime spotted an old black and white photograph, which had slipped out from the cover of a slim notebook. She reached down to pick up the vaguely familiar picture of a young woman wearing nurse's uniform. It was then realization dawned, she was holding a photograph of her mother. What was it doing here? She turned it over but there was no inscription. A frown creased her brow as she laid it on the desk then bent to retrieve the notebook.

Was it a diary? Jaime couldn't help wondering as her hand closed around it. Would it give her the answers she was looking for?

Well, it certainly wasn't a diary. Jaime glanced at the page she'd selected at random then, with wide eyed surprise, she flicked quickly through the rest. It was a collection of poems – love poems to be precise – All penned by the same distinctive hand which she easily recognized as belonging to James Montagu-Fyre.

So he'd been a poet too, as well as an able photographer and an accomplished artist. Not the sort of pursuits one associated with soldiering but, one lived and learnt and Jaime was definitely eager to learn more about the man who had left her almost everything he possessed.

When Jaime began to read the poems, her sense of bewilderment grew. It was pretty obvious, after she had read the first few, that the inspiration behind them was her own mother.

At first she was angry, then puzzled, and finally just sad. James had bared his soul, committing his most precious thoughts to paper, in an outpouring of passion that bore comparison with the great poets of the nineteenth century.

It prompted Jaime to wonder how much her mother had known. Had she been in love with James too, or was this a secret passion, something that no one else knew about? Either way, there was a host of probably unanswerable questions buzzing around in her head for all the people who might have given her the answers were dead. With a sigh of regret for the loss of those close to her, she closed the book and slipped it into her purse to read later, then began to gather up the remaining papers.

Three long hours later, Jaime returned the final drawer to its runners and sat back in the chair. If there was anything more to find then it certainly wasn't in the desk and she didn't know where else to look. Unless there was a safe. She glanced around the library, annoyed for not thinking of it sooner. Yes, a safe was a distinct possibility.

There were several, as yet unidentified, keys on the ring that might fit a safe. However, where to find it was a totally different matter. Jaime spent a long time examining all the likely places, looking behind pictures and moving furniture about, without success then, thoroughly disheartened by the lack of progress, she gave up the search and after a final look around tidied everything up again and set off back to London.

The next few days were frantically busy. A meeting with her agent, Darla Cookham, increased the pressure. Her forthcoming release, Undiscovered Truths, was due out at the end of the month and Darla informed her that the publisher had proposed advancing the release date of, Restitution, the next book in the series by three whole months. Something about optimizing the schedules. Unfortunately that meant an extra workload just at the time when she least needed it.

With all this and the recent events in Whitby, she was finding it increasingly difficult to concentrate on her writing. Especially those scenes relating to Granby which were the mainstay of her work. Kimberly's image kept appearing before her eyes and, every time it did, she would stop what she was doing and dream, which played havoc with her normally structured routine.

Kimberly occupied her thoughts by day and by night. Jaime kept wondering how she was, worrying if her shoulder was still hurting and what the consequences of that unfortunate incident might be. Above all that was a longing to relive the exquisite pleasure of Kimberly's lips on hers.

It wasn't just a simple kiss though. The element of both shock and surprise had somehow given it an added mystery, a sense of excitement that might not have existed had she expected it to happen. Plus the fact that it went against everything she believed in. One didn't kiss or receive kisses from somebody one disliked as much as she did Kimberly and yet she hungered for… No, the whole idea of repeating the process was too preposterous for words. It's not likely to happen again anyway, she told herself firmly, Kimberly wasn't interested in her or not in that way and she… Well, she certainly wasn't going to let the bitch use her for self-interest or amusement. Somehow, though, that thought had a hollow ring to it.

After some considerable time, during which she had stared at the monitor screen but failed to write a single word, Jaime gave up. For the first time, her usually sharp powers of thought deserted her and the words she sought just wouldn't come.

With a sigh of frustration, Jaime reached out and turned everything off. She'd take a break, go out somewhere or do something different; she could make up the time tomorrow, when she was in more settled frame of mind.

However, when she came to consider what to do with her unexpected holiday, Jaime found herself equally at a loss for ideas. After wandering restlessly around the room for several minutes, she finally arrived at the window seat. Without thinking she picked up the book of poems and began to leaf through the pages.

Reading the outpourings of love, made Jaime feel even more lonely and bereft. She longed for the sort steadfast love that these poems portrayed but, so far, it had eluded her. *I haven't even got a proper girlfriend,* she shook her head grimly. *True I go out on dates – if one could call a visit to the theatre or a concert a date – but Nigela Toleman,* her usual escort on these occasions, *could hardly be classed as a girlfriend and certainly not a lover.*

Hell, no! In the six years she'd been seeing her, they'd never progressed much beyond a kiss and a brief, unsatisfying, fumble in the car. Until now, Jaime had been happy for things to stay that way but something had happened to her in Whitby, something so powerful and potent that she knew she could never again be satisfied with Nigela's peculiar brand of bland friendship.

I don't want Kimberly either. Jaime shivered with a mixture of suppressed desire and fear at the thought. *Kimberly was just the catalyst, the instigator of my awakening. I want... Oh, damn!* Jaime cursed her inability to describe her feelings. This business with Kimberly had turned her usually razor sharp brain into something that resembled cotton wool. The only thing, about which she was certain, was her dissatisfaction with the status quo. If she was ever going to discover that special something, that vital spark of wild ecstasy, then Jaime knew she'd need to make some very drastic changes to her life. The prospect of slowly drifting into old-maid hood, without ever having experienced love or even the ecstasy of being caught up in the heat of passion, a previously undreamt of state, but hinted at by her brush with Kimberly, made a complete mockery of everything.

With a heavy sigh she turned the page and began to read the next poem then, suddenly, she wasn't reading anymore because the words had sparked an unexpected and serendipitous thought. If her idea was correct then she'd been looking in the wrong place for the information she sought. She closed the book and set it down her eyes bright with speculation. It was a long shot but, Jaime reasoned that the hand of fate was, at last, on her side. She couldn't contain her curiosity she had to check, now, at once. Although, if the information she sought was where she expected to find it, then it most certainly wasn't going to disappear.

Her mother had stored her most treasured possessions in an old, rather battered, black tin trunk.

Jaime had never seen inside because her mother always kept it securely locked even wearing the fancy brass key on a chain around her neck, like a pendant. Jaime wondered now, as she went to fetch the key from the jewelry box in her bedroom, why she'd never before thought to question the fact but when one grows up with something one tends to accept it as perfectly normal. Now, however, the particular reason behind her mother's almost obsessive need for privacy was becoming clearer by the minute.

With the key safely in her pocket, Jaime went in search of the trunk and that proved a much trickier operation. It was stored in the cupboard underneath the stairs but, over time, had moved backwards by the addition of new items. She had to unpack most of the cupboard to get at it.

The best part of an hour later, hot, dusty and tired, but also triumphant, she finally pulled the trunk from its resting place and dragged it across the hall and into the lounge.

After the accident, that had decimated her family, she had not felt able to poke and pry into their personal possessions. Now however, it was a different matter, she had a valid and pressing reason for doing so. Taking the key from her pocket Jaime inserted it in the lock, turned it then slowly lifted the lid and viewed the contents. A slight frown creased her brow as she contemplated the task ahead.

Did she really want to do this? What if… She could just shut the lid and put the trunk away again. No. That was the coward's way out, she wanted some answers and this was definitely the place to look for them.

A faint aroma of lavender drifted up from the interior and caught Jaime unawares. The perfume evoked vivid memories of happier times and the beautifully scented bags her mother had made and distributed all around the house each year. Jaime quickly wiped away the tears filling her eyes; this was not the time for tears. She steeled herself to pick up the first item, a tissue wrapped bundle, in which she discovered her christening robe. After carefully re-wrapping the parcel, she set it aside and removed the next item, then the next and the next, until the trunk was almost empty.

Once she'd made a start, Jaime felt a lot better. This was her family history, a part of her life. She had a perfect right to look through these things and discover any secrets hidden there. Not that she expected to find anything much. They had been a very ordinary family with, as far as she knew, no skeletons in the closet. Her father Edward, who'd taught maths at a nearby college and her mother Kay, a retired nurse, had lived simply with a local church at the center of all their activities and social life.

By the time she stopped to get some lunch, Jaime had sorted through almost half the contents without coming across anything out of the ordinary, except a bundle of her school reports, which had brought back several happy memories and some not so happy, and a sizable box.

Whilst she ate a salad sandwich, Jaime investigated the box which had intrigued her greatly since she'd disentangled it from an old curtain. Was this the thing she had been looking for? Although unremarkable in itself, somebody had wound a ribbon several times around the box and tied a knot so tight she needed a pair of scissors to cut it. Once released from its tie the box fell open and a pile of envelopes, presumably the ones she'd been seeking, spilled out onto the table.

There were more than a hundred, at a rough guess, all addressed to her mother in the same bold hand which she immediately identified as the one that had penned the poetry. The letters her mother had tried so hard to hide and to which James Montagu-Fyre had alluded in the poem.

Jaime regarded her discovery with mixed feelings and a little uncertainty. Although most had been opened a few were still sealed and now, suddenly, she wasn't at all sure how mother would have viewed the prospect of her reading them.

Jaime soon discovered a pattern when she began lay the letters out in order using the postmarks – although admittedly some marks were too indistinct to decipher. The earliest dated envelopes, those addressed to Miss K Simpson, were all open but the others, addressed to Mrs. E Fyre, were not. Jaime gained some comfort from the knowledge her mother hadn't actually cheated on her father, not that she had really considered it as a possibility. Cheating wasn't in her mother's nature and probably not in her vocabulary either. However, Jaime still couldn't understand why she had risked holding on to the letters all these years.

With her lunch finished Jaime rose and went to make some coffee whilst debating the ethical problem that she faced. There were several puzzling aspects which reading the letters might solve. However, did wanting answers give her the right to invade the privacy of others, even if those involved were all dead?

Jaime selected one of the already opened envelopes. Her heart fluttered to match her trembling hands as she extracted the contents. It was, as she had suspected, a love letter. Three pages long, written in the same flowing style and in similar vein to the poems. As she read it, Jaime began to understand why her mother had kept them all these years. One couldn't summarily dispose of something so precious and beautiful.

Putting the letter aside, she gazed dreamily out the window. This was the image of love she'd always regarded as a fantasy – a cruel, roses-around-the-door sort of joke, perpetuated by writers of a certain brand of slushy romance to dupe the lonely and gullible.

Maybe, Jaime decided finally, that special kind of love did exist after all but, if so, and if James and her mother had discovered it, why had they split up?

It was a complete enigma. James had cared deeply, that much was obvious, but what of Kay, had she been a silent partner in all this. No, she must have felt the same way or she wouldn't have kept the letters. And, James had referred to things in her last letter which proved they had a two way exchange.

Jaime shook her head in dismay, convinced that true love didn't just fade away and, for James, it hadn't, he'd continued writing even after Kay was lost to him forever. However, Jaime realized that she was running ahead of herself. She'd picked this letter at random. If she wanted the true picture then it was essential to go back to the beginning and start again.

Returning to the stack of letters, she began to read them in order.

She was struck by how beautifully written they all were and, by the time she'd read the first batch, she realized that James and her mother had forged a deep loving relationship. Although from the tone, she gathered that they didn't manage to meet up very often, which, perhaps, went some way to explain the nature of the correspondence.

Jaime sighed. It felt rather strange, reading about her mother's past. A past that didn't include her father. She had always imagined her parents, as teenage sweethearts, fulfilling the promise of first love. Now it seemed that mother had another great love before she met and married Edward but wait, Jaime remembered from the family tree that Edward and James were cousins. Maybe everything wasn't quite so clear cut as it seemed.

The afternoon disappeared in a flash. Jaime was very surprised when the old mantle clock struck four. She paused to make some tea before tackling the last six of the opened letters. As for the others, she wasn't sure what to do about them. It didn't seem right to open them but she was curious. Why had James continued writing even after he knew that Kay had married and, when presumably, she didn't reply to any of his letters?

With a pot of tea by her side, Jaime began on the final group and immediately some subtle changes struck home. James didn't specify the problem, other than the fact that he was to use his own words, *"stuck in some godforsaken outpost, as far from civilisation as it is possible to imagine, trying to prevent the savages killing one another"* but it was evident that one existed. His love for Kay continued to shine through the correspondence which had lasted now for three whole years but, in the last letter, she sensed the poignancy between the lines of love.

With a melancholy sigh, Jaime returned the final letter to its envelope and put it with all the rest back into the box. She would, she decided, sleep on the dilemma of whether it would be right to read the unopened letters.

Those she had read confirmed without doubt that a bond had existed between James and her mother but it didn't even begin to explain why he decided to leave his entire fortune to her, Jaime. Someone that he'd never met and presumably, based on the information gleaned from Henry Carr, never intended to meet.

Jaime was sure, absolutely certain in fact, that there must be a lot more to this story than she'd so far been able to discover. More letters, or even some diaries, maybe right here in the trunk. Or if not here, then hidden somewhere in Rykesby. A bunch of one-sided correspondence couldn't tell the whole story.

She resumed her interrupted search for information amongst the remaining papers. However, when another hour of concentrated effort had produced nothing else, she gave up the search and dumped everything back inside the trunk then sat back on her heels with a sigh of frustration.

The search through her mother's treasure chest had successfully occupied her thoughts for the remainder of the day but, that night, when she retired to her bed; it was another, very different, matter that kept her wide awake well into the small hours.

Kimberly Marshall certainly had a lot to answer for, Jaime decided as she pummeled the pillows in a last desperate attempt to get comfortable. No matter how hard she tried, she just couldn't get the bitch out of her head and it was driving her slowly mad. Had she fallen for Kimberly, then it might have been an understandable reaction but, as it was, she couldn't see why her image and the increasingly explicit sexual fantasies plagued her so incessantly.

At four o'clock, she abandoned any hope of sleep in favor of an early start to her day. After she had brewed a pot of coffee, she began work and with a determined effort managed to finish editing the final chapter by mid afternoon. With a sigh of pure relief, Jaime pressed the save key. Now, or at least when she'd emailed a copy to her editor, she could devote all her time to planning for the future.

Quite a lot was already in hand, like getting the telephone reconnected to Rykesby, and arranging for a whole host of people to advise her on the best way to renovate the fabric of the sadly neglected building. Although it didn't just end with the Rykesby, there was the move to organize, and a decision to make about this house. That she never wanted to live here again was the only certainty to emerge during the last couple of weeks, but she was still undecided whether to sell up or rent it out. That decision could wait, she had enough on her plate right now. Then there was the ever present problem of Kimberly Marshall.

No! With grim determination, Jaime took herself in hand. She would not allow Kimberly to disturb her peace of mind. She'd already done enough damage, by forcing her way uninvited into Rykesby and there was probably a lot more she could do to make life unbearable, if she wanted to and, if Jaime gave her the satisfaction of knowing she'd provoked a reaction.

Now you're being paranoid, Jaime muttered, angry with herself for dwelling on the subject. Kimberly was nothing more than an annoying tick. One that needed squashing admittedly, but after she'd put Kimberly firmly in her place a couple of times, then surely she would get the message. She needed to keep busy, keep her mind occupied so it didn't wander. With that resolution to the fore, she grabbed a notepad to make a detailed list of all the things that she must do before she could leave for Whitby.

Two days later, the car loaded with possessions and her nerves strung out almost to breaking point, Jaime finally set off for Rykesby and a month's vacation. Well, perhaps vacation was a bit of a misnomer because ahead of her was the source of her present unsettled mood and, four weeks of hard work. However, it would be a nice change of scene, and they do say a change is as good as a rest.

Rest! Jaime was not sure whether to laugh or cry at this thought. Real rest, and the consequent peace of mind it brought, was something she craved. All she asked was a few hours peaceful sleep, without any more vivid dreams about Kimberly. Although, as the days and nights progressed, she'd become resigned to her present parlous state, it was not easy to live with and, Jaime knew that eventually she would have to put a stop to it, by breaking out of the vicious circle in which she'd become trapped. The answer definitely lay with her. She could do it, if she really wanted but, and that was the crucial question, did she?

Jaime set aside all distractions while she maneuvered through the interchange between the M25 and the M1. Once on the motorway the miles sped by whilst she debated this vitally important point. Did she seriously want Kimberly right out of her life, or was she really torturing herself in the vain hope that one day… No! Jaime ground out a savage denial through clenched teeth. Kimberly was not the woman for her and she'd be a fool to think otherwise.

She knew, with absolute certainty, that Kimberly didn't do anything by halves. With all her actions and reactions governed by one desire to get her hands on Rykesby, rather than because she found Jaime attractive, there was little hope of building a relationship of equals. If she was stupid enough to let Kimberly gain a foothold in her life then she must be prepared to face the consequences.

Jaime left the motorway pushing any remaining thoughts of Kimberly from her mind to concentrate on her driving. She by-passed York and took the A64 to Malton, followed by the A169 through Pickering which would take her across the moors toward Whitby. Coming by this route there was no need for her to venture into the narrow confines of the town. Instead, she could cross the A171 and cut across to Rykesby from there. What Jaime hadn't bargained for however, was the fact that using this route would mean she'd have to drive right by Kimberly's cottage. The very place she'd sworn to avoid at all costs.

On rounding a bend, she caught sight of a distinctive dark shape ahead. Was that Kimberly's Range Rover, parked just a hundred yards away near the end of the short straight? A momentary frown creased her brow as she slowed down almost to a halt undecided, uncertain as to its identity. After all, she reasoned logically, this is rough country, so there must be quite a call for rugged vehicles hereabouts. Maybe it was another one, just like hers. Then she recognized Aspen Cottage and her heart started hammering.

Her immediate thought, was to turn around and find an alternative route but the road, well, little more than a lane, was far too narrow for such a maneuver.

This is absolutely ridiculous! Jaime expelled a sigh of frustration. Why can't I just drive on and ignore the fact that Kimberly may be there. Whilst easily expressed the decision was not nearly so easy to accomplish. She knew that Kimberly was unlikely to recognize the car or her, for that matter, in the seconds it would take to drive around the bend and be out of sight but something still held her back. Reluctance, she admitted finally and grudgingly, that stemmed from an overwhelming hope that Kimberly might actually appear. No. Jaime refuted the thought with every fiber of her being. That was the last thing she wanted. It's time she stopped behaving like a lovesick schoolgirl. With that thought firmly in the forefront of her mind she stirred herself into positive action, engaged first gear and released the brake.

Despite her avowed determination to keep moving, Jaime discovered a compulsive urge to brake when she neared the cottage. The car slowed momentarily then speeded up again in response to a guilty stab on the accelerator which propelled it on around the bend at a hair-raising pace.

Jaime chastised herself for her reckless behavior, acutely aware that it might have resulted in an accident had another vehicle happened along, and reduced her speed to a level more suitable for the narrow winding lane. Driving sedately now, she continued on toward her destination, acknowledging that she'd been fortunate to avoid trouble and the certain embarrassment of a face to face meeting with Kimberly. The memory their last encounter still made her hot and bothered. Jaime turned off the road into the long drive and her heart drummed with excitement. This felt like coming home, as if she belonged here not in London. Whatever trials the future held Jaime knew she would always want to be here. This wasn't just a flying visit, like last time, now she had a purpose, a reason to feel settled and content.

For a few minutes, Jaime just stood with her back to the house and stared at the view whilst easing the tension of the long drive out of her neck and shoulders. Then, with a feeling of complete peace, she began to unload the car. First, her laptop, although she hadn't planned to work while she was here, she hated to be without her link to the outside world via email and the internet, both made possible now she had a landline plus the accompanying wireless broadband hub. Once the computer was safely set up in the library, she concentrated on the remainder of her bags.

After several reviving cups of tea and a snack, she set about the unpacking with renewed energy. Humming a little tune as she worked, the job was finished in no time, aided by the fact that she had brought just the bare minimum in the way of clothes with her. Next, she went in search of the linen cupboard and made up a bed, choosing one of the large bedrooms at the front. It was by far the nicest, situated over the drawing room and having windows facing both east and south so she would wake up to the sun. Standing by the east window, Jaime could appreciate why her ancestor, Osbert Fyre, had chosen this site for his home. The rolling moorland, a patchwork tapestry of faded gold, purple, and green, was a perfect foil for the sparkling blue of the distant sea and sky. After she'd sorted out her bedroom, Jaime went on a tour of the house, happily discovering all its little secrets.

Jaime completed her tour, all except the library, which she'd deliberately left until last because she wanted plenty of time to explore it thoroughly. She was almost certain that, somewhere within its walls, there was a safe, or some other secret hiding place. There must be, if her assumption was correct, a bundle of letters from her mother to James, surely he wouldn't have thrown them all away. Perhaps there might be some diaries too. Jaime thought it quite likely that James was the type man who would keep a diary – faithfully recording the details his life for posterity. If only she could discover where he'd hidden those letters and diaries they would, she was sure, enable her to fit the missing pieces into the jigsaw. The only problem was that she had no idea where to look.

With supper out of the way, Jaime carried a tray of coffee into the library and sat at the desk. Whilst she pondered the problem she her found her gaze idly traversing the room searching for an answer that was so maddeningly elusive.

There was so much she wanted to know and nobody to turn to in her time of need. Even Henry Carr, who might possibly have provided some of the answers, was staying tight-lipped. Jaime sighed.

I'm on my own and, if necessary, I'll have to turn the whole house inside out to find what I'm looking for.

The idea was daunting, mainly because there was a wealth of potential hiding places. However, Jaime decided, first things first. A systematic search of the library should keep her busy for now. Then maybe…

The strident tone of the newly installed telephone invaded the silence.

Oh! Jaime jumped, knocking her cup of coffee over the desk.

CHAPTER SIX

Other than it was a local number, Jaime didn't recognize the caller ID but there couldn't be many people who knew this number or would bother to call it. She grabbed for a box of tissues to soak up the mess, a mixture of fear and joy churning in her stomach.

Kimberly?

It had to be Kimberly – she'd probably recognized Jaime's car pass her cottage earlier – and now… Jaime hesitated, caught in the crossfire of conflicting emotions. The strident ringing continued unabated, forcing her to concede the caller's perseverance. Finally, with her breathing under firm control, she lifted the receiver and said hello, without giving either name or number.

"Ah, Miss Fyre!" Henry Carr's voice carried a faint trace of amusement. "I thought I would try Rykesby on the off chance I might find you there."

"Mr. Carr..." Nausea burnt Jaime's throat making speech difficult. Something had gone wrong, she was convinced of it. Maybe he'd discovered she wasn't legally entitled to her legacy after all or, even worse, Kimberly had put in a valid counterclaim.

"I...Is there some problem?"

"No. No problem at all."

The lawyer's voice rang with reassuring conviction. Relief swept the nausea away allowing Jaime to breathe properly again.

"Now probate is completed there are a several things that need your signature so I wondered, providing you are free, if you would care to join us for dinner tomorrow?"

Dinner sounded very formal. She cast her gaze skyward. "Thank you for the invitation but I'm afraid I didn't bring many clothes with me, and if you dress...?"

"No. It's quite casual." Henry Carr paused then, as though he sensed her wavering. "Just a few close friends and, Margaret, my wife, who is longing to meet you. She knew both your parents."

His last remark did the trick. Jaime knew he was manipulating her by dangling a carrot on a stick but so what? He'd no doubt anticipated her reluctance and worked out a strategy to overcome it.

"Well, if you're sure. Yes, please, I'd love to accept."

Jaime cast a mental eye over her meager wardrobe, mainly jeans plus an assortment of shirts and sweaters, none of which she considered remotely suitable, casual or not. No, she would have to go shopping.

"Please do not worry too much," Henry interrupted her deliberations. "I am quite sure that you will look delightful whatever you wear.

Jaime noted the directions then replaced the handset with mixed feelings and not a little apprehension. Admittedly she had got what she wanted, somebody who knew her parents and, with whom she could talk, but, Margaret Carr might not be able or, like her husband, willing to fill in any of the gaps and it would be difficult, unless Margaret volunteered the information, because Jaime no idea what questions she needed to ask.

There were so many imponderables. A host of oddly conflicting facts that didn't make any logical sense and yet, somewhere, there must be a key to unlock it all.

Her eye fell upon the battered box which contained all the letters from her mother's treasure chest. It formed one small part of the complete puzzle but not enough to solve it by any means. What she needed now was to find the rest of the pieces.

I might as well make a start.

Getting up from the desk, Jaime wandered over to the first bank of shelves and began removing the books. Nothing there, she emptied the next shelf then the next and so on until the end, still nothing. Shaking her head, she began tapping at the paneling without any appreciable success, although there was a moment where her hopes rose. One panel next to the fireplace sounded different, sort of hollow, as though the wall behind was not solid. A careful examination gave her more reason to celebrate when she discovered what appeared to be a hairline crack between two panels. With eager hands, she pushed, pulled, and prodded at anything that might conceivably be the secret catch only accepting defeat when, after wasting absolutely ages, the panel remained stubbornly unmoved.

Now what? Once more Jaime scanned the room, her eyes registering every tiny detail, in the hope that she might spot something previously missed.

There was nothing behind any of the pictures or in the desk because she'd checked them out already and the same went for the rest of the furniture. She'd moved all the lighter pieces without result and she doubted that a safe would be hidden beneath or behind the any of the larger pieces. That would rather defeat the purpose. No, Jaime sighed, if there was a safe then it had to be in an easily accessible place, like behind those panels. If only she could discover the secret catch.

Maybe I'm looking at things all wrong, she thought. Just suppose this was one of my novels and Granby faced the problem of a secret hiding place. What would I do then and how would I go about it?

Grabbing up pad and pen Jaime began by drawing a detailed diagram of the room and then listed all the most important features. Writing fast she soon had a whole sheaf of notes then, fired up with enthusiasm and, almost before she realized what was happening, she found herself working on a comprehensive outline for a new book.

It always happened like this, out of the blue, the germ of an idea would spark off a period of frenzied activity from which there was no escape until it was all set down on paper. Everything else forgotten as she scribbled on, way into the small hours, her brain totally absorbed with the plot. Jaime finally crawled into bed at three fifteen, exhausted but ecstatic that she'd got the bulk of it out of her system. She drifted in and out of sleep now and then as more of the plot resolved itself in her brain then woke with a start a seven o'clock.

Granby had solved the problem she'd discovered the hidden catch, unlocked the secret door and found the missing papers. If only it were that simple…

Jaime rocketed out of bed and dashed barefoot down to the library to test out her theory. The ornately carved fire surround bristled with knobs and bumps, just the place to disguise a handle for a secret door. She stood for ages studying the intricacies of the pattern then, in a moment of sheer frustration, she gave the right hand pillar a sharp thump. There was a soft click. Jaime held her breath and waited. For a second or two nothing happened then, when she'd almost given up hope of a breakthrough, a boss on one of the shields moved sideways and revealed a small brass handle. For several minutes, Jaime just stood and stared. The discovery meant so much and yet she hardly dared turn the handle in case nothing happened.

Whilst she was debating the issue, the clock in the hall struck the hour. Eight o'clock, Jaime thought of all the things she needed to do today and decided the investigation could wait awhile. Once she began, there was no telling what she would find or how long it would take and it didn't feel right to treat this with disrespect. After a shower and breakfast, she drove into Whitby to buy something suitable for the Carr's dinner party.

Jaime found the ideal thing in a chic little boutique tucked away down a narrow cobbled alleyway. The silk two-piece in a subtle shade resembling dark sage bore a horrendous price tag and, by the time she had added a pair of high heeled sandals, a clutch purse and a silver choker necklace, it had nearly doubled. Feeling slightly guilty for spending such a lot on just one outfit she headed back to Rykesby to meet the first of the interior designers whom she had arranged to see that day.

As the evening approached, her nervous tension grew. Despite Henry Carr's assurances and her smart new outfit, the prospect of having to spend the evening making polite conversation with total strangers was somewhat daunting.

There were already several cars parked in the Carr's drive when Jaime arrived including a very familiar black Range Rover. The shock of seeing it there clenched her stomach into a tight knot. No! I can't do this, she thought. She didn't want to meet Kimberly with the memory of their last meeting still fresh in her mind, not here, not tonight, or in front of witnesses. What had Henry Carr been thinking of, to invite both of them together without warning her first?

She was about to turn around and flee when another car pulled in behind her. Trapped, with no chance of escape, Jaime scowled, quickly realizing that she had no choice but to make the best of it and face up to Kimberly. Unless she wanted the Carr's and their guests to witness her public humiliation, her only option was to put on a brave face and behave with total nonchalance.

Somehow, although she wasn't sure how, Jaime got herself out of the car then across the drive toward the door. Timing her entry to perfection behind the other new arrivals – a couple in their late forties. She hung back a little as both Henry and Margaret Carr welcomed the couple warmly. Jaime felt rather awkward arriving alone until Henry glanced up and spotted her in the doorway. He smiled then said something to the couple before coming over to greet her.

"Ah, Jaime, you found us! Do come in."

Drawing her into the group, he introduced her first to his wife Margaret. Who, after welcoming Jaime in a rather abstracted manner, excused herself on the pretext of seeing to dinner. "We will have a long talk later." Margaret promised before hurrying away. Henry then introduced Jaime to the other couple. The man, another Henry, turned out to be the Carr's son accompanied by his wife, Myra, who was definitely mutton dressed as lamb. She accorded Jaime a brief condescending smile, as she flicked a cursory glance over the new outfit, which was clearly not to her taste.

I don't believe I shall like her, Jaime decided quickly. They observed the ritual of a brief touch of hands and a few murmured pleasantries before following the men into a vast, well appointed, drawing room.

Glancing around, Jaime was immediately glad that she had taken the trouble to dress, despite Henry's assurances to the contrary. The other women all wore cocktail dresses, excluding Kimberly who'd teamed a dark purplish-red shirt, the shade of ripe plums, with black evening trousers, although the men sported lounge suits rather than tuxedos.

Henry senior took charge, leading Jaime around the room and introducing her to the assembled company most of whom were professional people. Two bank managers plus wives, an accountant, another solicitor and finally Kimberly.

No introduction was needed there. Jaime summoned up a smile then offered her hand which Kimberly shook rather offhandedly. This brief contact was cool and yet, it left Jaime feeling just as though she'd plunged her hand into boiling water. The heat spread, radiating through her entire body in a matter of seconds, a fierce all consuming fire, its flames licking at the very core of her being in a sensually disturbing manner. Rapidly pulling herself together, she went through the motions of being polite and totally unconcerned, although her voice did sound a trifle strained when she enquired casually as to Kimberly's health. Remarkably, or so it seemed, her shoulder appeared to have made a miraculous recovery, a fact for which Jaime was indeed grateful when one considered the possible consequences. Presumably, it had just been a case of some bruises or, more likely, a clever bit of play acting.

Having done her duty and, satisfied her host that peace had broken out Jaime began to edge away from Kimberly but Henry forestalled her move with a neat one of his own.

"Good, I will leave you two young people to get to know each other properly."

Jaime glanced frantically around her, seeking a means of escape but the other guests were all occupied, reluctantly, she turned back to Kimberly.

"I'm sorry about this. Had I known you were here I wouldn't have come."

Kimberly's gaze swept fleetingly over their fellow guests before returning to Jaime. "I think we were invited together for a purpose." She raised her brow in a faintly amused gesture. "Take a look around you. There's nobody else under fifty and they're all in neat couples. See what I mean?"

Jaime had to admit Kimberly had a point and she wasn't very happy with the discovery. The idea of spending almost an entire evening in Kimberly's company sent shivers of apprehension rushing down her spine.

"What say we give them something to think about?" Kimberly grinned. "I should imagine most, if not all of them, know about the feud. Let's enjoy some fun at their expense. What harm can it do to pretend we are the best of friends just for this one evening?"

"I…I hate lies," Jaime protested weakly. The idea of being friends with Kimberly terrified the life out of her. Lovers maybe, she'd been fighting that particular urge from the first second she'd clapped eyes on Kimberly but friends… No. Friendship was very different. The fellowship that stemmed from trust and mutual respect was noticeably absent from any equation in which Kimberly figured. She might exude charm and sex appeal from every pore but that couldn't possibly compensate for her less than generous nature. No, Jaime doubted that they could ever be friends.

"You won't have to lie." Sardonic amusement danced in Kimberly's eyes. "Just be yourself. It shouldn't stretch your inventive powers too far to put up a smokescreen, one convincing enough to fool the stuffed shirts here. Believe me, it would be a pleasure to watch you in action. Come on, let yourself go, relax that stiff little body, and show me what you can do."

"How dare you!" Jaime immediately wished her angry retort unsaid. She realized, too late, that it had played right into Kimberly's hands. The focus of her anger shifted, settling back upon herself, for rising to the bait. Granted Kimberly was the most irritating woman she'd ever had the misfortune to meet and, to cap it all, had a habit of always putting her down but, no matter how hard she tried to ignore it, Kimberly was proving too sexy for her peace of mind. That single, devastating, fact was enough to cloud her judgment.

Saved by the bell, so to speak. Before Kimberly could respond to her outburst, Margaret announced that dinner was ready. Jaime followed Kimberly into the dining room praying all the time that they would not have to sit together and, for once, her prayers were answered.

She was seated on Henry Carr's right with Clive Allard, another lawyer, on her left and Kimberly on the opposite side of the table well out of harm's way.

"When is Mrs. Plews returning?" Henry Carr asked once Margaret had served the first course, of smoked salmon pâté and Melba toast.

"I don't need a housekeeper."

He frowned. "You cannot be contemplating living in Rykesby alone?" He sounded aghast at the idea.

"Why not." Jaime shrugged. "I like living alone. Besides which, I'm planning quite few alterations and I wouldn't expect anyone to have to endure the dust and upheaval." Offering up one of her best smiles, she added. "Once the work is complete, and I am ready to move in permanently, maybe I'll rethink the situation."

Thankfully, Henry seemed satisfied with that. He nodded absentmindedly, before going on to remark that "They might discuss this matter in greater detail after dinner." Adding in an avuncular manner that. "He hoped she would accept his help and guidance."

To keep him happy Jaime nodded agreement, then steered the conversation to safer topics dividing her attention between Henry and Clive Allard for the remainder of the meal.

Jaime returned to the drawing room after leaving Henry's study, where they'd spent a considerable time arguing about her plans for the house. Henry had put up all sorts of objections, most of them so trivial that it reinforced her view that his prime objective was to dissuade her from living there at all.

She paused in the doorway, scanning the room for Kimberly. No sign of her. Jaime released her pent up anxiety, then smiled warmly as Clive Allard hurried across the room toward her.

That smile was a big mistake because he mistook it for genuine interest and, before she was fully aware of his intentions, he'd steered her across the drawing room and out onto the patio. The night air was mild for mid September. Strategically placed lights illuminated a well tended garden with many of the shrubs beginning to glow with rich shades as the leaves turned color.

Under more normal circumstances, a balding, fifty-something, man wouldn't have been her choice of after-dinner companion but this situation was far from normal. Jaime listened politely, whilst Clive held forth on what was clearly his favorite topic, himself, or, to be more precise, his recent divorce. Although why he imagined she would be interested in such a sordid tale of woe was beyond her.

"Ah! There you are."

Kimberly suddenly materialized next to her, both looking and sounding furious. Without a by-your-leave, she grasped Jaime firmly by the arm and forcibly dragged her away from Clive.

"Let go of me!" Jaime protested through heavily clenched teeth. Anger rippled through her body but her resistance proved futile.

Kimberly took absolutely no notice of her protest, and continued to propel her on, marching her swiftly across the lawn, without a thought for her precarious heels, until they reached a secluded gazebo. There was just enough light from nearest shrubbery to give the structure a soft glow. Kimberly swung her around, transfixing her with a hostile glare.

Jaime glared right back. Fury forced the blood through her veins at speed until the pressure drummed like a pneumatic drill in her head.

"How dare you embarrass me like that!" Jaime's breathing registered in short rasping gasps as she tried to shake herself free.

Kimberly held on, even tightening her grip a little, and inclining her head.

Fear gripped Jaime. The mere thought that Kimberly might kiss her again brought time to a complete halt whilst she battled conflicting emotions. She was torn between intoxicating desire and the real fear of falling victim to Kimberly's devious machinations. Thankfully, the moment passed and she found the strength to dismiss her more wayward urges.

"Simple expediency. You never let up, do you?" Kimberly's soft laughter mocked Jaime. "I thought that fool, Clive, needed rescuing. Give the poor guy a break. He certainly doesn't deserve to be taken for a sucker again. Also, since his divorce settlement, he's in no position to pander to your very expensive tastes."

A sense of powerlessness gripped Jaime's throat in a stranglehold rendering her momentarily speechless. Despite everything, Kimberly was still hell bent on branding her a fortune hunter. Not only had she appointed herself judge and jury, to make matters worse, she had also both tried and convicted Jaime, all without one single shred of credible evidence.

Bitch!

Jaime snatched a sharp breath and tore herself free from Kimberly's grasp. She flexed her arm then took a couple of paces backwards before her legs gave way forcing her to take refuge on the slatted bench that ran around three sides of the structure.

Damn! Now she has me at a disadvantage.

Jaime raised her sight to meet and match Kimberly's icy gaze before wading in, guns blazing. "You've gone too far this time! I will not stand for being bullied or assaulted, by anyone, and especially not by you. Bitch!"

"Temper, temper!" Heavy sarcasm dripped from Kimberly's lips. "You've got nothing to complain about, yet." She let this implied threat sink in for a moment before adding. "I thought it was high time we got at the truth – and don't insult my intelligence by pretending you don't understand. We're two of a kind, you and me, the sooner you admit that fact then the easier it will be for us to reach a mutual understanding."

"Really? I cannot imagine us ever doing that." Jaime shook her head. "You're not my type."

"I am pleased we agree on one point." Kimberly fixed Jaime with a contemptuous glare. "You obviously prefer men – old, rich, men. How can I possibly compete?"

"It is not a matter of competing." Jaime shrugged, stung by Kimberly's accusation. "It is simply that we have nothing in common, and are never likely to…"

Kimberly laughed. "That is where you are wrong! We do have one thing in common – Rykesby – and that's not going to go away."

So we're back to that are we?

A renewed surge of disgust, made Jaime all the more determined to regain the initiative. "You're wasting your time and mine." She got to her feet with the intention of bringing this futile conversation to an end and returning to the house but Kimberly was ahead of her. With lightening reflexes, she shot out an arm and barred the way.

"Let me go!" Jaime called upon the full might of her anger to reinforce the demand.

"All in good time." Kimberly's voice held a note of unquestionable authority. "I haven't finished with you yet, not by a long way. Before we're through, I will know everything about you. What drives you, your strengths and your weaknesses and, most importantly, your breaking point."

An insidious terror crept through Jaime's veins wiping everything else from her mind. Kimberly clearly hated her, so much so that she wanted to hurt her – to break her will.

Suddenly, in an amazing volte-face, Kimberly reached out and gently trailed one finger down the line of her jaw, then across her lips and on down into the hollow of her throat.

With a gasp, Jaime jerked away from her touch, from the fierce burning sensation it left on her skin. This abrupt switch from cold to hot left Jaime trembling, confused, and very angry.

"We have unfinished business." Kimberly held Jaime's gaze as she backed her very firmly toward the darkest corner of the gazebo.

"No." Jaime struggled fruitlessly to withstand her advance. Frightened by the intensity of her need whilst, at the same time, despising herself for being so weak.

"Don't fight me." Kimberly pinned Jaime against the wall with her body. "I'm not in the mood for games."

"I…I'm not the one playing games." Jaime heard the tremor in her voice, and hated that nervousness threatened to betray her vulnerability. She risked a brief glance at Kimberly's face, wondering if she'd heard it too but, thankfully, it appeared she hadn't. Not that that was particularly reassuring, because it meant also that Jaime hadn't made any impression. She had to get through to Kimberly, make her understand that she didn't want this, convince her there was no point in forcing her to capitulate.

If only I didn't, Jaime shuddered. The trouble was her body found Kimberly all too desirable, responding eagerly to her potent sexuality, without reference to either head or heart.

"Let me go!"

"I had a rather different idea," Kimberly suddenly dropped her head cutting Jaime's gasp of protest short as she demonstrated exactly what she had in mind.

Kimberly's demanding mouth and tongue caressed Jaime's unresponsive lips into submission. She fought valiantly, battling the rising tide of passion that threatened to engulf her before surrendering her mouth. Still Kimberly kept up the pressure, sliding her hand down Jaime's spine, molding her softer curves into full contact with her hard frame. They were both decidedly out of breath by the time Kimberly finally lifted her mouth away.

Heart pounding with a combination of suppressed desire and fury Jaime struggled free of Kimberly's body. She averted her face, to prevent the bitch reading her expression and gulped in a great lungful of air before turning back to face Kimberly.

"How dare you!"

"Me?"

"Yes you!"

"Oh, no." Kimberly shook her head in disbelief. "You're not going to pull that one you sly little bitch. I didn't do a thing to which you weren't an equal and willing participant."

Jaime blenched, her insides contracting tightly, nauseatingly, hardly registering the awful import of what she was hearing.

Did I really encourage her?

Just framing the question caused Jaime acute embarrassment. She examined her own behavior in minute detail, blushing to the roots of her hair as the scene unfolded in her head, before deciding that, in fact, she'd done just the opposite.

Kimberly had made all the moves, dictating the pace, forcing her to submit to her will and now she had the cheek to accuse her of complicity.

Typical! Jaime sighed. Kimberly's desire to punish her in order to avenge the past knew no bounds. It appeared the only way she could achieve the satisfaction she sought was to degrade and humiliate.

Admittedly, she had responded. What woman wouldn't, given the circumstances?

Jaime fixed Kimberly with an icy glare. "I didn't invite you to kiss me. Nor did I welcome it. Maybe you should learn to recognize the right signals otherwise you'll find yourself in serious trouble."

"A brilliant performance!" Kimberly's harsh tone cut Jaime to the quick. "You'll be the one in trouble, take my word for it, if you make a habit of leading women on, as you did with me. Women like you get just what they deserve in the end!"

"That's not a very fair or balanced view," Jaime retorted angrily. "I've never given you, or any woman, cause to regard me in such a light, nor would I."

The injustice of Kimberly's comment forced Jaime to take up defensive stance. Kimberly clearly had no idea of the very real anger such warped opinions provoked, and it was not the first time she had expressed them either. She distinctly remembered Kimberly voicing similar views the first day they met.

So what if some woman had given her a rough deal, Jaime didn't see why she should be the one to pick up the tab. On the evidence to hand, she thought it quite likely that Kimberly had created the problems herself. Although it would not be an easy task to get her to admit that. Why should I anyway? Jaime rejected any prospect of reconciliation. I don't want to win her around. As far as I'm concerned, she's an unpleasant complication, one that I could without at this moment.

One thing was certain. She must put a stop to this nonsense before it got completely out of hand. Other people mustn't become involved. She couldn't endure the shame if this became public knowledge. However, Jaime wasn't prepared to allow Kimberly to walk all over her. She must accept responsibility for her crass behavior and stop trying to foist the blame unjustly onto Jaime.

"Why don't you admit it?" Kimberly's sneer cut through the air. "You're nothing but a cheap little tart that uses her body as bait to get what she wants. Is that how you got your grubby hands on Rykesby? Did you come across to Uncle James? Tell me, is that how you got him to add your name to the family tree. Or, maybe it was Henry Carr who falsified the records? Is that why you spent so long in his library? Were you giving him a blow job as his reward? Perhaps I should have you checked out more thoroughly."

Propelled by the force of explosive rage, Jaime's hand shot out and made contact with Kimberly's face. Unable to believe she had just physically hit somebody, Jaime let a gasp of surprise escape her lips. Then she assuaged her guilty conscience with the thought that Kimberly had deserved it.

Jaime couldn't comprehend what Kimberly had just said, she must have lost complete control of the plot if she genuinely thought Jaime remotely capable of such baseness. The idea of her and James – bile rose in Jaime's throat almost choking her. There was something particularly obscene in the very suggestion. The same went for Henry Carr. Although recognizing she still had a few lingering doubts about him, she also thought it extremely unlikely that he could be bought in that way. Kimberly must be possessed of a very twisted mind if she actually believed, deep down, that Jaime was that mercenary.

"I am not listening to any more of this rubbish." Jaime drew on all her inner resolve. "If you can't be reasonable then I am going back inside and… Ouch!"

Once again. Kimberly's hand closed around her wrist, cutting her off in mid-sentence and forestalling any movement.

"Let go. You're hurting me!" Jaime ground her teeth against the pain. It was nothing less than the truth. Kimberly's vice-like grip was indeed hurting because it was driving her watch-strap into her wrist.

"Not until we have this out!" Kimberly had returned to a hard uncompromising stance that brooked no refusal. "I plan to find out just how devious you are and you're going to stay here until I'm completely satisfied."

"I'm not. You've got it all wrong." Jaime tried really hard to keep control of her voice but Kimberly's continued aggression was taking its toll.

A derisive snort signaled that Kimberly had picked up the tremor in Jaime's voice and seized on it as indication of guilt. Jaime sighed. She'd obviously made up her mind on the subject and nothing would change her opinion.

"I don't think so." Kimberly's eyes glittered like fire in the moonlight. "You're the one that has got it wrong

– very wrong – if you think I'll swallow the clever little fairy story you've concocted." She pushed Jaime backwards, forcing her down onto the seat whilst still keeping a tight hold of her wrist.

"You're going to tell me exactly what you did, and with whom, every little detail." Kimberly told her harshly.

"No! You've totally lost the plot." Stinging tears filled Jaime's eyes blurring her vision. She hated the pleading note that had crept into her voice, hated the feeling of impotence and sheer desperation that forced her to beg – however demeaning it was to do so. Above everything she wanted, needed, to stop this right now. "I didn't do anything. I couldn't. How can I prove to you that I knew nothing about James, Henry Carr, the will, you, or anything else, until a few days ago?"

"You can't." Kimberly ground out contemptuously. "This is not a game and you're no innocent child. Far from it!" Her mouth tightened in an expression of total disgust. "You may use your doubtful charms to hoodwink some people but I'm not that gullible. I've got your number and there is no way I'm prepared to settle for anything less than a full and frank admission of your guilt."

The picture Kimberly painted horrified Jaime. Her stomach contracted forcing her, once again, to fight back the nausea. What defenses did she have against such foul lies? Nothing.

Also, if she was totally honest, she did feel a twinge of guilt. Not that she'd done anything wrong, the legacy was rightfully hers. But, it was such a lot and, she conceded, there were still far too many unanswered questions surrounding it.

Silently cursing James, for putting her in such an invidious position, Jaime turned her thoughts back to the current problem of Kimberly. If she really did believe Jaime to be responsible for the loss of her inheritance then she probably believed she had a legitimate score to settle. Jaime hadn't forgotten the story Henry Carr recounted, nor did she discount the disappointment that Kimberly must have felt when she discovered another claimant to the estate, but that didn't excuse her current behavior or her apparent aim to humiliate and discredit Jaime. Kimberly had also failed to grasp one essential point – Jaime had the might of unquestionable evidence to back her case.

"This is getting us nowhere!" Jaime opted for attack as the best form of defense. There wasn't much point in arguing her case against such a biased view. With one fluid movement, she stood and wrenched her arm free from Kimberly's grasp. "I refuse to play your sick game and if, in the future, you've got anything further to say to me then please do it through my lawyer. Now I suggest you get lost!"

Without waiting for a response, she turned away and fled. It was the cowardly way out, but she didn't care. The house and the safety of numbers within seemed suddenly very attractive.

Kimberly glared hard at Jaime's back before she flung one final retort after her. "You can run but you can't hide." She watched Jaime streak across the garden as if the hounds of hell were after her. Those fragile heels looked barely capable of supporting Jaime's weight let alone coping with a sprint over unstable terrain, like grass and gravel.

That went well.

Anger formed Kimberly's lips into a tight line. Once again she'd blown a good chance to resolve this issue by letting things get out of hand. Kimberly fought the urge to bash her head against the framework of the gazebo in despair. Until she'd witnessed Jaime getting up close and personal with Clive, she'd fully intended to keep her cool, to befriend Jaime, to draw out the truth bit by bit, while keeping total control of the situation. Instead, she'd allowed her fluctuating emotions to highjack her common sense and dictate the following events.

Jaime wielded the power to instil jealousy, anger, and pure lust that no other woman had in a long time. Not since Rebecca nearly fifteen years ago. That relationship had faltered, smashed to death on the rocks of a physical and emotional trauma that had threatened to wreck both their lives. In the wake of the furore Rebecca had fled, leaving Whitby behind to make a life for herself with Karla, the designer for whom she regularly strutted her stuff on the haute couture catwalks around the globe. With the passage of time the intensity of their shared emotions had faded and nowadays, on the rare occasions that their paths crossed, Kimberly was able to greet Rebecca as a friend.

The situation with Jaime posed a whole new set of problems. Kimberly sat down on the wooden seat and let a long drawn sigh escape her lips. She'd barely had time to come to terms with the passing of Uncle James before she'd been thrust into the unpleasant reality of Jaime and her false, or fraudulent, claim to Rykesby. That both Henry Carr and the Probate Office had apparently accepted the will as genuine was another worrying aspect. Although the possibility of Henry's involvement in the fraud would explain the smooth passage of probate. Eva, her own lawyer, hadn't been able to find any chink of light in the paper chain, though both of them suspected there must be one somewhere. Something, that would debunk the sudden appearance of Jaime Fyre complete with a perfectly crafted life history that matched the will and gave credence to her claim. So far, all Eva's inquiries into Jaime's background had checked out but Kimberly wasn't convinced, there were still a few areas that didn't stack up as neatly as she would like. The lack of any work history was certainly suspicious. As far as Eva could ascertain Jaime had not worked for a single day since she graduated with honors in computer science. That was a red flag in itself. What did she live on? How did she pay her bills? There was no evidence of inherited wealth to explain her lack of income. Uncle Edward had had no money other than his teacher's salary, and possibly a life insurance policy but that wouldn't have kept Jaime all these years. Then there was the emotional and sexual trap. Kimberly wasn't ready to fall into that one again anytime soon.

Sure, Jaime was sex on a stick. A real cutie. She certainly had the attributes that attracted Kimberly's interest – the very same qualities exhibited by all the women with whom she forged a relationship. Very femme, and almost virginal – although in Jaime's case it was probably just a clever act – she certainly kissed like a novice, but she always appeared to be struggling to control an underlying hunger.

Kimberly shook her head. There were still too many unanswered questions surrounding Jaime and her involvement in this claim for Rykesby. The problem clearly wasn't likely to be resolved any time soon, not without a lot more digging into the backgrounds of all those involved. She must update Eva on developments. Kimberly clicked her cell phone on but there was no signal. Damn! She would have to go home and use the landline.

Kimberly skirted quickly around the house to reach her vehicle rather than going inside to say goodbye as polite convention dictated. She knew she wouldn't be able to trust herself, or her emotions, if she came face-to-face with Jaime again tonight.

A little over ten minutes later she had reached Eva at home.

"Calm down, Kim," Eva said firmly. "You're not making any sense. Take a deep breath and tell me what happened again, one fact at a time."

"I'm just so frustrated," Kimberly growled. "The bitch is running rings around us, I know she is. When I saw her making eyes at that poor sucker, Clive, I lost it and I..."

"I hope you didn't do anything stupid."

Kimberly laughed out loud. "Well, Eva, I suppose it all depends how you define the word stupid. Right now... I think I might have seriously messed up."

"I warned you not to get involved. There are plenty of other avenues available to resolve this without resorting to actions that may make matters worse or even land you in court for harassment."

"But she was there, at the Carr's, flaunting herself and her position. That old fool, Henry, was flapping around her like a mother hen with one chick. Not that she needs any encouragement. They were closeted in his study for ages after dinner and I have a pretty good idea what they were doing. She has the perfect mouth for sucking–"

"Really! You must be careful what you say. I do hope you haven't mentioned this to anybody else."

"Only to Jaime or whatever her name is. I got slapped across the face when I accused her of giving him a blow job as his reward for services rendered."

"Ouch!" Eva sighed.

"Exactly!"

"What else?"

"Well... Apart from dragging her across the lawn, holding her against her will in the gazebo, and kissing her again... Yes, I know I said I wouldn't but she looks so kissable when she's angry – and boy, was she angry tonight."

"I can imagine."

"You sound like you're sympathizing with her." Kimberly huffed loudly. "What about me? I'm the injured party in this."

"I know, Kim, but in the end it all comes down to proof. The legal facts need to be established beyond any doubt and right now there isn't enough evidence to disprove her claim."

"Are you saying that she's going to get away with her fraud?"

"No, I'm not saying anything of the sort, or that the evidence it isn't there to be found, only that I haven't yet uncovered the necessary documents.

"Maybe I should engage another lawyer, somebody younger who has both the experience and the resources to find the evidence against her. Or, better still, save myself a fortune in legal fees and do the job myself."

"Now you are just being silly. You know I have the necessary resources to tackle this and, although I may be old, I'm not yet in my dotage. I also have an advantage a stranger wouldn't have I know both you and a lot about the family history from working with your mother."

"I'm sorry, Eva. You're right, I'm not thinking coherently. This business has all come as a tremendous shock, on top of the bombshell of losing Uncle James. I can't think why Henry Carr never even bothered to tell me that he'd died."

"You know why, we've already been through this. Henry Carr had no obligation to inform you because you weren't mentioned in the will with which he is working."

"Yeah! Tell me about it. I just want to see some action."

"Please. Kim, do me a big favor, take a step back. Keep away from Jaime Fyre. I know what I'm doing leave the legal stuff to me. Just be patient and it'll all come good."

"Okay, I'll try to do what you ask but she's here, at Rykesby, I'm bound to bump into her socially or around town."

"I know... Passing her on the street is one thing but don't go near Rykesby, or make any more trouble."

"Yes, ma'am, I hear you loud and clear. I'll be good." Kimberly grimaced at the promise she knew she couldn't keep.

"That's all I want to hear." Eva replied. "Now I'm going back to my book. Goodnight Kimberly."

"Night, Eva, and thanks for listening. I appreciate all you do for me."

Kimberly cut the connection, and grabbed a beer from the fridge. She paced her lounge, beer in hand, debating her next move. Eva needn't know what she had in mind and, anyway, it was a legitimate business practice. Nobody could object to her doing her job.

CHAPTER SEVEN

Out of breath and stamina after running the length of the garden, Jaime paused at the darkest end of the patio, in order to wipe the heels of her shoes with a tissue and regain her composure. Then she found something else to worry about and her heart almost stopped beating.

Had they been missed? She'd completely lost track of time, since they'd left the house, but it had to be quite a long while, half an hour at the very least and maybe a whole lot more. How these people, in particular the Carr's, might view such a prolonged absence prompted Jaime to devise a strategy to divert any unwelcome attention. Once satisfied that she had got her story right she approached the French doors, and was immediately glad that she'd taken those extra minutes to put her thoughts in order.

Margaret gave her a searching glance when they met just inside. "Jaime... I wondered where you were. Is everything all right?"

"Yes, thank you, I'm fine. I just needed some air." Jaime met her concerned gaze. Then, using her prepared story. "I took a stroll around your beautiful garden."

Fortunately, Margaret seemed happy to accept her explanation without question. Jaime sent up a silent prayer of thanks to her guardian angel for saving her from an acutely embarrassing situation. She was determined, always providing she had a say in the matter, that no one else would ever learn the sordid details about what had gone on between her and Kimberly that night.

"Henry tells me that you are planning to renovate the Hall." Margaret guided Jaime into a cozy sitting room well away from the main drawing room. "I must say I am delighted. Rykesby used to be such a fine house, in the old days before…" She hesitated a moment, a slight shadow crossed her face as if the memories were difficult to recall, and then continued dreamily.

"When we were younger, Henry, Edward, James and us girls, we had such grand parties, formal dances, with a proper orchestra… Not the sort of thing you would have nowadays. I am afraid James let the house fall into ruin. He became a bit of a recluse after…"

Her voice tailed off and she fell into a contemplative silence.

Jaime waited, longing for more, yet unwilling to appear too eager in case her enthusiasm put Margaret off. She'd listened to Margaret's vague reminiscences with growing interest. Admittedly, they hadn't told her much about the people involved, yet it had helped, giving her an overall picture of the period.

"I always think it is such a shame." Margaret began again quietly, almost to herself. "When a lovely old property, like Rykesby, is allowed to fall into disrepair. However, I am sure you are going to change that and restore the house to its former glory." She flicked Jaime a meditative look, and added wistfully. "It is such a pity you are not married."

I'll bet it is.

Jaime wanted to make it clear that marriage would never be an option for her but she held her tongue. Margaret's attitude to life appeared similar to Henry's. Namely, a mere woman is incapable of managing her own affairs. Well this woman was, and she certainly wasn't going to allow these old fuddy-duddies to push her into what they would probably term 'a suitable marriage' nor even a marriage of convenience.

"Did you know my mother too?" Jaime seized the opportunity to change the subject. She'd noticed that

Margaret had omitted Kay's name earlier, and now seemed as good a time as any to catch her off guard.

"Yes, I did." Margaret paused, frowning as though she found detail hard to recall. "Although not very well. We only met briefly on maybe one or two occasions.

Jaime sensed a slight reluctance, on Margaret's part, to elaborate but, fired up with a growing need to find some answers, she ploughed on regardless.

"I believe James and Kay, my mother, were friends before she met my father?"

Margaret, it appeared, found some difficulty with this idea. Shaking her head in obvious denial, then immediately retracting it.

"Yes, I suppose they must have known each other," Margaret conceded, albeit reluctantly. "I believe it was James who first brought her to Rykesby. He was a major in those days, so very handsome and a good catch. I understood that she was a nurse from a public hospital near his barracks – but you must already know that."

Jaime thought she detected a note of snobbery in Margaret's voice. It appeared that a lowly nurse wasn't considered a suitable companion for James.

"Anyway," Margaret continued speaking, oblivious to the implied insult to Kay and the nursing profession in general. "James brought her home one weekend and,

I suppose, that is when she met Edward because I do not recall her coming again."

Even if you did you wouldn't tell me, Jaime thought. She was sure Margaret Carr knew a lot more but, like Henry, was unwilling to open up. There seemed to be a conspiracy of silence surrounding James and Kay. At every turn, she found blank stares and brick walls but, there was still a slim chance, one presumably, that nobody else knew about.

"Oh! I must have got it wrong." Jaime feigned innocence in a last ditch attempt to pries information out of Margaret. "I understood… Somebody mentioned something… and, well, I suppose, it led me to believe that James and my mother had been friends for a long time – several years in fact.

Margaret reacted instantly and negatively, casting Jaime a horrified glance, before stating very firmly and confidently "I am sure your information is incorrect. James would not have… We would have known. Now, I really think we should rejoin the other guests." Her tone held a note of finality that precluded any further conversation.

Jaime followed Margaret back to the drawing room and circulated like a good guest making polite conversation with those who remained. Whilst all the time she longed to escape. She couldn't wait to get home and check out that handle. Mercifully there was no sign of Kimberly. Jaime gave a sigh of relief for that small blessing. Kimberly must have taken her advice and departed whilst she was talking with Margaret.

Turning the details over in her mind as she drove home, Jaime decided the evening had been both a limited success and a total failure. Henry and Margaret were most definitely out as sources of information. Getting anything, however small, out them would be like extracting blood from a stone, although Margaret had confirmed that James had brought Kay to Rykesby on at least one occasion. Kimberly too had proved uninformative, if that was the right word to describe her strange behavior.

Thinking about Kimberly, Jaime had initially formed the opinion that she was nothing more than an opportunist who was out to feather her own nest at Jaime's expense. Then later, when she'd reverted to type and begun abusing her, she'd revised her opinion. The situation was more complicated than first impressions suggested. How much of a threat Kimberly's attitude was likely to pose was impossible to gauge, there were so many ways it might impinge on her life but, Jaime reasoned, it was bound to have some bearing, not only to her peace of mind but also on her chances of making new friends.

Whitby was a relatively small town and its social life would, most likely, revolve around a fairly close-knit group. It therefore followed that Kimberly might be in a position to make things very difficult.

Jaime was, she had to admit, rather surprised that the Carr's had invited her tonight. Did Henry see himself as a peacemaker? If that wasn't the aim of the exercise then what was? Anything else was too awful to contemplate. It was Henry's task, as her lawyer, to protect her interests. Now, after tonight, her doubts about his competence had resurfaced with a vengeance.

After locking the doors firmly behind her. Jaime went upstairs to change, whilst still pondering the problem of whether or not to rely on Henry Carr's integrity. It was possible, although unlikely, that he'd had no ulterior motive for inviting Kimberly. However, combined with the earlier coincidences, like the way Kimberly turned up at Rykesby so promptly on her first visit there and then again the following morning. The fact she'd had access to a key and actually used it, on at least those two occasions, prompted Jaime to view the situation with concern.

There were, however, Jaime reasoned, some curious inconsistencies. If Kimberly and Henry were in league then surely Henry would surely have given her all the relevant details, outlining exactly how Jaime came to inherit. Yet because Kimberly seemed so singularly ill informed, particularly in regard to the actual will, Jaime had to discount collusion.

It might, however, be a wise move to consider engaging another lawyer. Somebody from a large city who had no connection with Whitby, the Fyre's, or with Ms. Marshall. Then, at least, she would know for sure that her private business remained private.

As for Kimberly… After tonight's little performance, Jaime was at a loss to know what to think. One part of her never wanted to set eyes on Kimberly again but there was still a small corner of her mind that found this decision hard to swallow, and that confused her.

Jaime could not see the prospect of there ever being anything more than armed neutrality between them and, bearing that in mind, the sensible thing would be to cut and run now but she didn't want to. She wanted to stay on here and to make it a proper home full of warmth and happiness. Kimberly wasn't going to spoil it for her, because she wouldn't give her the satisfaction. When Jaime took a long hard look at the problems she might encounter they boiled down to the chance of bumping into Kimberly socially. She could solve that problem by not accepting any invitations, no matter who they came from, without first checking who else was on the guest list. It was a depressing prospect but her freedom to live in peace was at stake and, like anybody else, she had a perfect right to that.

Whilst cleaning her face of make-up Jaime turned her attention back to the exciting prospect of the secret cavity. Would it yield up the information she sought?

Dressed comfortably in leggings and a sweater, she made her way downstairs again, this time, making for the kitchen, where she brewed a large pot of coffee. Then carrying it and a plate of biscuits, she headed for the library. Her search could take all night or even longer depending on what she discovered behind the paneling. Because she had not known how to reverse the cover Jaime had left the brass handle exposed all day. A slight risk, if anybody had broken in but definitely one worth taking, as she wasn't exactly sure how the mechanism operated.

Now, as she regarded the handle, Jaime felt just a little apprehensive. This was the moment of truth, the time she found out what secrets lay in store for her. Standing on tiptoe, she just managed to grasp hold of the brass handle but it wouldn't budge. She tried turning it both ways without success. Frowning with annoyance, she stepped back and considered carefully what other options there were.

Deciding that the handle must be stiff from little usage, she reached up again putting all her strength into trying to shift it and in doing so, she lost her balance. Jaime put all her weight on the handle to save herself from falling. Then she heard an eerie creaking sound and, wonder of wonders, the section of paneling actually moved.

Eureka!

Jaime laughed out loud. What had appeared to be a handle was, in fact, a cleverly designed security device – a sliding spigot to be pulled out not turned. Although her euphoria was short lived. On pushing aside the section of paneling, Jaime discovered, yet another obstacle, a solid looking door. Grabbing the large bunch of keys that Henry Carr had given her, she began the task of trying each one in turn. Only to face severe disappointment when all the keys were exhausted without any of them opening the lock.

It was so unfair, she thought, tossing the bunch of keys onto the desk in disgust then slumping down in the chair. Having built up her hopes only to have them dashed seemed, in some perverse way, to sum up her present luck. Jaime turned her attention to the large box of keys but there were so many jumbled together, more than she'd anticipated, they would need sorting into categories and she hadn't got the energy to do so tonight.

The long case clock struck the hour; Jaime counted the chimes, twelve, midnight. There wasn't much point in staying up any longer since there wasn't any hope of finding the key to the safe. Not that she really expected to get any sleep but, one had to go through the motions and anyway, she would at least be resting her body.

Pulling her diary toward her, Jaime checked her appointments for the following day. Tomorrow morning at ten o'clock, she was seeing the surveyor for an initial consultation. She'd decided on a local firm on the basis that they would be more used to dealing with this type of property. Her main objective, at this point, was to check the internal fabric of the building. One wall in the dining room, and in the bedroom above it, was giving her real cause for concern. There were probably many other problem areas too, which would show up in the external survey later in the month.

She also wanted to consider the renovation of the entire below stairs area. The dark passages and smell of damp would definitely not attract a housekeeper if she decided to employ somebody full time. Returning her coffee tray to the kitchen, she took a final look around, making sure all the points that she wanted to raise were firm in her mind.

****

Jaime responded to the doorbell at precisely ten o clock the following morning with no premonition of disaster. After all, she was expecting the surveyor, Ann Chambers, and her punctuality was a good sign.

The welcoming smile died, wiped instantly from her face, when Jaime found Kimberly standing where she'd expected another. Fear and apprehension vied with intense curiosity as to what had brought Kimberly here.

"Good morning, Ms. Fyre."

For a split second, she found Kimberly's formality gravely disconcerting, until she noticed the ghost of a smile flit across her face. That smile spelt trouble.

"Go away!" Jaime made to shut the door firmly in her face but, Kimberly forestalled her move, thrusting her laptop bag into the gap. "You're expecting me. Surely you remember making the appointment?"

Jaime reeled, almost fainting, dumbfounded by the sudden realization that, of all people, it was Kimberly who had come to advise her. What a nightmare!

"No I'm not. I'm expecting a surveyor, Ann Chambers. Where is she?"

"Oh dear… Didn't you get her letter?"

Kimberly's casual manner confirmed she knew very well that Jaime hadn't had a letter. She'd probably held it back deliberately just for the pleasure of catching her off guard.

"Ann is away on maternity leave." Kimberly smirked. "And I'm in between jobs, so how could I refuse when my old firm invited me back for the next six months to cover for her."

"Not with me! Anyway, you're an architect not a surveyor." Jaime couldn't imagine a worse scenario. Kimberly was the last person with whom she'd dream of doing business. Aside from the fact that she didn't trust Kimberly, there was an insoluble conflict of interests to consider. Convinced, beyond any doubt, that Kimberly would delight in condemning anything and everything outright in order to promote her own plans stiffened Jaime's resolve to send her packing.

"Don't you think you're being rather childish?" Kimberly's eyebrow quirked. "I'm fully qualified to deal with a repair and conservation survey. The very least you can do is give me a chance to prove my worth. Also you need to be aware that since I've driven out here, at your request, my fee stands regardless."

Put like that Jaime had to admit it sounded quite reasonable. However, that didn't lessen the feeling that Kimberly was railroading her down a certain track for her own devious ends. There was little doubt in Jaime's mind that Kimberly saw this situation as an ideal opportunity to worm her way in and disrupt Jaime's life. The question was should she let her? The risks were legion. She dithered, concerned that letting Kimberly into her house and her life might backfire and leave her much worse off, in every sense of the word. On the other hand, however, she did need advice and if Kimberly was the only available choice, then perhaps… "Isn't there somebody else, a colleague, who could come instead?" Jaime gave it one last shot, still unsure about the wisdom of giving in.

"Sorry, no. Everyone else is busy with ongoing commissions. I've taken on Ann Chambers' client list and, as you're on it, it's me or nobody."

This smooth response threw Jaime's world into confusion Kimberly had got everything all neatly sewn up. Jaime realized the futility of further debate she was in a no-win situation with Kimberly as her only choice. Unless she contacted another firm, but even that presented difficulties. Time being the big enemy. She wanted to get everything arranged, before returning to London.

"Very well." Jaime gave Kimberly a steely glare. "I suppose you'd better come in. First, though, I want an assurance that you'll behave in a professional manner, at all times, no matter what your personal thoughts, or opinions, might be."

"Always." Kimberly moved a step closer. "You've got nothing to worry about on that score. Before we start, however, I owe you an apology. Last night – I'm afraid I allowed my feelings to get the better of me – I was way out of order."

"Really?" skepticism dominated Jaime's tone. "Do tell me Kimberly, which specific bit of last night's exchange are you apologizing for?"

She wasn't in the mood to be generous, when Kimberly appeared to be under the mistaken impression that it was perfectly okay for her to behave badly – so long as she apologized afterwards. Yet she was not disposed to extend the same freedom to Jaime.

Kimberly shot her a slightly surprised glance then looked away. Leaving Jaime to congratulate herself on her tactics. It seemed, for once, she had managed outmaneuver her adversary. Although she was under no illusion that this state of affairs would last.

"All of it, I suppose," Kimberly admitted eventually, after a lengthy silence. "When I saw you there, with Clive, I was so eaten up with jealousy that I wanted to kill him, or you – and, what happened later… well, it was all tied up with that."

Kimberly jealous? Of her and Clive? The idea was so preposterous Jaime couldn't contain her laughter.

The sound echoed hollowly around the hall. Or was it inside her head? Jaime was not sure. In fact she wasn't sure of anything anymore.

Nevertheless, she released the door then stepped back to allow Kimberly inside. In her opinion, Kimberly had agreed to her demands far too readily, almost as if she'd anticipated Jaime's reaction and then formulated a plan to block any moves to dismiss her.

Jaime regarded Kimberly with suspicion, while she tried and failed to assess her hidden agenda. There had to be one, it stood to reason. Women like Kimberly always operated on the principle of personal gain rather than altruism. With a heavy heart, she closed the door then led the way through to the dining room. Time would tell, but instinct warned her to be very careful.

"I want to start with this room." Jaime adopted a cool businesslike tone. "That wall doesn't look right to me." She pointed to the wall in question.

Kimberly took a small black meter from her bag and homed in on the problem area.

"Yes, you've definitely got some real trouble here." She frowned and probed lower down. "You say it is like this in the room above as well?"

Jaime nodded.

"Then I'd say this is penetrating damp, caused by moisture getting in either through the roof or the wall, rather than rising damp. We'll find out for sure when we do the full external inspection. I'll take a look upstairs now if that's okay."

Do I have any say in the matter?

Jaime led the way. Although, Kimberly probably knew her way around the house without any help from her. Kimberly tested the bedroom wall in several places and noted the readings. Then they returned downstairs to the dining room.

"So what's next on the agenda?"

Jaime picked up her notes from the table, where she'd left them earlier, and turned to meet Kimberly's gaze. Unprepared for the electric shock which jolted her body, she quickly averted her gaze to consult the pages with a studied frown. She couldn't believe this was happening, not after last night and the fact that she'd identified Kimberly as a bitch of the first order. Why couldn't her body follow her brain in this matter?

This wasn't going to work. Jaime sought for a valid excuse to send Kimberly packing. If she couldn't even face Kimberly, what hope did they have of working together?

"Yes?" Kimberly prompted, clearly puzzled by her continued silence. When Jaime failed to respond, she snatched the notes right out her hand and began reading through them.

"Yes. I see what you're after." Kimberly's gaze rested briefly on Jaime then back to the notes. "You are aware that this is a listed building and, as a result, you'll require special planning consent to carry out conservation work and, more especially, for any alterations."

"That's what I thought." Jaime found her voice but not her equilibrium.

Thankfully, Kimberly seemed too busy to care. Having set the notes aside, she'd opened her briefcase and removed another oblong black box which she used several times, presumably taking measurements of the dining room.

Turning to the next page, she read it through quickly then raised her eyes, meeting Jaime's in a deceptively thoughtful appraisal that reduced Jaime to jelly. "Shall we?" Kimberly indicated the door to the passage with a casual wave of her hand, before gathering up both black boxes and notepad.

Suppressing a feeling of unease that everything seemed to be going far too smoothly and wondering where the catch was, Jaime led Kimberly through the door and down the steps into a narrow passageway. At the door to the housekeeper's accommodation, they halted briefly. Kimberly again consulted Jaime's notes and made some of her own then, having opened the door she stood aside obviously expecting Jaime to enter first.

This gentlemanly gesture flustered Jaime. Her heart raced into overdrive and her legs became unsteady. Deciding that she couldn't bear the prospect of being in such a small space with Kimberly, she stepped back signaling Kimberly to go ahead.

"Please excuse me a moment." In an effort to gain time and some much needed space to get her emotions under control, Jaime said the first thing that came into her head. "I've just remembered an important call I have to make. I'm sure you can manage without me."

Jaime didn't wait for a response before she fled back along the passage making for the library and comparative safety.

Kimberly's presence was having a disturbing influence on her equilibrium. Jaime flopped down onto the chair and dropping her head into her hands, searched for a way out of a mess, which she was finding increasingly intolerable. It wouldn't be easy, she decided quickly, unless Kimberly stepped out of line – which wasn't very likely in the present circumstances. It went right against the grain for Jaime to admit it, but Kimberly could not have been pleasanter or more professional in her handling of the situation this morning.

Quite atypical of the woman she had come to know. However, Jaime reminded herself warily, this sudden transformation did not necessarily put her on the side of the angels, or even signify a change of heart. Neither did it mean that she could take the gamble of softening her attitude toward Kimberly. If she valued her sanity, she couldn't afford to let Kimberly catch her off guard. Icy fingers gripped Jaime's heart, as she contemplated the awful consequences of letting Kimberly creep under her defenses. She had already experienced the result of a momentary lapse…

"Jaime?" Kimberly's voice penetrated her brain. Then, before she had begun to gather her wits, the library door flew open and Kimberly stood facing her.

"I wanted to ask…" Kimberly began speaking, then broke off, frowning, as she met Jaime's gaze.

"Oh! Um…" Kimberly shifted uneasily. "Am I disturbing you?"

Yes you are! Jaime wanted to scream, but didn't. It wouldn't serve any useful purpose to alert Kimberly to her unsettled state of mind. "No, not really." Although her distinctly icy manner said otherwise. "What was it you wanted to ask me?"

"It doesn't matter now. It can wait," Kimberly retreated, closing the door quietly behind her.

Jaime heaved a sigh of relief then relaxed back against the chair. Only another couple of hours, she reckoned, then Kimberly would be gone. Before that, however, she would have to find enough composure to face her and discuss the results of her inspection.

On balance, the risks of allowing Kimberly free rein outweighed those of being anywhere near her. By shutting herself away in the library she'd hit on a perfect defensive ploy and if she stayed in here as long as possible – another hour at least – the chances of escaping unscathed were even better.

When she finally emerged from her hiding place, it was twelve thirty. She had reckoned on Kimberly being through by one o'clock and quite reasonably, thought half an hour ample time to discuss her findings. She found Kimberly in the dining room, seated at the table using an expensive-looking laptop to write up her notes. A good sign? Jaime thought so, congratulating herself on her good timing, it looked as if Kimberly had completed her investigations. Kimberly glanced up briefly as Jaime entered the room then returned immediately to her task. Initially put out, by being ignored, Jaime soon became absorbed in watching Kimberly's nimble fingers fly over the keys. Admiration and envy for her dexterity overtook the irritation. Recognition of a razor sharp brain, and exceptional hand eye coordination, forced her, yet again, to revise her opinion of Kimberly. Perhaps she wasn't the spoilt rich bitch she'd first thought. It took dedication and hard work to succeed in ones chosen profession and, from what she'd seen so far. Kimberly appeared to have done just that.

"All done!" Kimberly folded her laptop and stood up. "I will send you a detailed report shortly but, in the meantime, I thought we might usefully discuss the broad outline over lunch?"

Lunch!

Jaime recoiled from the prospect of lunching with Kimberly. She didn't want to give any her encouragement. Having Kimberly in the house all morning had been bad enough, but going out to lunch with her would be even worse – it was unthinkable.

"We have to talk," Kimberly said, as though reading Jaime's mind. "And as I'm absolutely starving, I thought we could combine talk with lunch?"

Just imagining the scenario gave Jaime a bad case of the jitters. Aside from the fact that she feared Kimberly's motives, Jaime also doubted that she'd be able to eat a single morsel in her company. Even considering it was courting trouble – like supping with the devil without the advantage of the proverbial long-handled spoon. No, she gave a convulsive shudder, the idea was unthinkable and she would tell her so.

"Where did you have in mind?" Jaime silently cursed her wayward mouth for uttering the words. The direct opposite of what she'd intended. A tacit acceptance rather than a blunt refusal.

"There's a decent bar just up the road from here." Kimberly frowned, clearly irritated by her question. Then, without any further explanation, she brushed Jaime aside to concentrate on collecting her things together and returning them to her bag.

Jaime found it rather disconcerting that Kimberly hadn't forced the issue but, instead, left her free to make up her own mind. She dithered, torn between a desire to learn what Kimberly had worked out and her fear of having anything to do with her. Her careless mouth had dropped her right into this potentially explosive situation, one that she'd have much rather avoided but, given the circumstances, it didn't seem she could escape. Although a bar lunch sounded safe enough – there would be other people around to offer assistance if Kimberly turned nasty again. Jaime hesitated over her decision. Admitting fear, even to oneself, always promoted a sense of vulnerability and in this instance, she had a very good reason to be concerned. Kimberly had already demonstrated just how volatile she could be, not once, but on several occasions.

"Well, I'm off now," Kimberly snapped the catches on her laptop bag, picked it up, then made for the door. Only turning her head to enquire, "Are you coming?" as an afterthought.

She'd done it again! Jaime realized, a second too late, that Kimberly had pulled off another coup. Anger replaced the feeling of apprehension, making her blood boil and her brain whirl. As usual, Kimberly had dealt herself all the right cards leaving Jaime to make the best of the rest. Her strategy was crystal clear now. If she didn't go to lunch with Kimberly then she wasn't going to get a chance to discuss the situation or have any chance to input her own ideas.

Jaime saw that Kimberly didn't intend to wait whilst she dithered. She'd reached the door and was almost through it before she found the voice to respond. "Give me two minutes." Jaime threw caution to the wind. Urged on by a feeling of reckless euphoria, she raced upstairs to tidy herself. Having successfully suppressed her remaining fears, she took some comfort from the thought that little harm could ensue from joining Kimberly for a working lunch?

CHAPTER EIGHT

Coming more slowly down the staircase five minutes later, she found Kimberly in the hall studying the suit of armor. She glanced up smiling, and that fleeting smile all but took Jaime's breath away.

"What are you going to do with all this stuff?" Kimberly waved a hand over the collection.

With supreme effort, Jaime forced herself to complete her descent of the stairs before she responded.

"I haven't decided yet, although I'll probably donate it all to a museum." She deliberately kept her response vague so as not to give Kimberly any ideas.

"Best place for it." Kimberly turned and made for the door.

Biting on her lip, an annoying habit she was prone to in times of stress, Jaime forced her feet to move.

That Kimberly hadn't disagreed, was a sign of real progress. Although Jaime's suspicious mind still mistrusted Kimberly's motives. What had brought about this morning's astounding change of attitude? After last night, when Kimberly had questioned her morals, and her honesty, so forcibly, Jaime had given up all hope of proving to her that she was a completely innocent victim of circumstance.

Kimberly had decided, right from the outset, without an ounce of proof, that she was a conniving, mercenary bitch with doubtful morals and nothing Jaime had done or said, so far, had made her alter that view.

Once outside though her pace slowed, faltering, as a new concern surfaced. Jaime came to an abrupt halt, alongside her own car, casting a worried glance at Kimberly waiting by the Range Rover. This is so stupid. Jaime chastised herself for the inability to make one simple commitment, that of traveling with Kimberly. The idea of being confined in a vehicle with Kimberly for however long it took them to get to this bar and back – always supposing that she brought her back – set her nerves jangling.

If previous experience was anything to go by there was considerably more than a fifty-fifty chance that Kimberly would delight in provoking yet another fight and the prospect of being ditched, somewhere in the back of beyond, certainly did not appeal. "I think I'll take my car." Jaime called out, keeping her tone neutral. "Then you won't have waste your time bringing me back here."

Kimberly's reaction was predictable. Her relaxed pose transformed instantly into a glacial scowl. Expecting yet another ugly scene, Jaime hesitated expecting Kimberly to argue the point in her usual aggressive manner, but, unexpectedly, she didn't. Instead, she merely shrugged dismissively then turned away and slid into driving seat of the Range Rover.

Expelling a long drawn out sigh of relief, Jaime waited until Kimberly started her engine before following suit. A moment later, the Range Rover sped away down the drive, trailing a cloud of dust and gravel.

Following Kimberly gave Jaime valuable time to think.

There were so many facets to Kimberly that she didn't understand – her erroneous opinions, her fluctuations of mood and her obsession with some long dead feud – to name just three. Every time they met, Jaime discovered some new trait which served to confuse her more. Kimberly was a complex mix of fire and ice, and, rather like a chameleon, she seemed able to adopt a new persona without warning.

Deep in thought she was nearly caught off guard as Kimberly slowed, the indicator flashing right, before turning into a narrow lane. Jaime followed, negotiating the bends with care, unsure what lay ahead.

The Ship Inn, as its name suggested, was right by the sea. Kimberly brought the Range Rover to a halt at the end of the lane, slotting in neatly between a Honda and a battered orange truck parked alongside the short stretch of sandy beach. Apart from the inn, the other vehicles, and a couple of upturned rowing boats, the place was deserted.

After parking on the other side of the truck. Jaime stood gazing out to sea for a few moments. Then having gathered her thoughts and her courage, she turned and followed Kimberly into the bar.

The barman greeted Kimberly by name, clearly knowing her well then, turning his gaze to Jaime, eyed her with open speculation.

"What can I get you?" Kimberly made no move to introduce her. Jaime fumed inwardly at being treated so rudely, biting back the urge to declare she had changed her mind. Now she'd come this far, it made sense to stay put and see this thing through to the bitter end.

Bitter being the operative word she thought with grim presentiment. All their previous encounters had finished in slanging matches, why should this one be any different. Although there was always a chance, if only a slim one, that everything would pan out differently today. For once Kimberly was behaving with a measure of restraint but, for some uncanny reason that worried rather than reassured Jaime.

"Mineral water please." Jaime refused to look directly at either Kimberly or the barman. Then she sauntered nonchalantly over to a table by the window and gave her full attention to the menu.

She was dismayed to discover that they were the only customers – foolishly, she had expected it to be a busy crowded place. Although, thinking about it now, she realized that Kimberly had probably known all along it would be this quiet. It was rather late in the year for tourists and too far out of the town for the local lunch trade. Kimberly was very clever she had to grant her that, once again, she'd managed to put Jaime in a position of hopeless disadvantage.

"Seen anything you fancy?" Kimberly set her drink on the table then slid into the seat opposite. Adding, without waiting to hear Jaime's opinion. "I can heartily recommend the crab – they catch them locally."

Jaime was tempted. She particularly liked crab, favoring it above all other shellfish, but she felt too much on edge to enjoy it today. Maybe a sandwich would be a better choice. With a shake of her head, Jaime put the menu down then raised her gaze to find Kimberly regarding her intently. Her heart lurched, an uncomfortable, yet timely, reminder of her vulnerability where Kimberly was concerned.

"I'll just have a ham sandwich." Jaime looked away quickly so Kimberly wouldn't see her confusion.

"It's your choice," Kimberly remarked quietly. Then in a louder voice. "Two ham sandwiches, please, Andy!" Picking up her laptop bag, she extracted her notes and quickly scanned through them, before taking a sip of her beer.

"Right!" Kimberly broke the tense silence. "Where shall I start?"

"You're the expert. You tell me!" Jaime immediately regretted her tone. Deliberately provoking Kimberly was a very dangerous game to play. She was much too wily, and she didn't need any encouragement to turn nasty. However, she was the professional, and Jaime was employing her, so the ball was in Kimberly's court. It wasn't her place to tell Kimberly what to do it was up to her to prove her worth.

"Okay." Kimberly's gaze flicked briefly across her face, a deeply disturbing look that left Jaime's heart hammering. She shivered, feeling as though Kimberly had penetrated her innermost soul.

"Well, on the face of it, you had some very sound ideas. We just need to clear up a couple of points before I..." She broke off, to thank Andy for the sandwiches.

"What was I saying? Ah. Yes! Your ideas are very sound, I couldn't fault them but I think we might be wise to consider enlarging on the…"

Jaime nibbled abstractedly at her sandwich whilst listening to Kimberly. She hadn't felt hungry but, she suddenly found her appetite, once she started eating. The sandwich was surprisingly good. Fresh crusty home-baked bread, with generous slices of juicy ham. Real ham, nothing like the tasteless rubbery stuff one usually got. The good food had the effect of relaxing her and dispelling most of the apprehension that had accompanied Kimberly's unexpected arrival on her doorstep. Fears, which had grown, unabated, throughout a long and difficult morning, now seemed groundless.

Kimberly hadn't put a foot wrong, Jaime was loath to admit it but, she actually admired her ability to set aside her true feelings and get on with the task in hand.

"…Well, that's about it," Kimberly said, then leant back in her chair and finished her beer. "Is there anything that you're not entirely happy with?"

"No, it all sounds quite straightforward." Jaime said cautiously. "Although, naturally, I would like to vet your plans before we reach an agreement on submitting them for approval."

She wasn't prepared to take any chances.

"Certainly," Kimberly agreed blandly. "It might take about four to six weeks but I'll get them to you as soon as I can."

Four weeks or more! Jaime went cold. By then she would be back in London and the very last thing she wanted to do was let Kimberly have that address.

"I take it you won't still be at Rykesby?" Kimberly eyed her keenly. "Well that's no problem." She pushed the notepad across the table toward Jaime. "Just jot down your address then I can pop them in the mail."

Jaime recoiled from the notepad as though it was red hot. Every instinct warned of danger. She wasn't happy about it. London was her safety net, somewhere Kimberly couldn't touch her. If she caved in now, she feared that she'd be making a fatal error of judgment.

"I'm not too sure where I'll be." Jaime sought a believable excuse, one that would both satisfy Kimberly and gain her valuable breathing space. Besides, it really was half true. The research trip for, Ransom – currently in the planning stage – would take her away to various European countries over the next couple of months. The one obvious answer was to have her send the plans via Henry Carr but Jaime had reservations about the wisdom of even that. She wasn't sure she could, or should, put her trust in the lawyer.

"What about your London address?" Kimberly's tone carried a hint of irritation. "Surely it will find you there?"

Jaime barely suppressed her gasp of horror. "What makes you think I live in London?" There was an edge of panic in her voice. How did Kimberly know? Could she have tracked down her actual address?

"I know you do!" The hint of irritation developed into anger. "Why are you being so damned difficult?"

Why indeed? Jaime wondered. She raised her head meeting Kimberly's withering glare with a determinedly stony expression.

She'd known it was too good to last. What was their problem? Why were they unable to hold a civilized conversation for more than ten minutes without full scale war breaking out? Normally she got on well with everybody but Kimberly got under her skin – like a festering sore – there was no other way to describe it.

"Isn't this is becoming just a little ridiculous. What's wrong with you? Why are you so against giving me an address?"

Kimberly's cavalier attitude only served to make Jaime dig her toes in deeper. What gave Kimberly the right to question Jaime's reasons? Wasn't she entitled to keep, and protect, her privacy? Obviously not, as far as Kimberly was concerned. She had to be the most objectionable apology for a human being that Jaime had ever had the misfortune to meet. It was quite apparent that Kimberly expected her to jump through hoops, on her command, regardless of Jaime's own feelings in the matter. Although, in this instance, she was actually doing herself a disservice. The more pressure Kimberly applied the more determined Jaime became to keep her at bay.

"Here!" She thrust the notepad closer, ignoring Jaime's earlier adamant refusal completely. "Just write the blasted address down and be done with it!"

"I can't!" Jaime pushed back her chair and stood up, glowering. "Don't you understand plain English? I've already told you I have no idea where I'll be!"

Kimberly frowned, obviously puzzled but, true to her nature, unbowed.

Jaime savored the small but significant victory. Kimberly had tried, once again, to back her into a corner but, this time, she had managed to effect an escape.

"If you can't or won't give me an address then how am I supposed to send you the plans?" Kimberly's combative tone grated.

"Easy." Jaime hit on the perfect solution to her predicament. "If I call you in four weeks, you can tell me whether the plans are ready and, if they are, then I'll arrange for a courier to collect them."

Kimberly nodded, clearly stunned into silence by the neat maneuver and Jaime's stubborn refusal to give way.

Jaime observed Kimberly covertly. She shook her head, as though trying to stimulate her brain. She would, be eager to regain the initiative as quickly as possible. A circumstance, Jaime was equally determined, would never happen. Until today, Kimberly had been the one in total control of the situation using her not inconsiderable powers of coercion and persuasion to dictate events. Now it was proving immensely satisfying to turn the tables on her. Keeping up the pressure, Jaime glanced at her watch.

"I'm afraid I must go. Thank you for lunch."

Jaime left the bar without a backward glance, and drove home in a much more confident frame of mind. Now she had managed to overcome this latest attempt at domination, she was sure Kimberly would not be able touch her any more. Her ability to influence events and make life hell in the process was finished, kaput, along with any lingering ideas she might still harbor about getting her hands on Rykesby. Heartened by this conclusion Jaime swept like a whirlwind through the house, humming a catchy tune as she went. Content that she had won the battle, she savored her victory by dancing a little jig.

Feeling relaxed and at peace, she spent the rest of the afternoon exploring the upstairs rooms again, especially the studio where James had obviously spent many hours painting watercolors or developing his vast array of photographs in the attached dark room. His photography fell into two distinct schools, general landscapes and portraits. The landscapes depicted mostly foreign lands, scenes of Asia, Africa, and beautiful shots of a frozen wasteland, possibly Antarctica, but the portraits gave her pause for thought. Aside from a series of albums charting Kimberly's life from a tiny baby to adulthood, the remainder fell into one broad category: sexual gratification.

The subjects were all petite blondes, the very women Kimberly had described as his favorites, with poses ranging from virginal innocence, through artistically erotic, to the positively pornographic. Jaime studied them all with keen interest. The pornography wasn't a particular turn on but neither did it shock her. Explicit sexual content often featured in her stories as it went hand in glove with the underworld, where large scale fraud, money laundering, gambling, drugs, prostitution, and people trafficking were a fact of life. A world that sometimes impinged on an ordinary or naïve soul duped into some illegal act by clever crooks. Usually, but not always, Granby arrived on the scene, just in time, to save these unfortunates from themselves and expose the criminals.

Jaime spent quite a while trying to discover a link between the women portrayed in the photographs and her mother, Kay. There was something particularly disturbing in the similarity of them all. Why had James fixated on one type of woman? She decided that he must have been a very lonely man in later life, clinging to these images in place of the woman of his dreams.

Having had her fill of naked bodies, and the overt eroticism that made her acutely aware of her sexuality, Jaime called it a day. As an afterthought, she picked up the album depicting Kimberly from early teen to adult and carried it downstairs. Maybe studying these photographs of the milestones in the ordinary life of her adversary would help answer some of the questions buzzing through her head.

The following few days flew by in a whirl of activity most of it connected in some way or other to Rykesby. Jaime had meetings with various people including Henry Carr, her tenant farmers, and the local heritage group; it was they who shared Jaime's interest in both the preservation of the building and its protection from rampant commercialism. Sadly, very little of the original thirteenth century hall had survived a complete rebuild by James Fyre in the mid eighteenth century. Although remnants, like the inner hall, the staircase, and the long gallery gave some clues to the earliest structure. Jaime's aim now was to research what little did remain and preserve it from further decay by attacks from time, dry rot, and woodworm. From her observations, little in the way of conservation had taken place for years, and none at all during the last forty years. Margaret Carr hadn't exaggerated when she said, "James really let the property deteriorate." Jaime faced an uphill struggle to catch up with the major repair work.

Thankfully, she'd had no more unsettling visits from Kimberly. However, her absence and silence proved almost as disturbing as her presence. Jaime shook her head over this sad state of affairs. She needed to find something to explain this obsession with Kimberly that wouldn't go away no matter how hard she tried to shut the bitch out of her mind. To understand and resolve why an unbearable craving for sex, with a woman she hardly knew and didn't even like, dogged her by day and by night.

Other matters also added their weight to her state of sleep deprivation. Jaime still hadn't resolved the problem of the missing key. The large box of keys, for which she'd had such high hopes, proved a real disappointment. So far she'd discounted over one hundred keys already and with just a few possibles still to test, she had reluctantly come to the conclusion that the box was nothing more than dumping ground for redundant keys. The key she wanted must be somewhere more accessible, available for use at a moment's notice. With this in mind she had continued to comb the rooms, both upstairs and down, and every conceivable hiding place therein, without result. Much as it pained her to do so she finally set a deadline, if she didn't find the key by the end of next week then she would give up and call a locksmith.

There were still a few unexplored areas to tackle first, the master bedroom being one. Jaime had been putting it off for no better reason than it was the room James had used and still contained all his clutter, clothes, and personal possessions. Plus the fact she'd reckoned on the need to set aside a whole, uninterrupted, day for this room and such days were few and far between.

Indeed, emptying out the closets and drawers proved a lengthy task. She made two piles, one for taking to the charity shop and the other for recycling. All his suits and a good proportion of the shirts went onto the charity shop pile along with sweaters, shoes and several pairs of new socks.

Jaime felt the fabric of his dress-shirt, as she folded it and placed on the pile. It was good stuff, old, but well cared for, somebody would get a lot of wear out of it and the same went for the rest of the clothes. Having discovered a set of matching luggage in one of the closets, Jaime packed everything into the cases then carried them one by one down to the car.

The task had taken much longer than expected the long case clock chimed five as she dragged the last and largest bag along the gallery. With a weary sigh, Jaime halted at the top of the staircase, balancing the heavy bag on the top tread whilst she flexed her muscles. She felt decidedly hot and sticky and badly in need of a long relaxing soak in the bath. Thinking longingly of the warm scented water that awaited her, she stirred herself. Lowering the heavy burden down the staircase, step by step, restraining a natural impulse to hurry.

The light was failing as she approached the car. With one final heave, she thrust her load into the waiting gap. A contented sigh escaped her as she closed the tailgate.

"Running away already?"

Kimberly's mocking drawl sent icy shimmers racing down Jaime's spine and wiped the smile of satisfaction from her lips.

"No. Why should I?" Jaime felt the rush of blood to her cheeks as her heart went into overdrive. She was totally thrown off guard by this totally unexpected, and unwelcome, turn of events.

Surely she'd made it plain enough that Kimberly wasn't welcome and yet here she was again, as large as life, and still intent on hounding her. Jaime wanted to scream, hit Kimberly, throw something, anything to end this nightmare and send her packing.

She had vowed the last time Kimberly pulled this stunt that she'd never give the bitch another chance to take her unawares but all her good intentions had come to naught. No, that wasn't quite true, Jaime sighed. There's not much any person can do against such persistence other than lock oneself away, and that would solve anything.

Taking her time, she turned around slowly, praying that Kimberly wouldn't notice how flushed her face was or, at least, put it down to her recent exertions.

"I'm just tak—" Shit! Jaime stopped speaking abruptly.

No! Why should I justify myself to her? It's none of her business.

Belatedly, she did what she should have done in the first instance. "What are you doing here, Kimberly? I don't remember issuing an open invitation."

Kimberly shrugged. Dismissing the challenge with the contempt that Jaime had come to expect from her. No sign of embarrassment, no apology, nothing, other than wanton arrogance. "I didn't think I needed one." She moved forward, closing the gap to a mere couple of feet and scanned Jaime's face with hard speculative eyes. "I thought you'd got that nonsense out of your system."

Nonsense?

What planet is this moron from?

Jaime huffed in total disbelief, whilst attempting to contain her anger. Kimberly hadn't listened to a word she'd said her presence here this evening was proof of that.

"What do you want Kimberly?" Jaime barely kept her anger in check. "I am rather busy, so I'd appreciate it if you'd leave, right now."

Kimberly stood her ground, she didn't move a muscle. "We need to talk. I want to make you—"

"I'm sure you do!" Jaime interjected, giving Kimberly a contemptuous glance. "I'm sure you've got lots more insults to throw at me but, I'm afraid, you are wasting your time I'm not interested."

Without waiting for a reaction, she turned away, back toward the house and safety. If she could just make it inside and lock the door.

CHAPTER NINE

"Not so fast. We're not done yet."

Jaime's attempt to slam the heavy door and turn the key in the lock proved futile in the face of Kimberly's superior strength, and determination. She pushed hard, defying all Jaime's effort to keep her out.

"Get out of my house!" Jaime tried to assert herself as she moved quickly to bar the way through the inner door but that, too, became a fruitless exercise. Kimberly merely thrust her aside as if she were nothing more than a rag doll before she strode onward.

Bitch!

Jaime raced after her adversary, anger driving her forward, until they came face to face with each other in the center of the great hall where Kimberly had taken up a tactical position.

"You won't solve anything by constantly running away from me, and from the fact that I have right on my side." Kimberly fired her opening salvo in Jaime's face.

"No?" Jaime chose to deny Kimberly the satisfaction of being right. She refused to give an inch in this fight for the upper hand.

"No!" Kimberly caught hold of Jaime's arm. "This time, we're going to stay put and talk this through until I'm satisfied we've finally got at the truth – the whole truth." She returned Jaime's steely glare, then added. "I've had enough lies and evasive tactics to last me a lifetime."

"I've had enough of you, period!" Jaime wriggled hard, trying unsuccessfully to escape from the vice-like grip, her frustration with Kimberly's attitude growing apace. "Get real, Kimberly, we could both stand here until hell freezes over and I doubt that you'd ever accept what I tell you as the truth. You have a misguided, fairytale, notion fixed in your head and you'll refuse to believe anything that doesn't exactly fit that scenario."

"There is nothing misguided or fanciful about my right of inheritance." Kimberly let go of Jaime's arm and waved her hand to encompass the area where they stood, as if staking her claim. "I've known it was on the cards all my life, there was never any doubt until you came along with your false claim."

Jaime sighed. After all the hassles they were back to square one. Although she hated the idea of capitulation in the face of threats, maybe it was time to do as Kimberly wanted and call a halt to this ridiculous carousel of claim and counter-claim. Although, given Kimberly's intransigence, resolving their differences and sorting fact from fiction wouldn't be an easy task. She snatched a calming breath then waded in. "Who told you? Who led you to believe a myth? Who gave you false expectations? I'm quite sure it wasn't James, or Henry Carr. Think about it... By my reckoning, both men would have had more sense."

Kimberly looked startled by Jaime's challenge. She shook her head then, seemingly contradicting herself, she nodded. "Uncle James always promised he would look after me."

"He did..." Jaime struggled with her conscience. "Well, I'm sure he must have given you plenty over the years."

Kimberly huffed loudly. "You're way off beam if you think the... Don't forget, I was...no, *I am*, his only relative. You can't count the little gifts he gave me for birthdays or Christmas."

"Or just because you were a *good little girl*... No, I wasn't." Jaime didn't want to betray a confidence by revealing what Henry had told her but...

What the hell!

Jaime weighed the moral argument. Kimberly wasn't playing fair so why should she?

"I was thinking more about the big things, very big if my information is correct. What about the deeds to Aspen Cottage? Your substantial trust fund? The way James helped your career by buying you a partnership? Not forgetting the way he financed your degree? You didn't have to juggle two jobs to pay your way through college, like the rest of us. Oh, no! James handed it all to you on a plate."

"How do you know all this?" Kimberly's incandescent glare spoke louder than any words. "You have no right to poke your nose into my private affairs. I'm not the one who has to prove anything."

Such was Kimberly's vehemence that Jaime took an involuntary step back before recovering her equilibrium. "That's a matter of opinion..." Jaime allowed a hint of sarcasm to drip from her lips. "You are perfectly willing to pry into my life and to accuse me of all sorts of devious acts but you don't like it when you're confronted with your own tactics. Face the truth, Kimberly, you have done extremely well out of James one way and another. You had his company, and his support, while you were growing up, as well as the full benefit of his money. Don't begrudge me my share."

Kimberly's lips formed a tight line as her disapproving glare focused on Jaime. "What I do begrudge is you swanning in here after his death, claiming false kinship, and scooping the pot. You never once showed your face while Uncle James was alive. Let's face facts, Jaime, you wouldn't have dared, he would have seen through your little charade in a couple of minutes."

"That's where you're wrong..." Jaime knew her protest would fall on deaf ears. "However, as James isn't here now, there is no way I can prove that point."

Why did James leave me to face the full force of Kimberly's wrath without any protection?

Once again Jaime cursed James for putting her in this awkward position. He must have known, when he wrote and updated the will, how strongly Kimberly felt about Rykesby and her inheritance. Anybody who knew Kimberly well must have realized how she would react to the arrival of another legatee, a usurper to her presumption as the only beneficiary. What about Henry Carr? He, too, must bear some responsibility. Why hadn't he done his job and advised James to make the situation clearer to Kimberly? Of course, there was always a chance that he had done so and, for whatever reason, James had overruled him. Jaime could only guess at the sequence of events since she knew little or nothing about what had gone on in meetings between those parties.

There were so many unanswered questions. Things that Jaime desperately wanted to know about the past. Like where she, and her mother, fitted into this curious setup. No doubt the answers were there to be found, but until she discovered a way to open the locked door they would remain elusive.

Does Kimberly know how to get into that secret place?

Jaime resisted the temptation to enquire. Asking Kimberly could only complicate matters. With so much at stake, Jaime wanted to be alone when the door was opened and the contents were revealed —

"Of course you can't."

Kimberly's barbed response scythed through Jaime's deliberations.

"That, presumably, was part of your plan. As was waiting just long enough after his death so that the false claim you'd submitted through Henry Carr would clear probate within days of your arrival. My lawyer found the sequence of events extremely fishy, but she didn't have time to gather the evidence of fraud that she needed to halt the grant of probate. That's not to say she has given up. Depending what we discover over the coming weeks and months, we still have the option to involve the police."

Threats of police action sounded a bit farfetched, even for Kimberly. "I have nothing to fear on that score," Jaime said firmly. Indeed, Henry Carr had assured her, on several occasions, that everything was above board and that she had no reason to fear Kimberly or her legal team.

"I must say you sound very sure of yourself." Kimberly smirked. "I'd hate to be in your shoes when the shit hits the fan."

"Nor me in yours, Kimberly. Who will duck first?" The idea of them both ducking to avoid the fallout drew a burst of ironic laughter from Jaime, the sound returning as a dull echo off the wooden paneling. By pursuing this line Kimberly was riding for a heavy fall. "Indeed, if I were you, I'd change my lawyer since your woman seems to be falling down on her job. The will has completed probate so all the relevant information therein is available for scrutiny. Failing that, why don't you simply order a copy of the will for yourself? You'll find the answers all your questions in the document."

"That won't be necessary," Kimberly said. "We already have a copy. It's the contents that don't add up. The will reads exactly like your elaborate fairy tale. *The long lost relation discovered by chance at the final moment and made the heir at the expense of the rightful claimant*. That sort of thing is the stuff of fiction and doesn't happen in real life."

Jaime frowned. That was not how Henry Carr had described events. In fact she understood that James had written her into his will when she was a small child. Although she hadn't actually seen a copy of the original will, nor any rewrites. Perhaps the real problem here was that the final will looked different from earlier versions. Yet another puzzle to solve. A little digging into Henry Carr's archives was the next obvious step. Surely she was entitled to see, and have paper copies of, all the relevant documents since their existence played such an important part in her life and her peace of mind? From day one, Jaime had sensed that Henry Car was keeping something from her, something vitally important. Until now, Jaime hadn't wanted to rock the boat by insisting that he must divulge whatever it was. However, in the light of current events the information might well be the key to unlocking the secrets of the past and, more significantly, a way of giving Kimberly undeniable proof of her right of inheritance.

"You really need to do your homework, Kimberly," Jaime said, taking firm stand. "I'm hardly a *last minute addition,* as you put it. As I understand the situation my name has been in the frame for something like thirty years. The only *last minute* part, as I've already told you, is that I had no prior knowledge of my inclusion in or anything to do with the will until I received Henry Carr's letter. I came here, at his invitation, and discovered a branch of my family that I never previously knew existed: James, Rykesby, and *you.* How do you think the shock of these unexpected revelations affected me?" Jaime suddenly felt light headed, like the room was revolving slowly around her. The only time she remembered feeling this strange was during her first term at college when, egged on by the crowd, she'd taken one drink too many. Not a pleasant experience and one that she'd been careful never to repeat. Besides which, Jaime knew, it wasn't alcohol this time; she hadn't had a drink in days.

"Now you've strayed away from a fairy tale into pure fantasy." Kimberly sounded irritated. "Where's your proof? Where are the documents to back up this ridiculous assertion?"

"There is proof but I don't have it here, you'll have to—"

"I thought not!" Kimberly waggled her hand dismissively. "I suppose you expect me to wait patiently while you prepare another lot of dodgy paperwork?"

"If I could just finish..." Jaime sighed. She desperately wanted to sit down but that meant moving from the spot and she wasn't sure she had the strength to walk anywhere. "I was trying to say you'll have to speak to Henry Carr, he has the paperwork all the proof you need, I'm done with..."

****

Jaime moaned softly, reveling in the pleasure of being held and kissed. At least it felt like she was being kissed. Gradually, as the sensual message began to spread its candescent fire through her body. Then, suddenly, she came back to earth with an almighty bump. Her head cleared and she became conscious of her surroundings.

Why am I stretched out on the chaise longue?

The facts didn't add up. It wasn't just that Jaime couldn't remember anything, she felt as if a whole chunk of her life had gone missing.

Minutes? Even hours?

No, not hours, it was still only dusk outside.

Why is Kimberly bent over me as if she...we...?

The mere fact that Jaime didn't know what had happened between being in the hall and where she found herself now was particularly disturbing.

Had they...?

Kimberly moved closer, crowding into Jaime's personal space.

"Get away from me!" Jaime pushed her aside and tried to sit up but her body seemed reluctant to obey.

A vague sense of being in Kimberly's arms flitted into her head and was gone before it took on any substance. Flushed, trembling, mortified, and totally confused by the images that played through her mind, like ephemeral wisps of cloud in the sky, Jaime could not, dare not, meet Kimberly's gaze for fear of what she might see reflected therein. Smugness certainly, she decided unhappily, but what else? Cold indifference, scorn, contempt, revulsion? The list was endless.

What have I done?

An involuntary gasp of dismay and distress escaped her lips. How had things got so far out of hand?

Has she deliberately used my vulnerability to further her own nefarious ends?

"Jaime, Look at me." The unexpected softness of Kimberly's tone grabbed Jaime's attention. She met Kimberly's gaze, warily at first, then perplexed, because her eyes held none of the expressions she'd expected. Just concern. "You fainted."

"Did I?" The revelation caught Jaime completely off guard. She shook her head, rejecting the notion. "No..." She'd never fainted in her entire life.

"Yes, you did," Kimberly confirmed. "You gave me quite a fright keeling over like that. I carried you in here for your own safety."

And... What else?

How long was I out of it?

Once again, Jaime struggled to sit up and take stock of the situation, even though she had this strange floaty feeling when she lifted her head off the cushion.

Notwithstanding her wooziness, she was eager to get back on her feet as quickly as possible. This recumbent position put her at a distinct disadvantage and played right into Kimberly's hands. She'd have given anything to put the clock back to before – before Kimberly invaded her well-ordered world and turned it upside down or if not that far, then certainly the last half hour or so.

"Stay put." Kimberly pushed Jaime back down.

"Don't!" Driven by blind panic, Jaime brushed Kimberly's hand away. She couldn't endure Kimberly's touch on her bare arm.

"I won't hurt you," Kimberly remarked stiffly, and then her tone changed, softened. "I'm just concerned why you fainted. You should see a doctor and get a check-up. Are you pregnant?"

"No!" Jaime shook her head to reinforce the point and then wished she hadn't. "Pregnancy is the one thing I can rule out with absolute certainty."

"I only asked... No need to get huffy!" Kimberly smirked.

"What's so funny?" Jaime struggled to understand why Kimberly looked so pleased with herself.

"Nothing."

"Really?"

"If you must know... you sort of half answered the question that's been bothering me since we first met."

"And that is? Was?"

"Do I have to spell it out?"

"I think you do."

"Well, if you must know, I've been trying to decide where you stand... sexually that is. You are a bit of an enigma, always giving out mixed signals, and for once I can't trust my gaydar."

"You didn't know... yet you kissed me?" Kimberly was a devious bitch.

"I know... I couldn't help myself when you looked like you wanted to eat me, but then you reacted so violently and I began to have doubts."

"Ah! I see your problem." Jaime nodded. "Just for the record, my reaction to your kiss was based solely on your unreasonable behavior, it had nothing whatsoever to do with my sexual orientation."

Kimberly quirked her brow. "And that is?"

"I thought we'd established that point… I stand on the same side of the line as you. Now, can we change the subject?" She really didn't want to have this conversation with Kimberly of all people. Her sexuality was immaterial since, as far as she was concerned, they would never reach a stage in their relationship where it had any relevance.

"We still haven't come to a conclusion on the main question, why you fainted."

"I have no idea. I'm not prone to fainting." Jaime sighed. "Maybe I buckled under the strain of being bullied – trying to come to terms with and adjust to recent events has not been easy and your attitude has made things a hundred times more difficult. Or I just did too much – I've spent the whole day sorting through the master bedroom, packing James' clothes to donate to charity."

"That's what you were loading into the car?"

"Yes. Not that it is any of your business what I do, or why I do it. I just wish you'd go away and leave me alone."

"No, not yet. You're in no fit state to be alone. I want to ensure you'll be okay." Kimberly's voice was full of solicitude. "Have you eaten?"

"Eaten?" Jaime echoed the question, her tone full of blank amazement.

"Yes. As in putting food in your mouth." Kimberly gave a snort, of what sounded like irritation.

"No. I haven't, but…"

"Ah! That explains it," Kimberly muttered. "Your blood sugar is probably low. All you need is some food and you'll be as right as rain."

Little does she know?

Jaime opened her mouth to declare that food was the last thing on her mind but Kimberly forestalled her.

"We'll go into town and get a meal," Kimberly continued, taking Jaime's agreement for granted. "I know the perfect place; good food home-cooked plus a decent wine list. And, after we've eaten, we might be able to continue our discussion.

"I can't go out like this." Jaime protested with a glance at her ragged jeans. "At the very least I'd need to shower and change my clothes. Anyway, the point is redundant, I don't want to have dinner with you."

Nor any discussion.

"Too bad!" Kimberly dismissed her protest with a smug smile. "I wasn't actually giving you the choice. Let me see you stand."

Jaime ignored the proffered hand and got carefully to her feet. After an initial lurch, like she was on the deck of a ship, she recovered her balance and risked a couple of steps. Reassured by her progress she took several more, putting valuable distance between her and Kimberly.

"Okay, you look more stable," Kimberly said. I'll leave you to get changed. Make sure you're ready when I come back to collect you in half an hour."

Jaime followed Kimberly to the door, fuming silently over her arrogant attitude.

They were back to square one.

Well, perhaps, not quite. Jaime frowned, turning fractionally so that she could watch Kimberly until she disappeared from view. Her thoughts racing wildly as she attempted to put this disturbing turn of events into some sort of perspective.

Kimberly's insistence that they go out to dinner together, didn't make a lot of sense, given the antipathy between them. Why go to such extreme lengths, when she could easily have said what she wanted right away, without committing them both to a whole evening from hell.

Dragging her gaze away from the empty horizon, Jaime expelled a ragged sigh, then turned abruptly and went indoors to shower and change. There was no point in continued speculation, it was a total waste of time, in just a short while Kimberly would, undoubtedly, explain. The real question was what? Kimberly probably had some new and devious trick up her sleeve. Jaime grimaced at the thought, as she delved into the wardrobe looking for something suitable to wear.

Kimberly strode out toward her home, even in semi darkness the twists and turns of the narrow moorland track familiar territory despite her many years absence. In her mind she relived the encounter trying to separate fact from fiction, and truth from fantasy. She didn't get very far however, the image of Jaime crumpling like a slow-motion scene in a movie overwhelmed everything else. She'd acted instinctively, leaping forward to catch

Jaime milliseconds before she hit the floor. With the fragile body cradled in her arms Kimberly found the desire to do something, anything, to help Jaime had momentarily overcome her animosity and pushed their differences aside. Working on autopilot, and her sketchy first aid training, she'd deposited Jaime carefully on the chaise longue in the library then checked her pulse and breathing. Both, thankfully, appeared normal, which eliminated the need for a panicky triple nine call. Then in a moment of total madness she'd settled a gentle kiss upon Jaime's lips.

Oh hell!

Kimberly shuddered at the memory and immediately relived the sharp tingle of desire that invaded her body.

What possessed me to be so stupid?

Relief that Jaime appeared not to be in any immediate danger must have addled her brain. She'd promised herself it wasn't going to happen again. No more kisses. They were sworn enemies. The only saving grace, on this occasion, was Jaime being unconscious. Or almost so... Kimberly wasn't certain but she thought that Jaime had breathed a word, or a name, in the fraction of a second after their lips touched.

Who or what is Granby?

A place or a person?

With no answer forthcoming, Kimberly tucked that puzzle away for later to concentrate on the main issue.

What had prompted Jaime to faint?

Something I said or did?

Kimberly reviewed their conversation. No specific clue there, Jaime had held her own until the last when her voice faltered in the middle of a sentence.

When all the snippets were pulled together they added up to one simple statement.

Henry Carr supposedly had the necessary proof. Documents, going back something like thirty years, linking Jaime to both Uncle James, and to Rykesby.

Kimberly still couldn't credit that explanation. Thirty years ago, Jaime would have been a small child – three, four, five, at the most.

Could it really be true?

Had she misjudged Jaime?

Was she genuine?

No!

Surely Eva would have picked up on such an important fact when she did her research?

Anyway, there were insurmountable discrepancies to overcome. First, that of Jaime's parentage. Edward couldn't be her father. No way. Edward was unable to father children; he was completely infertile due to a childhood illness. The information was well documented in the family archive. He had even stated publicly he would never marry, claiming it would be unfair to deny a woman the chance to bear children. Then, in the space of a few years, he had gone back on his word.

Kimberly was glad her mother hadn't lived to hear Jaime's lies she'd suffered enough at Edward's hands as it was.

Secondly, she found it impossible to imagine Uncle James, her confidant, keeping such an important fact secret from her for thirty years. He had told her many times what he planned for Rykesby and his fortune, and each time he'd said something along the lines of, *"I'm going to leave it all to someone special, the closest family member left. I hope that she will cherish the inheritance and keep it safe."*

What could be clearer? Kimberly had always known he was really talking about her. There wasn't anybody else.

Why then had uncle James apparently gone against himself and everything he held dear by leaving everything to somebody outside the family circle?

Questions, questions, questions, and no answers – yet.

First thing tomorrow she must get Eva to dig deeper and, at the very least, approach Henry Carr for documentary evidence to disprove the latest outrageous claims. He had previously refused Kimberly's own request for copies of the vital documents citing 'client confidentiality' but lawyer to lawyer ought to be a different matter. Failing that, she would insist on Jaime taking a DNA test to prove her claim of paternal kinship. DNA didn't lie.

Back at Aspen Cottage Kimberly phoned ahead to book a table at the bistro, from memory it had always been busy, a popular place to eat even out of season, no point in taking chances. A quick shower was next on the agenda. Once dressed again she glanced at the time – With less than five minutes to spare she logged onto the computer and typed 'Granby' into the Google search box, not expecting much in the way of results, if anything .

Wow! So many entries… and they all appeared to point to one place – a series of crime novels by somebody called Corey Adams. Male or female? She'd never heard of the author, not that her ignorance was significant, she rarely read any fiction. Kimberly scanned the first few entries but there didn't appear to be any link between Jaime and what was listed. She sighed. This line of inquiry looked like a dead end.

Maybe I misheard her.

Kimberly logged off and hurried out to the car. She could always make a more thorough search later, when she had more time. Meanwhile, she needed to get her thoughts clear before she arrived at Rykesby.

Jaime held the key to whatever secrets were out there. Maybe she would unwind a little over dinner, although Kimberly doubted that anything Jaime said could be trusted without some corroborative back up in the form of verified paperwork. Sifting the truth from an abundance of lies, fact from fantasy, answers from the multitude of questions, and solving the mystery of whom and what looked likely to be a very long task. Kimberly didn't relish the time and effort involved to achieve a satisfactory conclusion but it had to be done if Jaime's ridiculous claim was to be disproved.

Despite the few minor points that niggled away in the background of her mind, Kimberly was totally convinced of a blatant fraud on Jaime's part. Her story just wasn't feasible from so many angles. She had failed to establish any connection to Uncle James, ditto to Uncle Edward – despite the family tree in James' own hand which in itself was suspect. Uncle James would surely have mentioned such a momentous event – the discovery of another family member to add to the line of which he was so proud. Then there was the way Jaime had popped up at the right moment with a background carefully crafted to match the will and the other documents she presented.

The whole story was bunkum. Lies heaped upon lies, upon more lies. Kim couldn't understand why it was taking so long to uncover the fraud. Henry Carr and the Probate Office were either complicit or blind to what was going on. Even Eva, whom she'd trusted with her affairs for many years, and who should have been 100% on her side, hadn't got a handle on the facts. All she ever got from Eva these days were lectures about taking a step back and being cautious.

Why doesn't anybody else see Jaime for what she is?

A voice in Kimberly's head answered.

Maybe because there isn't anything to find.

Kimberly took her growing frustration out on the steering wheel. She couldn't believe it was anything other than a giant conspiracy.

But what if...?

Had Uncle James chosen to take his secrets to the grave rather than be upfront about the truth and his intentions?

No! He'd had no reason to keep silent all these years, or give her false expectations. That wasn't his style.

No matter how one looked at the facts there wasn't a shred of evidence to support Jaime's claim to Rykesby. Kimberly sighed. This looked likely to prove a long and very trying evening unless Jaime let her guard down. Kim knew she would have to play this minute by minute, see how the conversation flowed and if there was a way to catch Jaime out in a deliberate lie.

Still undecided, and running out of time to consider an alternative way forward, Kim passed between the stone pillars that marked the entrance to Rykesby.

CHAPTER TEN

As the designated half hour wound down to a few final minutes Jaime's tension increased to fever pitch. The prospect of spending any time in Kimberly's company terrified her but curiosity triumphed. She was loath to admit it but, Kimberly's clever tactics had sparked her interest and now she desperately needed to discover what she was up to even if that meant spending the whole evening in her company. And they seemed to be spending a lot of time together. Everywhere she turned Kimberly was there. It was almost as if she deliberately set out to engineer their encounters. Yet why would she?

Jaime had just descended the stairs when she heard Kimberly's Range Rover pull up but not wanting to appear too eager she paused and let Kimberly ring the ancient bell before she went to open the door.

"Are you ready?" Kimberly asked, her voice unusually guarded, while her gaze traveled smoothly over the pearly gray silk shirt and black trousers that Jaime had flung on in desperation having run out of time to look for anything more suitable.

"Yes, I am." Jaime nodded. Kimberly had opted for her normal attire in which she looked good enough to eat – tonight a black vest under a patterned shirt, in several shades of red, and tight jeans that accentuated her long legs and neat ass. Jaime scooped up her purse and keys from the hall table, eager to be on the move, convinced that she'd feel more relaxed once they arrived at their destination and were amongst a crowd of strangers.

Although she soon had cause to revise that opinion when Kimberly escorted her into Appleyards some twenty minutes later. Finding that Kimberly's choice of restaurant was, in fact, her own favorite eatery proved strangely disturbing.

"I didn't realize you two were acquainted," the waitress remarked, wide-eyed, as she ushered them to the quiet corner table that Jaime normally used and handed them the menus.

"And if I didn't know you better," Kimberly remarked silkily, although her expression was wary. "I'd say you were verging on being Miss Nosy Parker."

Jaime looked from one to the other in amazement. They clearly knew each other well, but how well? Was this woman one of Kimberly's army of lovers? Hell's teeth! Jaime's horror at having posed such an unsettling question stuck in her craw. What was she doing, thinking in those terms, especially as she had no valid information on which to base her assumption?

"Oh, Kim, honey! You know I'm not like that."

Kimberly made a show of sounding unconvinced by these protestations. "Well then, maybe I should put you out of your misery and introduce you properly."

"Jaime, meet Rebecca Appleyard. Her family owns the bistro. Rebecca, this is Jaime Fyre. Apparently she is a very distant cousin and the new chatelaine of Rykesby."

The two women exchanged the briefest of greetings, before Rebecca turned swiftly back to Kimberly. Leaving Jaime free to speculate on the exact nature of their relationship.

"B...but I..." Rebecca stammered, her eyes popping in amazement, clearly demonstrating that she was fully aware of Kimberly's expectations.

"Yes, I know," Kimberly intervened smoothly, before Rebecca could continue. "I was surprised too, but now I am getting quite used to the whole idea. Uncle James clearly had his reasons for leaving everything to Jaime, so who am I to argue."

"Good. Well, I'd better leave you to it." Rebecca included Jaime in a vague, slightly glazed, smile before hurrying away to attend to another table.

"Why did you tell her?" Jaime whispered, the moment Rebecca was out of earshot. Her anger focused on Kimberly for taking the decision to reveal all out of her hands. "I don't want everybody to know my business."

Her criticism brought smoldering fire to Kimberly's eyes. She leaned across the table, her body language reinforcing the message.

"Rebecca isn't everybody, she's a friend, and besides, you can't honestly expect to keep this secret. It will be the talk of the town once Mrs. Plews gets wind of the situation."

Whew! Jaime exhaled with profound relief as the fire died in Kimberly's eyes and she relaxed back into her seat. Although she was still deeply disturbed by the prospect of her private life being hawked around to a horde of busybodies.

"I haven't met Mrs. Plews yet, but… Are you saying she's a gossip-monger?" If that was the case, Jaime decided, she would definitely be looking to engage a new housekeeper – somebody from outside the town.

"Well, to be fair, no more than most of the old biddies around here," Kimberly replied, nodding thoughtfully. "It's one hazard of living in a small town. Everyone knows everything about everybody else and, I dare say, what they don't actually know they invent."

"Thanks for the warning." Jaime replied tartly, then immediately tempered the tartness with a lighthearted laugh. Although, there was no reason to feel complacent, when Kimberly had just confirmed her worst fears.

"Oh, I'm quite sure you'll manage to survive," Kimberly remarked with pointed sarcasm. "After all you've had plenty of practice at keeping secrets, haven't you?"

Now it was Jaime's turn to be furious. What gave Kimberly the right to judge her so harshly?

She clamped her lips shut on a stinging retort and retreated, simmering with rage, behind her menu. There was no virtue in retaliation, when Kimberly always managed to twist things around so she came out the clear winner. It happened every time they had a spat and, without doubt, was a prime cause of her sense of inadequacy. The sound of Kimberly's voice, giving her order to a smiling Rebecca, jolted Jaime out of her reverie.

"…and the steak pie. Jaime?" Kimberly raised an interrogative eyebrow.

"I'll have the same," Jaime replied absentmindedly, fully aware that she was ordering blind, having only heard the final words of Kimberly's order.

Rebecca wrote down the order, enquired about wine, then departed, leaving Jaime none the wiser.

Studying Rebecca as she weaved her way through the maze of tables with grace and expertise, Jaime was beset by consuming envy. Rebecca was everything she wasn't. Willowy, beautiful, with shining auburn hair and lightly tanned skin. She certainly wouldn't have looked out of place amongst the world's top models.

Jaime swiveled her gaze between Rebecca and Kimberly thinking what a perfectly matched couple they made.

Meeting Kimberly's questioning look cost her dear, she gratefully seized upon the first thing that came to mind, to span what seemed like an unbridgeable void. "So, what did you want to discuss?"

"Later... Let's eat first." Kimberly favored her with a rare, bone-melting, smile. And, in the meantime, why don't you tell me what you do apart, that is, from acquiring valuable property. I presume you do have a job – a career?"

This abrupt transition from smiles to venom caught Jaime off guard. It was so typical of Kimberly, nice one minute and nasty the next. She quickly smothered the reciprocal smile and drew in a lungful of air.

"Yes, I do," she defended hotly. "I work in publishing."

"You do?" Kimberly's expression suddenly became more animated. She leaned forward and fixed Jaime with a hard enquiring gaze. "Doing what, exactly?"

What? Jaime frowned. Trust Kimberly not to be satisfied, as most people were, with her usual vague response. Now she was faced with a stark choice. Either risk the consequences of revealing all, thereby giving Kimberly another lever to use against her, or invent a plausible story.

"My role is fluid," she temporized, hoping that Kimberly had a hazy knowledge of the publishing world. "Mainly I liaise with the editorial staff and the production team, but I also read manuscripts and, occasionally, I even get to write the blurb on book jackets." It was almost the truth and near enough to what she actually did, aside from the actual writing, not to leave her exposed to questions she couldn't answer.

"Sounds interesting,"

"It is," Jaime affirmed, wondering how to change the subject to something less fraught with pitfalls.

"You must tell me more," Kimberly said silkily.

Rebecca saved the day. Her timely arrival with the wine – a Californian Merlot – gave Jaime the perfect opportunity to ask about Kimberly's time in the USA.

Surprisingly, Kimberly appeared happy to oblige, launching into an amusing narrative of her lifestyle and work. Jaime thought it sounded fun but worlds apart from England and, especially, a small town like Whitby.

"It sounds absolutely wonderful," Jaime enthused when Kimberly paused to sip her wine. Jaime followed suit, cautiously, she knew little about wine, but the silky taste of rich berries seduced her and lingered on her tongue almost like good dark chocolate. Kimberly had chosen well, she clearly knew her wine. "Aren't you missing the excitement? I know I would."

Kimberly gave her a suspicious glance, implying that she had no right to make such an assumption, before saying. "No, I'm not. Because I always intended coming back here. I had... have... a dream, to set up on my own."

"And I put paid to your dream. Is that what you're saying?"

"Not at all." Kimberly shook her head. "My plans for Rykesby were small beer in the overall scheme. I've got plenty of other options, most of them much more viable plus they come with the added advantage of no unexpected surprises to stop me achieving the results."

"I'm glad to hear that." Jaime was genuinely relieved that Kimberly's future prosperity did not entirely rest upon acquiring Rykesby. Although, it didn't go all the way to salving her troubled conscience.

"So tell me about your ideas," she continued brightly, hoping to keep Kimberly so busy talking about herself and her plans that she would forget about the discussion.

It worked, too, throughout their meal Kimberly talked animatedly, outlining various schemes, explaining in detail her views on present architectural trends and how she aimed to make her own mark.

Jaime hardly gave a thought to what she ate save that the creamy soup tasted of the sea and the steak pie melted in the mouth. She nodded, listened, smiled and chipped in with the odd question, whenever the occasion demanded. Just thankful that Kimberly seemed totally absorbed in her subject. It couldn't last.

The arrival of coffee broke the spell and the flow of relaxed conversation. "That's enough about me." Kimberly seized the initiative. "I think it's time we got down to the serious business."

Jaime sighed. This intervention gave her no chance to promote a new topic. Kimberly's incisive tone also dispelled any hope that their earlier rapport might continue and the certainty formed in Jaime's mind that she was bound to find any new solution Kimberly proposed totally unacceptable. She couldn't face another unpleasant scene, especially here, in public, with Rebecca Appleyard watching them closely. To the casual observer it appeared the other woman was absorbed in her work but Jaime sensed Rebecca had followed their conversation with more than a casual interest throughout the evening. There was something disturbing in her presence, to say the least, a subtle undercurrent of simmering emotion that spoke of unfinished business between Rebecca and Kimberly.

"Actually, I'm suddenly rather tired." Jaime stifled a yawn. "Could we postpone our discussion to another time?" Indeed, her fatigue was genuine. Jaime couldn't remember when she'd last felt so completely exhausted.

"Okay," Kimberly agreed without demur. "My fault... I should have realized you weren't up to a late night. We'll make a date for later in the week, when you're feeling better." Kimberly signaled to Rebecca. "I'll just get the check and then take you home."

That was way too easy. Kimberly was up to something but Jaime couldn't fathom what it might be. When it came to deviousness she was definitely no match for Kimberly. As Rebecca approached their table Jaime got to her feet. She acknowledged Rebecca with a brief smile, and moved swiftly on toward the exit leaving Kimberly and Rebecca alone to say their goodbyes.

Outside, the cobbled lane was cloaked in darkness and the evening air laden with a refreshing aroma of the sea carried inland on a soft breeze. While she waited for Kimberly to emerge from the bistro, Jaime leaned against a wall and tried to get her thoughts in order.

"There you are!" Kimberly's voice carried a note of mild irritation. "You didn't have to rush off like that."

"I thought I should give you and Rebecca some time alone to say goodnight." Jaime shrugged. "I didn't want to play gooseberry."

"What!" Kimberly's laugher rang out, multiplying several times as it echoed off the surrounding buildings. "Why on earth would you think that? There's absolutely nothing going on with Rebecca. We are simply old friends, that's all, we went to the same school a long time ago and—"

"It's none of my business anyway," Jaime interrupted. Any fool could see the two women shared a history that went way beyond 'just old school friends' and the fact that Kimberly felt the need to hide the true nature of that friendship proved the point. "Please, no more talk, just take me home."

"Yes ma'am!"

Ma'am?

Was that a hint of sarcasm? Jaime cast a quick glance in Kimberly's direction but it was too dark to read her expression. She resisted when Kimberly took her arm but after just a few steps down the lane that led to the parking lot near the harbor Jaime was forced to accept the need for some support. Her heels were totally unsuitable for both the uneven cobblestones and the steepness of the hill. Had she known their destination in advance she would definitely have chosen different shoes.

Fifteen minutes later Kimberly brought the Range Rover to a halt facing the front of the house, the headlights illuminating the heavy oak door. "I'll just see you inside."

"No need. Please don't bother getting out, I can manage from here." Jaime unclipped her seatbelt ready for a quick exit. "Thank you for dinner, and for bringing me home."

"My pleasure." Kimberly switched on the interior light then turned slightly to face Jaime. "I'll call you tomorrow to arrange date and time to continue our discussion."

"Sorry, tomorrow is not good for me, I'm out all day. Better make it the day after." Jaime registered the immediate look of irritation that crossed Kimberly's face and savored the small victory. Being the one calling the shots gave her the confidence to add. "Let's also make it late afternoon... If my meetings run on I may stay over rather than driving back in the dark."

"Very mysterious." Kimberly raised an interrogative brow.

"Just work."

"Ah, yes, your work in publishing..."

"Exactly." Jaime refused to be drawn by Kimberly's sarcasm, and the unvoiced implication that there was a question mark over her veracity.

Where she went, what she did there, and who she met was none of Kimberly's business. Jaime saw no need to make any explanation about her trip to York. Especially so, in view of one particular appointment. If Kimberly got wind that she was meeting with a forensic scientist, an expert in handwriting and document analysis, she would be bound to twist the facts to make trouble.

Professor Leta Rosselli had helped Jaime several times before with research questions. Ever a stickler for detail, Jaime made every effort to ensure Granby used proper procedures and the services of professional forensic scientists to identify perpetrators and solve crimes. Most experts were happy to help her, some for a fee, and others for the goodwill, or a mention in the credits. Leta fell into the latter category. Over the years they had formed a bond of friendship and respect.

"Goodnight, Kimberly." Keys in hand, Jaime opened the door and slid out of the vehicle.

"Night..."

Jaime shut the car door on Kimberly's somewhat abstracted response and hurried toward the house, her heels making a soft crunching sound as they sank into the fine gravel. She unlocked the heavy outer door, grateful for the beam from the headlamps, and then flicked the switch to turn on the hall light. Behind her,

Kimberly revved the engine, turned, and departed in a shower of loose chippings almost before Jaime had a chance to wave her thanks.

What was that all about?

Jaime opened the inner door and headed for the library to check her emails. Any mention of her work in publishing and Kimberly suddenly got all uptight and twitchy. It had happened in the restaurant and again just now. Jaime hoped that Kimberly didn't have an inkling about her being an author. That would be an absolute disaster. As would the discovery of her pseudonym, Corey Adams.

From the outset she'd guarded her anonymity, initially to hide the fact that she wrote lesbian fiction from her parents and their circle of bigoted chapel-going friends. As far as she was aware, her parents had never guessed she was 'sick and abnormal' – their obnoxious terminology for anybody who wasn't heterosexual. Jaime had tested their reaction just once, in her early teens whilst she was trying to come to terms with her feelings, and received a stern rebuff *'not to talk such filth'* together with a lecture on how the *'the Lord struck down those who went against His word.'* She had never visited the subject again. All her parents had known about her life was that she worked for a publisher and, rather than going into the office daily, she did her job from home. They had never shown enough interest in what she actually did behind the locked door of her bedroom.

After her parents died she'd continued to hide her identity out of habit, always refusing to do readings, book signings, or anything else that may expose her as the author of the Granby novels. Jaime couldn't begin to imagine how her private life might be changed by all the hype that Granby generated. The online blogs and fanzines totally blew her mind. She wasn't out to most people, just Nigela Toleman, whom she'd met at a lesbian drop-in center, and now Kimberly. Jaime winced, wondering how that *'outing'* had happened so easily. Not that Jaime was ashamed of being a lesbian, but her sexual orientation was deeply private and a very personal part of whom she was. She wasn't particularly interested in sex per se. In fact, she had wondered for a while if she fell into the asexual camp but eventually decided that she didn't. It was more a case of not having met the person who stirred her sexually – until Kimberly that is. Fate at its most unkind.

Why did it have to be Kimberly?

That question alone caused her to re-evaluate where her life was headed.

Jaime wasn't particularly bothered about her lack of friends or a social life in Whitby. She wasn't that keen on going out to clubs, bars, music venues, and the like. As a result there were very few people whom she classed as friends in London, so life here wouldn't be that different. In her Corey Adams persona, she had Leta and a small group of online friends, mostly other authors, with whom she chatted when time allowed. They supported one another through the hard times, when the words wouldn't flow, and celebrated when the dry spells evolved into days filled with crazy torrents of writing that made a nonsense of normal patterns of eating and sleeping.

What bothered Jaime more was the way Kimberly had invaded every aspect of her life, and even when she wasn't physically present she messed with Jaime's head.

Jaime closed the lid of her laptop and focused her attention on the panel behind which she believed lay the answers to so many other questions. There were still a dozen untried keys but she didn't hold out much hope for any of them. Half an hour later she was proved right. None of the keys fitted. She'd tossed each one back into the box until there were none left.

Okay, where do I go from here?

Keep looking or contact the locksmith?

Henry Carr had given her a name of somebody reliable and the number to call but she still hesitated, the key must be here, most probably somewhere in this room, it was just a matter of finding its hiding place.

Back at her cottage Kimberly grabbed a bottle of beer from the fridge and carried it together with a bag of her favorite savory crackers into the lounge. The fire had died down in her absence but the addition of a few peat briquettes and a couple of logs soon revived it.

She flopped down onto the recliner, operated the lever to raise footrest and set her mind to reviewing the evening. Not much progress certainly. Apart from dropping one golden nugget of information – namely that she worked in publishing – Jaime had manipulated the conversation away from herself, seemingly reluctant to touch on personal matters even when pressed. She'd been especially tight-lipped, about her trip tomorrow – something to do with work, but where and with whom remained a complete mystery. Kim sighed. Despite her optimism, earlier in the evening, she was no further forward in her search for answers.

Almost absentmindedly Kimberly tipped the bottle to her lips and took a long draft of beer, allowing the familiar smooth liquid to caress her tongue. All those years away she'd longed for her favorite, locally brewed, ale. It was the first thing she'd stocked up on, after her return home. Not that she ever drank to excess, getting rat-arsed every weekend, like some of her male colleagues, wasn't something she enjoyed.

What now?

Another look at Granby...?

Enthused by the idea of more research Kimberly moved over to the desk, logged onto the computer, and set to work. She scrolled through hundreds of listings for the books, plus various websites for digital downloads to eReaders, reviews, discussion groups, and fanzines. The series was clearly popular. Kimberly checked out some of the fan sites to get a flavor of what people found so compelling and came away with the impression that Granby was seen by some as a lesbian icon, just as Xena had been a few years earlier although without the Sapphic subtext. Granby was out and proud, a butch who embraced her sexuality as an integral part of life. She had a live-in lover, to whom she remained faithful, and they were already talking about the possibility of marriage when the legislation finally passed scrutiny. Maybe that was it... Jaime, like all these other sad women, was a fan of this character and...

Oh! My sweet Lord!

Kimberly gasped, barely able to comprehend the evidence on the monitor. The page of photos that had resulted from an unintentional mouse over – mainly cover images, promotional material, and other pictures relating to the Granby circus. Only one problem... All the pictures could easily have been of herself. The uncanny portrayal of not just her features, but her clothes, and even her stance was scary, like looking in a mirror. Or seeing a ghost of oneself on the screen.

This discovery put a totally different slant on the situation and destroyed her earlier notion: namely the possibility of Jaime being the author. Jaime didn't know her well enough to construct such a finely drawn picture. It didn't, however, preclude Jaime from learning a lot of the Fyre family history from whoever was responsible. Now Kimberly knew Jaime had connections with a publisher this scenario had become more likely. She made a note to check out the publisher and see if Jaime worked there.

Who could have got everything so right?

Somebody who knew her well.

Someone from Whitby?

Kimberly couldn't imagine who, or why anybody would want to use her as a role model.

Hell! It probably accounted for the number of strange looks she'd received from fellow travelers when she landed at Heathrow on her way back from America.

Okay, let's try to rationalize this.

Kimberly went back to basics. Back to the first book in the series, *Calculated Risk*, published some thirteen years earlier while she was still living here, to see if she could discover the identity of the author from the detail. The blurb and excerpt concentrated on the plot rather than Granby. The reviews weren't much help either. She tried the next, then the third with the same result. The earliest books hadn't received the same hype as later ones.

Frustrated by the lack of helpful detail, Kim installed the free desktop app for a popular eReader then bought and downloaded all eleven eBooks. She began a systematic search for clues, noting everything on a spreadsheet, sure that somewhere, in one of the volumes, amongst all Granby's personal character details, there would be a clue to her creator. A little fact about her personality that no stranger could possibly know something that, hopefully, might identify the author without shred of doubt.

When I get my hands on whoever...

By dawn she had reached book four, *Trojan Horse*, and the spreadsheet already ran into many pages of facts – from purely physical characteristics and mannerisms to Granby's preferences for certain clothes, foods, and entertainment, even down to the particular aroma of the soap and shampoo she used in the shower. Again, Kimberly found the number of similarities to her own preferences far outweighed those that didn't fit. But still nothing to identify the person responsible.

This is really scary.

Kimberly took a break, to snatch a quick nap before she had to head out for a day at the office.

Throughout the day she struggled to concentrate on the job in hand – planning rules had changed a lot, across the board, in the time she'd been away. Many new building regulations in regard to material specifications, energy efficiency, and insulation were now in force and needed to be studied in fine detail. Mid afternoon, while perusing a list of documents on the computer, something struck her, forcibly. She stopped work to put all her resources into considering this new and vital information.

Granby not only understood modern technology, it was second nature to her. She used it all the time to crack codes, hack into computers, and much more, all in the name of solving crimes and protecting the innocent from harm. In the real world, computer hacking, commercial espionage, and cell phone interception so much in the news of late, were all termed illegal but this was fiction. However, to be convincing, the author would need a good grounding in and knowledge of modern technology. Not only that, as time advanced so did the complexity of the technology. Computer coding, for instance, comprised several different languages, some relatively simple and others devilishly hard – the sort of meaningless jumble that fried ones brain. The hardware, too, was beyond most people. The author would have to understand so much that mystified the average man or woman in the street who cared little what went on inside their computer, tablet, or cell phone, as long as the thing worked when they switched it on. Kimberly thought of herself middle of the road in terms of technological ability. She could write simple code and knew a little about the workings of her computer, but she wouldn't have a clue how to put some of the more complicated procedures that Granby used into practice, let alone make a good job of weaving them into a story line. Whoever was responsible would have needed to keep up to date with the subject.

She could save herself a lot of time and energy, by sorting the sheep from the goats. Kimberly smiled. Uncle James would approve of her using one of his favorite sayings. This approach would enable her to quickly narrow down the field and to focus on those who had both the knowledge and the ability to put it into practice.

Kimberly left the office early, pleading a headache. She wanted to see if her ideas held water. If she made a list of all the people she knew, from here in Whitby and at the university in York, going back say fifteen or even twenty years, anybody whom she might class as a possible author, then in the light of this new theory, see how many she could eliminate. For the remainder she could maybe figure out some way to do background checks looking for evidence of unusual work patterns and wealth – the whole series of books must bring in a substantial income.

CHAPTER ELEVEN

York, as always, bustled with people – both tourists, here to view the iconic sights, and locals going about their daily business. Jaime found being away from Rykesby, even for a few hours, liberating. It gave her the chance to unwind and be herself without the ever-present threat of Kimberly's unwelcome intrusion destroying her peace of mind.

Hell!

Her stomach flipped at the mere thought of Kimberly and what she represented – her uncanny likeness to Granby and the resulting sexual attraction was totally unreal. No matter how hard Jaime tried to smother her feelings she could never shake off her desire for Kimberly. The all-consuming need for sexual release tormented her. If only... Capitulation was an outcome that she knew must never happen – it would be a disastrous mistake on every level.

By mid afternoon Jaime decided to extend her trip and stay overnight. She checked into the hotel, her favorite place in the city, and freshened up before heading downstairs for her appointment with Leta. They always arranged to meet in the comfort of a hotel lounge where they could enjoy a drink and a snack whilst they chatted. Today Jaime chose a secluded corner table, well away from the central walkway, where they could talk undisturbed and placed the folder of notes on the spare seat whilst she checked her messages using the hotel's free wifi.

A sixth sense made Jaime glance up from the iPad just as Leta walked through the arched entrance from reception and paused to get her bearings. Leta was petite, barely five feet tall. She bore her Italian heritage with pride, appearing strong and determined despite her slight build. Jaime waved to attract her attention.

Leta waved back then crossed the lounge to their table. "Hello, Corey. How are you?"

"I'm well, thanks." Jaime switched off the tablet and stowed it in her bag. "You look fantastic... I love the new haircut, it really suits you." Indeed, Leta's mid gray hair had been restyled into a soft feather-cut that framed her face and enhanced her neat elfin features. It took several years off her – Jaime wasn't sure of Leta's exact age but her guess was nearer sixty than fifty.

"Thank you." Leta's dark eyes sparkled. "I got so fed up having to gather my hair up into something both tidy and practical, and it would never stay put all day."

"Definitely a good idea then." Jaime noticed the lounge server heading in their direction and picked up the menu card. "Shall we order something?"

Leta nodded. "They do a wonderful veggie mushroom sandwich, I had it last time we were here, and it was really delicious."

"Yes, I remember. I'll have the same. Beer or wine?"

"Let's share a bottle of wine... Unless you have to drive?"

"No driving. I'm checked in for the night." Jaime grinned. "I'd prefer wine to beer but you choose."

"Okay, wine it is." Leta gave the order, stipulating the wine she wanted, and then she turned back to Jaime. "So, Corey, what engaging puzzle have you got for me today?"

"Something for you to get your teeth into." Jaime handed the folder over. "It hasn't got a title yet, I'm still toying with a couple of possibles – Rogue Dealer or Double Dealing – I've gathered the scenes and the relevant background notes together in here – you know best how this works – but as far as I'm concerned it boils down to a few questions. As part of the case she's working on Granby has uncovered some documents and a sheaf of bearer bonds but she has her suspicions that something isn't right. Bearer bonds can be notoriously difficult validate so that is one problem. Could the bonds be forgeries? Have the supporting documents been doctored to appear genuine? Who should she approach to verify them? What questions ought she to ask? What sort of tests need to be done? I'm particularly interested in how would you go about testing the evidence? In this instance it's important that the results will stand up in court."

"Sounds intriguing." Leta slipped the folder into her laptop bag. "I'll get back to you when I have all the answers."

"Thanks, Leta. I really appreciate all you do for me."

"It's nothing. I enjoy doing research and, when I see the finished book in the store, it's good to feel part of the story."

"You are certainly a big part of Granby's success. I couldn't imagine writing her exploits without your input. I just wish I had her on my side in real life."

Leta frowned. "What's wrong?"

"Nothing... Please forget I spoke."

"Come on, Corey, I can see there is something. Do you have another problem for me?"

"No, not really. At least nothing connected with the Granby stories."

"Are you in trouble?"

"It depends how you define trouble." Jaime tried for a jocular response but failed miserably.

"Now you're scaring me."

"It's complicated." Jaime paused as the server arrived with their wine. When they were alone again she continued. "To cut a long story short. Just over a month ago I inherited a property and some money from an uncle. Unfortunately the bequest came with a nasty surprise in the shape of a distant relative who disputes my right of inheritance. Before you ask, the will is legal – I didn't know anything about the legacy until the lawyer contacted me – and it's cleared probate, but the person concerned is still convinced that I'm a fraud and there doesn't seem any way I can prove I'm not."

"That's tough."

"It gets a lot worse, believe me, but I won't bore you with the sordid details. Suffice to say there's other stuff, including a missing key. I'm sure that my uncle left paperwork that may explain more and also reveal why he made the decisions he did – I found some letters elsewhere to back up that theory – but until I can get into the safe, or what looks more likely a secret room..." Jaime sighed. "Does all this sound like one of my plots? A case of life imitating art?"

"Yes, you have a point." Leta nodded. "If you ever need to get something verified I can put you in touch with a colleague – we know each other too well for me to be of any help to you on that score."

"Thank you, Leta. I appreciate the thought. I'm not in that position right now but I'll keep it in mind for the future."

"What about your lawyer, can he or she not help to sort this out?"

"He... No, he's too closely tied into the family history for my liking, and I'm not completely sure I trust his judgment. With that thought in mind, I had a preliminary meeting today with a lawyer, here in York, to discuss the possibility of her taking on my affairs. However, although she's interested in taking me on she advised caution, pointing out that any move would take time and may not, in the long run, provide the resolution I'm looking for. Seems I'm stuck with the status quo for now."

"That doesn't sound ideal." Leta said. "Why York? Are you living up here now?"

Damn! Jaime realized her mistake. Leta knew she lived somewhere in London, although not exactly where. She decided on evasion. "I don't think location matters so much these days, York is as good a place as anywhere, and I do visit fairly regularly."

"That's very true." Leta smiled warmly. "I'm glad you do, and that I get to enjoy your company."

"And I yours." Jaime returned Leta's smile whilst she determinedly smothered the pangs of guilt. She hated being economical with the truth but telling Leta the full story now, after all the years of being Corey, would prove difficult to justify.

"Please remember, I am always available if you need to unburden yourself. Just email me or we can even Skype if you want – I'm getting better at it all the time."

"Thanks... Ah, here's our food." Jaime welcomed the opportunity to change the subject, fully aware that she had stupidly put herself at risk of revealing too much personal information.

What is the matter with me lately?

First she'd allowed Kimberly to out her and now she'd almost made the same mistake with Leta – not in the same way, admittedly, but it set a dangerous precedent.

"That was so good." Jaime used the final piece of ciabatta to clean up the juices from her plate. "I'll have to try making this at home."

"Rather you than me, I'm hopeless in the kitchen," Leta admitted sheepishly. My husband, Paolo, does all the cooking. He has time on his hands now, since he retired from the university. Paolo is a committed carnivore, maybe I should bring him here to try this he's always looking to discover new dishes that satisfy us both.

"I'm sure he'd love it. The mushroom more than makes up for the meat. Or, as a last resort, he could grill a steak or a chicken breast to add to his portion."

"Very true." Leta grinned. "You are clever. Talking of clever... When is Undiscovered Truths due out, it must be soon?"

"In two weeks. And the release date for Restitution has been advanced to the end of November."

"Excellent! I'm looking forward to my copies and to seeing the books in the stores. I'm sure they'll both make the best sellers list."

"Thank you, Leta, you are very generous." Jaime felt heat invading her face. "I'm always amazed how many people buy the books and say nice things about them."

Leta glanced at her watch and pulled a face. "Sorry, I have to rush away tonight, Paolo will be waiting for me, – we're going to a concert at the Barbican."

"I understand." Jaime stopped Leta from picking up the tab. "I'll get this one. You go and enjoy the concert with your husband."

****

Jaime hit the shops to stock up with fresh ingredients before she left York and arrived back at Rykesby around midday. She carried her purchases inside and went to make a sandwich lunch before starting work on fleshing out some ideas she'd been mulling over during the trip. When Kimberly called just before five, Jaime was shocked to discover how quickly the afternoon had flown by.

"You're home..." Kimberly stated the obvious.

"So it would seem." Jaime saved the document then closed the laptop. She sat back in her chair and tried to dispel the butterflies dancing a merry jig in her stomach whilst she waited for Kimberly to say what was on her mind.

"Are you busy tonight?"

"I am, rather... got a lot of work to catch up on."

And I need more time to decide how I'm going to deal with you.

"How about tomorrow night? We need to finish our discussion."

"Maybe... It depends what you have in mind."

"Dinner at Appleyards?"

"I think not."

"Why not? I thought you liked eating there?"

"I did... I do... but..."

"You're not still harping on about my relationship with Rebecca?"

"So you admit you do have a relationship with her?"

"You're twisting my words. That's not what I said and you know it."

Jaime's lips parted in a smile. Winding up Kimberly was easy when they weren't face-to-face.

"Methinks the lady doth protest too much. I know what I saw."

There was a long silence before Kimberly responded.

"All right. We did have something going for a while but it was over years ago, long before I went to America. Rebecca has moved on and so have I."

"Are you sure about that? You may have moved on but I'm not so sure about Rebecca."

"Rubbish! Rebecca and Karla are... solid."

"You don't sound very sure. Anyway, I have no idea who Karla is—"

"Karla, the fashion designer," Kimberly chipped in. Her voice carried a distinct note of irritation. "Rebecca is the top catwalk model for all Karla's shows."

Ah, Jaime smiled, that explained her impression of Rebecca. Something she might have already known had she followed current trends but celebrity and fashion held little interest.

"The name doesn't mean anything to me, and it isn't relevant to our conversation. But if they are as 'solid' as you say then why is Rebecca here, in Whitby, waiting tables in her parent's bistro, rather than by her lover's side? Doesn't that tell you something?"

"Not really..." Kimberly said. "I guess Rebecca is just here on a visit."

"Whatever... I have no interest in Rebecca's private life. I just don't feel comfortable with her listening in to every word of our discussion."

"Now you're just being stupid."

"No! I value my privacy and want what we have to say to say each other to remain strictly between us. While I'm not implying Rebecca is a gossip I do have concerns, as I'm sure you'll appreciate, if you think about it. Please be honest, Kimberly... How would you feel if your private affairs were hawked around town for public entertainment?"

Another lengthy silence ensued. Jaime had almost given up waiting and was about to intervene when Kimberly spoke.

"Okay, I hate to admit it but you put up a valid argument against Appleyards. However, I would also add that any discussions we have in a public place are open to the same potential lapses of security. Where does that leave us?"

"No closer to solving our differences. Whatever it is you have to discuss had better be done in private."

"Where?"

Good question. It was Jaime's turn to pause for thought. She gritted her teeth and fought the conclusion that had emerged as front runner. Although it went against her better judgment, there really was only one sensible place.

"Here maybe? I could cook us supper, if you don't mind a scratch meal in the library – I live in here – I can't stand to eat in the dining room it's so gloomy and the kitchen smells of damp."

During the week she had swapped several pieces of furniture to and from the library to make her life more comfortable. Until the renovations were complete she would be camping out in here – not that *camping out* was any hardship. The library was both beautiful and big enough to accommodate her needs with a large window that looked out over the garden to moorland and the distant sea beyond.

"You're inviting me over for a meal?" Kimberly sounded incredulous.

"Not from choice. It's more a matter of self preservation."

Kimberly laughed. "Okay, I accept. Tomorrow night?"

"Yes. Seven o'clock sharp."

"May I contribute some wine? Or maybe beer? I don't know what you're cooking?"

"Nothing fancy. Jaime was glad she'd restocked her fridge. "Steak and salad. I'm not really fussed about wine, or beer, but feel free to bring something for yourself." Her brain switched to planning mode. They wouldn't need a starter, apart from a bowl of nibbles. The broiled steak alongside a toasted ciabatta roll topped with a portabella mushroom, tomato, red onion, roasted red pepper, and salad leaves would do for the main and she could whip up a quick dessert out of a can of cherries, some crushed amaretto biscuits and a dollop of thick cream fraîche. Simple!

"Thank you, I'll bring both. Have you tried the local beer?"

"No, I haven't."

"You must, it's a very smooth brew, I'm sure you'll love it."

"I doubt it... I've never really developed a taste for beer."

"Then we'll definitely have to test your palate."

Not if I have any say in the matter.

Jaime was determined not to let alcohol dull her brain or be caught out by any other underhand tactics Kimberly chose to employ – a clear head was essential. Right now, Kimberly was keeping tight-lipped about the actual detail although Jaime had little doubt that it involved her and Rykesby. Time to end the conversation before Kimberly set any more traps.

"I'm sorry to cut this call short, Kimberly, but something just came up that I have to deal with right away. I'll see you tomorrow night."

"Sure thing. Bye!"

Kimberly was gone before Jaime had the opportunity to say goodbye. She replaced the handset then got to her feet and crossed to the window. The sunshine of earlier in the day had faded into a leaden sky with the promised heavy rain imminent. In the distance a large oil tanker battled against the choppy waters of the North Sea and closer to home a strong gust of wind whipped a flurry of leaves across the grass. Jaime shivered, not a pleasant evening to be outside, she decided to forego her daily walk. She closed the shutters, added another couple of logs to the fire and picked up her book.

Later, around seven o'clock, Jaime prepared a quick meal of lemony chicken and artichoke pasta which she carried through to the library. Tomorrow looked like a hectic day. She had a conference call on Skype with her editors in the morning, an appointment with Henry Carr after lunch, and in the evening, Kimberly. How that would pan out was very much in the balance. There wasn't any way to prepare herself in advance since everything depended on the line Kimberly chose to follow. She was so unpredictable;

Jaime rarely if ever knew where she stood or how to react.

Hopefully her visit to Henry Carr's office would have resolved all the outstanding issues surrounding the will and other documents. Once she had copies of everything in her possession she would be on much firmer ground in this ongoing dispute with Kimberly.

Kimberly cut the connection, a frown creasing her brow. *What is Jaime playing at now?* The latest development had her puzzled and she didn't know what to think. An invitation to supper at Rykesby was the last thing she'd expected to come out of the call. And Jaime had sounded different, more relaxed, and more confident. The trip away had obviously given her a lift.

Had she met somebody?

A lover?

Kimberly's gut clenched at the thought and she struggled to dismiss an erotic image of Jaime naked in the arms of another woman her gorgeous skin glowing in the dying throes of an orgasm.

I want it to be me!

Kimberly's body thrummed, adding its own message of hope.

Not that it was ever likely to happen.

Hell! No way, unless one of them capitulated, or something else occurred to resolve the dispute, they were destined remain apart. But, hey, a girl could dream.

Another point had come out of the call. When Jaime voiced her concern about privacy she had highlighted Kimberly's own struggle to discover who had used her as a model for Granby. The person responsible for such a brazen breach of trust must be somebody close, very close to her. When all the probabilities were factored in only two names had remained on her list – Amy, her housemate from uni, whom she'd now eliminated, and Rebecca. Not that she really believed Rebecca capable either on the technical side nor, for that matter, on a motivational level. Researching and writing eleven successful books required the sort of dedicated work ethic that Rebecca lacked, but every avenue was worth checking. To that end she planned to have her dinner at the bistro tonight – it would also give her a chance to test Jaime's theory about Rebecca's relationship with Karla.

She didn't book, banking on the element of surprise as her the best chance of assessing how things stood with Rebecca, and timed her arrival to scrape in below last orders.

"Kimberly!" Rebecca rushed to greet her with a brief kiss on both cheeks. "On your own tonight?"

"Yes, I am." She wasn't giving anything away.

The bistro was quiet, even for an out of season week night, with just three of the twelve tables occupied. Rebecca got her seated and fussed around like a mother hen with a single chick. Kimberly sensed she was building up to something.

"Are you and Jaime Fyre an item?"

Wow! Kimberly smothered her gasp of shock. Rebecca certainly didn't mess about; she'd dived straight in leaving no room for misunderstanding. "No, nothing like that, we have a few things to fix up, family stuff to be worked through, but we are not in a relationship."

Not yet... possibly never.

Rebecca brightened visibly. "What can I get you to eat?"

"I'll have the crab soup with the steak pie to follow."

Left alone Kim mused on Rebecca's behavior. Jaime had been right, damn the bitch.

Why didn't I see it the other night?

Probably because she hadn't been looking. The surprise of finding Rebecca back in town, and in familiar surroundings, had dulled her senses. It had taken a fresh pair of eyes to connect all the dots, and make the result add up to something tangible.

Rebecca was clearly on the hunt with her sights firmly fixed on at the very least renewing their friendship and probably more. Kimberly shuddered. She didn't want to go there again, not after last time, besides which she had outgrown Rebecca and her manipulative games. If, sometime in the future, she ventured into being a couple with anyone she'd want honesty and a grown-up relationship of equals. Kimberly deliberately lingered over her meal. She'd come here seeking answers, and now it looked as if she was going to get more than she'd bargained for. At the very least she might discover what Rebecca was up to and how far or fast she'd try to move things forward.

Eventually Rebecca showed the last couple out then locked the door and turned out most of the lights before coming across and taking the seat next to Kimberly. "Alone at last! I thought they'd never leave. It's so good to have you to myself – like old times."

Kimberly refused to take the bait. "I got quite a shock to find you back home, waiting tables, are you and Karla...?"

"We split up. About a year ago. He took on a new model, a younger version, and I became surplus to requirements."

"I'm sorry."

"Don't be, I'm over it... and over modeling, too. Seems I'm no longer employable, at thirty nine, nobody wants me on their books."

"That's tough."

"Tell me about it. All my agent can offer me now is catalog work."

Kimberly quirked her brow. "It's work, and probably a good income, better than nothing."

"You honestly expect me to lower my standards to...?" Rebecca pulled a face. "Yuk!"

"Waiting tables is hardly top of the job stakes..."

"Maybe not, but it's hassle-free pocket money, and my parents don't throw a fit if I take a few days off work to have some fun. I tried signing on but... the job center took away my benefit after I refused to take a job cleaning holiday chalets. Can you imagine it; they actually expected me to do menial work for the minimum wage."

"So what are you planning to do with the rest of your life?"

"I don't know..." Rebecca gave her a questioning look. "Settle down with... somewhere local; maybe have some children before it's too late."

Kimberly almost threw up in disgust. Rebecca was one heartless bitch, she'd had the chance of a home and a family fifteen years ago and she'd tossed it all away to chase her dream of fame and fortune. Kimberly didn't think she could ever really forgive or forget the events of that year. She had stood by Rebecca through all the drama, despite knowing that she frequently played away by using her body as currency or to advance her career. And when Rebecca fell pregnant, Kimberly had stepped in to offer her a home and financial security but she'd turned it down, aborted the baby, and then rushed headlong into Karla's arms and his bed.

"What?" Rebecca huffed. "You don't think I'm serious?"

"Did I say that?"

"You didn't have to... the expression on your face said it all."

"Can you wonder? As I recall you were very specific, and I quote. *'Getting stuck in this godforsaken town with you and a screaming brat is my idea of hell'* that was quite lot to take on board."

Rebecca laughed. "Come on, Kim... honey... I didn't mean *you*... Well not like that anyway. I was upset, not thinking straight, I thought you understood."

"Oh, yes, I understood all right." Kimberly removed Rebecca's hand from her arm. "We'd been a couple for close on six years, and because I loved you I'd turned a blind eye to your shenanigans – yes, I knew you slept around, with both men and women – stupid me, I thought it was just a phase that you needed to get out of your system."

"That's all it was, I swear. None of them meant anything."

"I can believe that. Not even the father of your baby. Just out of interest, did you ever work out who he was?"

"Not for sure..." Rebecca shook her head. "The only thing I knew for certain was that Karla would dump me as his number one model if he discovered I was pregnant. I'd just hit the big time... What was I supposed to do?"

"What, indeed..." Kimberly shrugged. "I suppose when it comes to making decisions like that it depends to a large extent on how one values life."

"That's not fair!" Rebecca whined. "In my place you'd probably have done the same."

"I doubt it. Our outlook on the important issues is totally different – always has been."

"Anyway..." Rebecca waved her hand in the air dismissively. "That's all in the past. I'm more interested in the future – our future."

Whoa!

Rebecca's bold assumption that they had a future, any sort of future, was way off beam. Nausea burnt the back of Kimberly's throat. She pushed her chair back and stood. "Sorry, I have to go now." She needed some fresh air, fast.

Rebecca followed her to the door. "When will I see you again?

"I don't know."

Never might be too soon.

"How about tomorrow night? I could get off early and we could—"

"I'm busy tomorrow."

"The weekend then?" Rebecca snuggled closer, angling her face as if asking for a kiss. "I'm so glad you're finally back in Whitby and we can pick up where we left off."

"No!" Kimberly firmly put Rebecca away from her. "We are done. Finished!" She opened the door and strode out of the bistro without a backward glance.

How could I have been so blind?

Kimberly gulped in some fresh air as she stumbled down the hill toward the parking lot with Rebecca's plaintive cries ringing in her ears. Hell, not just her ears, half the town could probably hear what was going on.

Shut up, you stupid self-serving bitch!

Had she been too harsh? No. She'd had no choice but to stop the fantasy before it got out of hand. Their relationship was over already, they hadn't spoken more than half a dozen times in fifteen years. How could Rebecca even believe they might have a future?

The landline had been busy by the time Kimberly got home, with a string of messages already recorded on the answer machine. She noted the caller ID and, just to be sure, listened to the start of one message before deleting it and all of the remainder unheard. Thankfully Rebecca didn't know her new cell phone number, although that wasn't really a problem since the phone only worked in a very few locations in and around town and outside the immediate area.

The next few days were likely to be difficult to say the least. Other than switching the landline ringer to mute so all her calls would automatically go to the answer machine, Kimberly hadn't got a plan, it was very much a case of wait and see what transpired. She hoped that Rebecca would soon get tired of pleading her case, harassment, or whatever else, and accept that "we're finished" really meant the end and not a bargaining tool.

Kimberly had enough bargaining of her own to do. Tomorrow night's supper with Jaime was likely to prove pivotal in that little saga. Like an evenly matched pair engaged in a game of table tennis, they had batted claim and counter-claim to and fro but, at the end of the day, neither party had scored a single point.

Eva was getting nowhere with her enquiries, and although Henry Carr had allowed her sight of some documents they hadn't proved or disproved anything. It actually appeared there may be nothing untoward to find but... Kimberly sighed.

Why then do I still have niggling doubts about Jaime?

Because the facts just don't add up. There was a gaping hole in the story. Somewhere buried deep in the myriad of information, and misinformation, was the one vital piece of the jigsaw that would reveal the full picture.

Picture!

That one word pulled Kimberly up short and started a new line of thought.

Why didn't I see the answer before?

Kimberly paced her lounge examining the possible new solution from all angles. Put simply she was considering a radical shortcut that might resolve one of the issues between them. Right now Jaime was probably in possession of something that Kimberly coveted even more than she did Rykesby. Not that she didn't care about Rykesby, she did, it was the center of her world, but one had to be realistic. If – and right now that little word still loomed as a large question mark over everything else in her mind – if there wasn't anything amiss with Jaime and her claim then the picture would prove a perfect consolation prize. Monetary value wasn't the issue here – she would never dream of selling something so dear to her heart – this was about righting a wrong, and restoring a valued heirloom to its rightful place in the family.

From the outset Kimberly had found it odd that the portrait in question wasn't mentioned specifically in the will, or in the probate valuation. However, since the picture had remained hidden for something in the region of two hundred and sixty years, she assumed that nobody but her now knew of its existence. Her mother had handed down all the paperwork that provided indisputable provenance; letters, documents giving full details of the original commission, and the receipt for full payment from the artist. Now all she needed was the portrait itself. She knew it wasn't hanging in any of the rooms at Rykesby, nor was it buried under all the discarded artwork in the studio, because she'd searched for it many times over the years. Uncle James, bless him, had pleaded ignorance when she'd asked him outright, but the twinkle in his eye said that he knew exactly where the painting was. This was her opportunity to get it back where it belonged but the scheme would only work if Jaime had the painting in her possession and agreed to play ball. Then... Kimberly's heart beat a little faster in anticipation. Maybe they could settle their dispute over Rykesby to everyone's satisfaction.

The real problem lay in how to initiate the proposal. Any sign of weakness or uncertainty would give the wrong signal. Kimberly wanted to appear strong yet benevolent in making a deal that would see them both come out on the winning side. The last thing she wanted was to give Jaime the opportunity to seize the painting for herself or to hold it hostage in a bidding war.

The portrait would mean nothing to Jaime, personally, other than a means of adding to her already considerable fortune, but without the necessary documentation to give provenance it would probably be more of a white elephant and fetch a fraction of its true value at auction. Whereas Kimberly could prove ownership without doubt, and that the painting had been stolen from Ralph by his brother, James, in the late seventeen fifties.

Kimberly spent a little while mentally preparing her pitch and sorting out some props from the safe in her bedroom. These items would, hopefully, give her a way into the topic and provide proof of ownership if or when the portrait came to light.

Meanwhile, she still had a lot more research to do on the Granby novels.

Kimberly had tried the publisher earlier in the day. First asking to speak to Jaime Fyre which drew a blank – apparently no person of that name worked in any department. She'd tried again, by making a general enquiry on current releases that included Corey Adams along with several different authors. Then, much later, posing as a freelance journalist who was writing a piece on Corey Adams and wanted an interview with the author. When her requests drew a blank refusal to give any detail, apart from stock publicity releases, she gave up. All she did get from the publisher on the last call was a generic response. "Put your request in writing and we'll pass it on to the author."

With a pot of coffee to help keep her awake she settled at her desk and began on the next book, number eight, Guilty Secrets – the aptness of that title wasn't lost on Kimberly. She worked on, into the night, through nine, ten, and finally eleven, Hush Money.

As she'd worked her way through books five, six, and seven, the original spreadsheet had morphed into a full-blown searchable database of facts, now not just about Granby but also the technical and geographical details of each book. Kimberly continued to be amazed by the complexity of the plots and the smooth yet gripping way Corey Adams moved from scene to scene. The books were real page turners, keeping the reader on the edge of their seat, often with a surprise twist at the very end. Kimberly refused to admit that she was hooked on the Granby novels. Although her pulse definitely quickened with the news that there was a new title, Undiscovered Truths, due for release at the end of the month making twelve books in all.

At the end of the night Kimberly queried the database for specific information and printed off the results to study at her leisure. Somewhere, amongst all the facts, there must be the clue to unlock the secret of Corey Adams real identity.

Meanwhile she needed to perfect her approach to Jaime so she had all her bases covered when she arrived at Rykesby for supper later.

CHAPTER TWELVE

Jaime arrived home from town a little after five o'clock still fuming that Henry Carr had refused to release or even give her sight of most of the documents she'd requested. It was hardly a helpful meeting, given her need for information and the fact that, in her opinion, she was entitled to see everything that related to her inheritance. He'd justified his reluctance to comply with her wishes as, *"it not being in her best interests"* whatever such an obstructive phrase meant, which added fuel to the fire of her original suspicion that he was keeping something important from her.

Henry had hemmed and hawed then finally relented, after a fashion, when she told him point blank of her intention to take her affairs out of his hands unless he co-operated. The slim folder of photocopies, that she'd insisted on waiting for, was a fraction of what she'd expected – a small but nevertheless significant victory. Pity it had taken so long which meant she didn't have time to go over the paperwork in detail before Kimberly arrived but a quick scan might give her some valuable ammunition.

Damn! This is useless!

Her frustration and disappointment boiling over, Jaime swept the papers off the desk. All she appeared to have was the latest will and a cut-down version of an earlier one with several vital pages missing, plus several somewhat obsolete documents relating to the disposal of property, and various tenancy agreements. From her point of view there appeared nothing of interest. Certainly nothing with which to challenge Kimberly's assertion of fraud.

With time short Jaime collected the fallen items back into the folder and stuffed it one of the drawers in the elegant highboy that stood on the opposite side of the fireplace to the secret panel. Then she set about tidying away her notes, the box of letters, and anything else she didn't want Kimberly to see leaving just the laptop on a clean desk. Food preparation took less than half an hour which left Jaime ample time to shower and change before Kimberly arrived. Calming her frazzled nerves proved a more difficult task but with minutes to spare she achieved some sort of equilibrium.

Kimberly arrived on the dot of seven. Jaime opened the door, unprepared to be confronted by a bunch of roses and the carefully schooled mask of cool vanished from her face.

"For you," Kimberly added, somewhat unnecessarily, as she thrust the flowers into Jaime's hand. "I trust you like roses?"

Jaime's fingers closed automatically around the paper-wrapped stems, drawing the flowers to her like a lifeline, her brain a turmoil of indecision. The implications behind Kimberly's choice of flowers, mainly red roses – a universally accepted token of love – sent her brain into confusion. Could Kimberly really be trying to convey a message or, a sudden chilling thought evaporated her euphoria, perhaps she gave red roses to every woman

It would be dangerous to draw any conclusions from them Jaime's high hopes sank like a stone, very dangerous indeed. Mortified, she took refuge in the flowers, burying her face and her abject misery in their midst. Thank goodness she'd remained silent and had not betrayed herself or her errant feelings with some stupid remark.

"No perfume, I'm afraid."

The sound of Kimberly's voice reclaimed Jaime's attention. Lifting her gaze, she focused it upon Kimberly. Tonight she wore a deep amethyst colored shirt over a black vest and dark gray pants. The impeccable tailoring was indicative of Armani, expensive and exclusive.

Jaime's mouth went dry.

As usual, in Kimberly's presence, Jaime felt hopelessly inadequate. But now, her emotional see-saw teetered on the brink leaving her floundering for words.

"T…They're lovely anyway. Thank you." she managed finally, deploying the roses as a defensive barrier between them.

"Just like you."

Jaime couldn't believe her ears. The unexpected compliment, so softly spoken, caught her totally unawares. Then she felt the tell-tale rush of warmth to her cheeks and sought, instinctively, to hide her discomfort from Kimberly by lowering her head and, in the process, lost her grip on the roses. The flowers would have fallen to the floor, but for Kimberly, who stepped in and saved them.

"Perhaps you should put them in water." Kimberly's voice carried a trace of amusement.

"Yes, I should," Jaime answered quietly, seizing the opportunity to escape.

Arranging the roses in a crystal vase gave her a few vital minutes to recover her composure. Then, with head held high, she carried the vase of roses to the library and placed it on a low table by the window.

When she turned around, Kimberly was standing close to the desk. Instantly wary, Jaime registered a change in her expression. She looked slightly anxious, as if she had nearly been caught doing something wrong. Had she been prying?

Jaime's gaze flew to the desk in panic but, everything appeared perfectly normal. The laptop was closed and the tooled leather desktop just as she'd left it earlier, clear. Jaime heaved a sigh of relief and decided it was merely her imagination playing tricks. Anyway, she'd better get over her funk because, unless she could think up a viable solution, she'd have to leave Kimberly alone in the room whilst she went to get the food. As things turned out Jaime had no more cause to worry. When the time came, Kimberly volunteered her help so they went down to the kitchen and carried the food back together.

Jaime had brought two chairs from dining room and arranged them on either side of a small oval table that she'd discovered in one of the bedrooms so they could sit to eat in comfort.

"That was absolutely amazing." Kimberly pushed her empty plate aside then leaned back with a contented sigh. "Where did you learn to cook like that?"

Jaime shook her head. "It was nothing special, just a scratch meal, and there is still dessert to come."

"I need a break first." Kimberly smiled. "More wine?"

"Not for me." Jaime covered her glass when Kimberly picked up the wine bottle. I'll just clear these dishes and get the dessert. Would you like coffee?"

"Not unless you do, I'm happy with wine."

Jaime stacked their used dishes on the tray and carried it down to the kitchen. She retrieved the prepared dishes from the fridge, placed them on a new tray then added a pitcher of iced water before returning to the library.

Kimberly was prowling, glass in hand, examining the shelves of books that took up one whole wall. She turned and said. "Do you suppose anybody has ever read all these?"

"Some of them, I imagine, I've read a few myself." Jaime set the tray down on the table and crossed the room to stand next to Kimberly. "This section contains mostly first editions, although I doubt any of them are particularly valuable. The reference works are a mixed bunch – some of them well used others in pristine condition. Whoever collected the library had eclectic tastes in both fiction and scientific research – there are also a lot of eighteenth and nineteenth century medical works. I wonder, maybe you'd know if any of the family connected to the medical profession?"

Kimberly shook her head. "Not to my knowledge. Most of the men of that period followed a military career, like Uncle James – the family has had strong military ties to The Green Howards since the regiment was created in the mid seventeen hundreds, and before that to the Regiment of Foot formed in sixteen eighty eight under Francis Lutterall to support William of Orange in his invasion of England. The men who didn't sign up for military service, with the regiment, were primarily landowners or dabbled in business connected to The East India Company and later in the city."

Jaime was amazed how easily Kimberly could draw on the family history. "So medicine must have been a side interest for one of the family?"

Kimberly nodded. "Yes. Most probably in conjunction with his travels to India or some other far flung place where access to even rudimentary medicine was not available. Having the knowledge and a guide to current practice would have been a godsend to keeping fit and healthy in remote places."

"I hadn't thought of it like that." Jaime realized that she hadn't really thought at all. She had a lot to learn about the history of the family. And much more to discover about Kimberly who, now she wasn't hell bent on throwing accusation or scoring points, clearly had some very interesting stories to tell. What a pity Rykesby, and all the sordid fighting over the will, had destroyed any chance of them forging a lasting friendship. Or more – much more. Jaime sighed, and pushed the sex genie firmly back inside its box, she mustn't go there. In another life, maybe, but not in this one.

Time to change the subject. "Are you ready for dessert now?" Jaime moved to the table and set out the dishes then she poured herself a glass of water.

"What have we here?" Kimberly followed and zeroed in on the glass bowl that Jaime set before her.

"Dark cherries, with amaretto biscuits, and crème fraîche, it's a favorite of mine. I hope you like it."

"I'm sure I shall." Kimberly conveyed a spoonful of cherries and crème fraîche to her mouth. "Mmmmm... Yes! This is heavenly. You're spoiling me."

Not intentionally, but if you want to think that I certainly won't argue.

Jaime smiled. "It's no secret that I enjoy good food from every point of view both cooking and eating." And keeping Kimberly in a good mood was an added bonus.

"You can cook for me any time you like." Kimberly scraped her dish clean. "I love eating well but living on my own, I mostly eat out or rely on microwave meals."

"Living on your own is no excuse for not eating well – that's just a cop out."

"Maybe it's different for you, I'm not clever that way, I've tried to cook but the preparation and following a recipe is beyond me."

Jaime shook her head. Kimberly wasn't stupid, far from it, more like lazy.

"I want to show you something." Kimberly dug into her pocket and produced a small black velvet pouch. She tipped the contents onto the table and used one finger to separate the items. Then she picked up a ring and held it out for inspection.

"Oh!" Jaime smiled. "That is really beautiful."

"I think so – It belonged to my mother. She gave it to me just before she died."

Jaime became suddenly breathless, overcome with emotion, she forced her attention upward from the ring to meet Kimberly's gaze. Was it her imagination or did she detected a momentary spark of tenderness reflected in those dark eyes? Blinking surprised, she looked again, but it was gone. Wishful thinking. Jaime reminded herself not get too carried away with romantic notions.

"It looks old."

"It is... At least three hundred years old, maybe more." Kimberly sighed. "The jewels are an heirloom, handed down through the family"

"That's amazing. Think of all the women who have worn these beautiful things."

"Indeed." Kimberly said. "Not that I would ever have cause to wear the jewelry – although I believe there is a portrait of Phoebe, Ralph's wife, which shows the ring and the rest of the jewels."

Jaime glanced briefly down at the ring then to the other jewels before her gaze traveled back to Kimberly. "I wonder where the picture is?" she mused aloud. "I'd love to see it."

"Yes. So would I," Kimberly said, her voice grated harshly. "Apparently the picture was left behind, by mistake, when Ralph moved out and, although it was of no real value to him, James took a stand by refusing point blank to hand it over."

"Was that how the feud started?"

"Ah! There you have me." Kimberly shrugged. "I don't know – although I imagine it went a lot deeper than a mere dispute over a portrait. But, that's all in the past." she stated, closing the door on further speculation. "I'm more interested in the present, and tracing the portrait."

"I can't say I've seen anything like you describe around the house."

"I'm sure you haven't," Kimberly said. "Nor have I, but I'm certain it's here somewhere. Probably locked away in one of the secret places."

"Places? Plural? I only know of one."

"There are three to my knowledge although there may be more. What was in the one you discovered?"

"I don't know. I haven't found the key yet."

"Ah! How frustrating for you."

Jaime ignored the perceived hint of sarcasm. "I'm actually thinking of contacting the locksmith – Henry Carr gave me his number – but if there are more places to discover maybe I'd better wait until I know where they are and do all the locks in one go."

"There should be a key in here somewhere." Kimberly stood and moved across the room toward the highboy. "I recall Uncle James mentioning it on one occasion."

Jaime panicked. "No! I checked all the drawers already." She racked her brain, trying to recall if there was anything in the drawers of the highboy that would give away her identity. Maybe not. Her notes and the box of letters from James to her mother was safely locked in one of the desk drawers. She'd moved the original contents from the desk to the highboy to free up the drawer space.

"It's not that simple," Kimberly said. "You definitely aren't likely to find anything in the drawers themselves, what I'm talking about is some sort of secret compartment. Uncle James made a joke about a lever you have to pull but I never actually saw him work it so we'll have to hunt around."

"Ah! In that case I think I know what he meant. He wasn't talking about the highboy." Jaime got to her feet and crossed to the fireplace, intent on diverting Kimberly's focus, she thumped the pillar to operate the mechanism that revealed the small brass handle. "This is what I've discovered so far. See..." She reached up, pulled the lever out, and then pointed to the open panel.

"Cool!" Kimberly stepped into the gap to examine the door. "Just think, I've spent a good part of my life in this house and I've never seen this hidden door before. Maybe you're right and Uncle James was deliberately leading me astray."

"It doesn't help us much; I still can't find the key that opens the inner door." Jaime sighed. "Henry gave me a big box of old keys in addition to the bunch that opens all the usual locks but I've exhausted all of those."

"We need to think about where Uncle James would hide a key." Kimberly glanced around the room. "Consider the most likely places – let's assume he used the key regularly, he would have wanted somewhere easily accessible like the bookshelves or his desk."

"Been there, done that," Jaime said quickly. Things were moving way too fast for comfort. Jaime wanted, needed, to keep her identity hidden and Kimberly was getting too close to finding the information that would unmask her. "What about the other places you mentioned do you know how to get into them?"

"The one in the hall is easy; all it needs is a bit of ingenuity and manipulation. Come, I'll show you." Kimberly led the way to a spot on the right of the staircase.

Jaime frowned. She couldn't see anything, rather like initially she hadn't with the panel in the library, but here there wasn't a handy pillar or any neat little carved symbols behind which the means of access might be hidden. Kimberly had said ingenuity and that meant something even less obvious. After studying the panel for some time she gave up and asked. "Where is it?"

"There." Kimberly pointed to a section of the original plain oak paneling underneath the overhang of the gallery. "You must push on the panel both top and bottom at the same time to release the catches like this." She reached up to press firmly against the wood with the palm of one hand whilst her foot rested on an area near the bottom. There was a creaking sound and the whole panel opened like a door.

Jaime leaned in and counted the flight of rough-hewn stone steps until they disappeared into a dark void then her gaze returned to Kimberly. "Looks awfully creepy... Where does it lead?"

"I'm not entirely sure..." Kimberly shrugged. "As I recall after the steps that you can see there is a long passage carved out of the solid rock – it must have taken ages to achieve with primitive tools. I only went down there once when I saw the door open – I was about twelve at the time and hooked on stories related to hidden treasure and smugglers – it seemed like a big adventure but my torch gave out before I got to the end. Uncle James had to come down and rescue me. He was really cross about it so I never dared try again."

"That's a shame. I'm not sure I'd like to venture down there by myself but I'd love to know where the passage goes."

"So would I." Kimberly grinned mischievously. "What say I come back tomorrow with a strong flashlight and we go exploring?"

"You can, if you want, but I'd rather stay safely above ground."

"Coward!" Kimberly laughed. "It's not as cramped as one would imagine. Although the passage is fairly narrow, just wide enough for one person, it's a good height, Uncle James was a big man, but he didn't have to bend down at all."

"Whatever... I'm not comfortable in confined spaces." That was an understatement. Jaime had experienced a major panic attack during a school visit to a cave system in France and she didn't want to display that sort of vulnerability in front of Kimberly. "So this is one secret place, where are the other two?"

"One is in the drawing room – there's nothing in it, hasn't been as long as I've known about its existence – and the other one is upstairs, in the studio. Uncle James kept his naughty pictures hidden in there – he probably thought it was a safe hiding place, somewhere I couldn't access, but I soon worked out how to get inside. As a randy teen I used to get off on his girly pics when he wasn't around – it fueled my fire. Come with me and I'll show you where to look and how to open them."

Jaime followed Kimberly across the hall and into the drawing room. The secret cavity, hidden behind one of the shutters was, as Kimberly had said, empty. Upstairs was a different matter. Kimberly demonstrated how to operate the catch that allowed a shelf unit to swing open and reveal a recess, inside which they discovered a large number of photographs, some books, and even a few DVDs.

"Whew!" Kimberly whistled. "I knew that Uncle James was into girl on girl erotica but some of this is definitely hardcore porn."

"It would seem so." Jaime examined the DVD she'd picked up. "This one is for sure."

"Are you okay with these?" Kimberly pointed to the pile of photos. "I could take them away or burn them if they worry you."

"No, I'm not bothered. I'm more interested in the history behind this particular collection. I'd already discovered a lot of other photographs similar to these. As you already said, James appeared to have a fixation on the same type of woman. What I'm trying to fathom is why?" Jaime wasn't ready to divulge how like her mother all these models looked.

"I suppose he needed sexual release, and he used his imagination to conjure up a perfect woman."

"Didn't James have a woman in his life?" Jaime kept her tone casual. She wanted to see if Kimberly would volunteer any useful information.

"No, he didn't. Leastways I never heard tell of anybody special. Although to be honest I know little about his life before he went away, and when he came back..."

"Went away?" Jaime picked up on the strange turn of phrase.

"I don't know all the details. I was only a small child at the time so our paths didn't cross as much. Apparently, sometime in the late seventies I think, he went missing in Africa. There was a lot happening around then with ex-colonial states flexing their independence muscles. As

I understand the situation he was sent there by the British government as an intermediary to help one of the leaders negotiate peace with the opposition, or something like that, but a rebel faction captured him and held him hostage for months. My mother reckoned he was a broken man when he returned. He certainly never talked about that lost time to me, and in later life he became something of a hermit hardly ever leaving Rykesby or meeting people outside the family and his select group of women."

"That's so sad." Jaime frowned, recalling a sentence in one of James' letters to her mother about *'being stuck in some godforsaken place, trying to prevent the savages killing one another'*. Did this refer to the same *'went away'* that Kimberly had just mentioned? Could it explain why the relationship ended and her mother married Edward? If only she could find those missing letters, or even James' diaries.

"What's up?"

Jaime blinked, startled by Kimberly's question.

"Nothing."

"You could have fooled me..." Kimberly quirked her brow. "You went as white as a sheet back there. Do you need to sit down?"

"I'm okay, really, I was just thinking about something..." Jaime realized that time was running out for the truth to emerge. The letters formed a big part of the mystery surrounding Rykesby and the will, as did the friendship between James and her mother. Did she really have a choice about telling Kimberly?

"Mmmmm. Clearly not a nice thought. I think we ought to go back downstairs away from this stuff."

Jaime put up token resistance when Kimberly stepped in, took her arm, and steered her downstairs. They reached the library before she came to a firm decision. "Kimberly, please. I..."

"What?"

"...I may as well tell you, since you are as likely to stumble across them as me; I've been searching for some letters... Letters from my mother to James – I already have a number of his letters to her that I discovered amongst my mother's possession, plus a book of his poetry that is based on their friendship, but I wanted to get the full picture... to unravel what went on between them. I am sure James would have kept her letters and maybe some of his old diaries but I've drawn a complete blank."

"Are you saying Uncle James and your mother knew each other?"

"Yes, they were once close friends... it was a long time ago, before I was born." Jaime almost said 'in love' but she didn't want to give Kimberly any excuse to twist what she said or denigrate the relationship.

"Before she married Edward?"

"Definitely. The envelopes bear her maiden name." Again, Jaime didn't mention that there were also three unopened letters address to Mrs. E Fyre.

"Well, I'll be...

"I know..."

"How long were they...?"

"In a relationship?" Jaime wanted to bite her tongue, or withdraw the word relationship, but now she'd started the ball rolling there wasn't an easy way to halt the process. "The letters that I have cover a period of three years – although they may have been together much longer than that. The correspondence relates to time spent apart while James was posted to distant places."

"Why didn't you say something earlier?"

It was a valid question. Jaime sighed. "Would you have listened?"

Kimberly had the grace to look embarrassed. "You may have a point."

"You also have to remember that I when I discovered the letters I was still shock after being told I'd inherited Rykesby and all the money. I couldn't begin to fathom their friendship, it went against everything I thought I knew about my parents and even now I don't fully understand what it all means."

"What did Henry Carr tell you?"

"Nothing." Jaime shook her head. "Well nothing useful anyway. Henry and Margaret both deny knowledge of my mother although I'm certain they're being somewhat economical with the truth – and I'm also certain that Henry is keeping something important from me because, as he sees it the information, *is not in my best interests*. It's so frustrating not knowing. And you haven't helped..."

Kimberly nodded. "With good reason. I couldn't see where you fitted into the picture. There are still gaps but I'm beginning to decipher a hazy outline."

"I'm glad somebody is because I'm still firmly in the dark."

"Maybe we can solve this mystery if we work together?" Kimberly turned Jaime to face her. "Will you trust me? I know that I haven't exactly given you reason to do so up 'til now but... We have a common interest in our search for the truth."

"Yes, I'd like that very..." Jaime met Kimberly's gaze and the breath caught in her throat cutting off the rest of the sentence.

Kimberly nodded. "Just for the record, Henry is keeping stuff from me, too. He refused me sight of certain documents and did the same to my lawyer, Eva. I thought he was on the take, in cahoots with you and what I can only describe as a dodgy will."

"Snap!" Jaime found her voice. "Right from the first time we clashed, I thought there was a real possibility that you and Henry were in it together."

"Oh, Jaime... Honey... I'm so sorry."

"Don't! Please don't say s..." Jaime fought to stem the tide of moisture welling up in her eyes but it overflowed anyway. Her vision obscured, she tried to move away but instead found herself held firm in Kimberly's arms and for once she didn't resist.

Kimberly couldn't bear to witness Jaime's distress, nor the tears staining the delicate skin of her cheeks. Jaime tried to turn away but she stumbled, and would have fallen if Kimberly had not scooped her up and carried her to the safety of the chaise longue.

This is getting to be a habit.

"Hush, honey, everything is all right now." She stroked Jaime's hair.

"No..." Jaime's voice was almost inaudible, drowned out by her sobbing.

What have I done?

Kimberly berated herself for her insensitivity, and her bull-headed approach. Sure, there had been and still were a multitude of questions with no apparent answers, but she hadn't needed to behave like an avenging harpy to get at the truth.

This new information about Uncle James and Jaime's mother went a long way to explaining some of the things that had puzzled her since day one. Once the pieces of the jigsaw began to emerge Kimberly had easily added two and two to arrive at a very surprising total, unlike Jaime who still appeared not to see the conclusion or where it was taking her. Kimberly sighed. The sensitive nature of the upcoming disclosures meant she'd need to use extreme care so as not to make matters one hundred times worse. If they could find the letters then the information within may help ease Jaime into full realization of the facts.

The letters and more must be somewhere in this room. Like Jaime, Uncle James spent a lot of his time in here – he had a real gift for writing and had penned several volumes of historical fiction centered on Rykesby and the surrounding area which had sold moderately well. Kimberly glanced across the room to the locked door, behind which she was certain lay the answers to all the missing pieces of the jigsaw, and then to the desk. Her fingers itched to investigate every nook and cranny. She eased away from Jaime who had fallen into an exhausted doze. Working quietly, she removed the desk drawers, all except one deep drawer which was locked, and stacked them neatly beside the desk – she wasn't interested in the drawers themselves or in the contents but what might be hidden in the cavities.

She slid her hand, palm up, as far as it would go into the shallowest opening in the center and felt around – nothing – frustrated she tried again, palm down, with the same result. The drawers on either side were deeper and offered better access but none produced the expected result. Kimberly replaced the drawers and circled the desk, idly running her fingers under the overhanging rim of the desk top. She'd nearly completed the task when she discovered a small depression, hardly more than a subtle difference in texture. She explored the small dimple until it finally gave under pressure.

Got it!

A section of beaded molding, barely two inches deep, between the desk top and the base slid out forming a shallow drawer inside which nestled three keys – a large ornate one that might fit the secret door and two smaller ones more suited to deed or jewelry boxes. Kimberly smiled, satisfied that, hopefully, she had solved one more piece of the puzzle. She longed to try the large key out, but restrained herself, she'd already overstepped the mark by poking into the desk. She hoped that once the good news about the keys sunk in Jaime would overlook the intrusion into her privacy.

Kimberly pushed the secret drawer closed then she got up, crossed over to the table where she emptied the remaining wine into her glass, before she moved to the armchair by the fire. She would leave Jaime to sleep, for now, while she let the events and revelations sink into her brain. The evening certainly hadn't gone according to plan, leaving her with presumptions to revise or discard and totally new areas to explore. Her carefully crafted proposal, to relinquish any claim on Rykesby in exchange for the painting now looked incredibly shaky and unworkable.

The one area where she faced the most trouble was Jaime herself. After Maxine, and before her Rebecca, Kimberly was naturally relationship wary. She had no appetite for sharing her life with another woman any time soon but however hard she tried to quell her physical reactions Jaime proved a potent aphrodisiac. A purely sexual relationship was off the cards for all sorts of reasons. The main one being that Kimberly doubted Jaime was into no-strings sex and if truth be told neither was she. However, it was way too soon to consider anything deeper or more permanent. They both had issues to resolve before there was any chance of moving forward to make the sort of life changing decisions currently churning in her brain.

CHAPTER THIRTEEN

Jaime drifted into consciousness and several tense seconds of confusion before she made any sense of her surroundings. The library was in semi-darkness, a single lamp cast more areas of shadow than light. Other than the soft crackling of the fire not a sound disturbed the silence, but Jaime knew instinctively that she wasn't alone. She sat up and glanced around the room, her vision slowly acclimatized to the gloom, and finally she focused on a figure dozing in the big armchair by the fire.

Granby?

No stupid, Granby is fictitious, so who?

Fear gripped Jaime's insides when she couldn't identify her companion. It took several more scary seconds to recognize Kimberly then recall the events of the evening before full understanding dawned.

Why is Kimberly still here?

What's the time?

Jaime felt as if she'd been asleep for hours. She couldn't see the clock, from her position, but she guessed it must be late – easily later than ten o'clock – they'd finished supper some time before exploring the secret places downstairs followed by the trek up to the studio where they'd spent around an hour. Jaime reviewed the outcome, trying to make sense of the new developments.

It would appear, from what Kimberly had said tonight, that they were in fact both batting for the same side – albeit from slightly altered perspectives – with Henry Carr playing a different game entirely.

What is he hiding from me... from us?

Maybe Kimberly's suggestion, that they as work together as a team to find the missing key and solve the mystery surrounding the will, wasn't such a bad idea after all. Two against one may increase the chances of persuading Henry to play nice. She certainly hadn't made any significant progress by working alone and time wasn't on her side. The only problem with this plan was her attraction to Kimberly.

Was it possible for them to work together without sex getting in the way?

Jaime couldn't begin to answer that question, she'd never been in this position before, but from her limited experience she feared her sexual attraction to Kimberly may blight any chance of them forging a platonic friendship. Anything else, like them becoming lovers, was out of the question as long as the unfinished business between Rebecca and Kimberly lay unresolved.

An unexpected loud crackle from the fire, as two logs collapsed into a shower of sparks followed by a bright flame that lit up the room, and roused Kimberly from her doze. She stretched then turned to look at Jaime and her lips parted in a smile.

"Hi honey. Are you feeling okay now?"

"Yes, much better, thank you." Jaime nodded.

"Good." Kimberly stretched then stood and moved swiftly across the room to the desk. She beckoned. "Come... I have something important to show you."

Although puzzled by this sudden and somewhat cryptic command Jaime obeyed and having seated herself at the desk as per Kimberly's instructions waited for the revelation.

Despite her barely restrained excitement Kimberly appeared in no hurry to get to the point. Instead she slowly circled the desk, moving in a clockwise direction, until she reach the opposite side from where she'd started then she paused. Jaime struggled to understand what was going on in Kimberly's mind.

Suddenly a section between the desk top and the base slid out. "Oh!" Jaime gasped, pushing back in her chair as the shallow drawer advanced. Jaime focused on the contents, overwhelmed by a swirl of emotion that left her feeling totally unreal. She couldn't believe the key that had eluded her for so long was within her grasp.

Several seconds elapsed in silence before she lifted her gaze to Kimberly. "How long have you known about this?"

"Just tonight... I found it whilst you were asleep."

Jaime glanced back down to the key, her brain still refusing to function at normal speed. "Did you...?"

"No. It wasn't my place."

"Thank you." Jaime's hand shook as reached for the largest of the three keys. "I suppose we'd better see if it fits before we get too excited." She got up and walked over to the door. The key slid smoothly into the lock, she drew in a long breath then released it and turned the key. The door opened onto what turned out to be a small room some five feet wide by at least ten feet long but it was difficult to see the exact size for all the clutter. One long side had floor to ceiling shelving also crammed with items.

Kimberly whistled from somewhere behind Jaime.

"Indeed," Jaime agreed, smiling, somewhat bemused by the sudden turn of events. "This looks like a long job. I don't even know where to start."

"I'll help, if you'll let me," Kimberly said. "Let's move the table closer to the window then we can stack the stuff in that area ready for sorting later."

"Look at how much there is." Jaime sighed. "I think I'd prefer to put everything out in the hall, where there's more room to spread it out." James, and possibly others before him, had clearly used the room as a dumping ground rather than somewhere to store important documents and valuables.

Kimberly nodded. "Yes, you're probably right."

"Okay, let's do it, if you're sure you don't mind – it's getting late.

"It's only just gone eleven. I'm good for a while. No work tomorrow."

They worked in harmony, exchanging a word or a smile as they passed each other en route between library and hall. The initial small pile of miscellany soon accumulated into a sizable mountain. Jaime kept an eye open for anything that may contain the letters, or the painting that Kimberly had mentioned, but nothing she handled looked remotely likely. Those special items, if they existed at all, were probably buried right at the back.

"Whew!" Kimberly paused to dust off her hands and grab a bottle of beer from the bag she'd brought. She snapped the top off and took a long draft. "Want one?" She held a second bottle out to Jaime.

Jaime shook her head.

"Go on, it's refreshing." Kimberly urged, pushing the open bottle into Jaime's hand.

Jaime took a cautious sip of beer and then another longer one. Kimberly was right, the beer was refreshing and more pleasing on the tongue than she'd expected. She drank about half the bottle then put it down.

"Thanks. Was that the local beer you mentioned?"

"Yes, it was. You can't get it anywhere apart from a couple of local bars and the micro brewery right here in town." Kimberly grinned. "Have I converted you?"

"I wouldn't go that far, but it's nicer than I imagined..." Before she could say more the long-case clock in the hall struck the midnight hour. "Do you want to stop now?" Jaime glanced at room, delighted with the progress so far although there was still quite a way to go before they reached the back wall.

"No, Let's carry on for a while." Kimberly's voice oozed enthusiasm.

Jaime smiled, and willingly returned to moving the detritus of years.

It was gone one thirty before they cleared the floor area but despite their joint effort neither of the searched for items had come to light. "We're not going to find anything." Jaime sighed, close to despair. She'd had such high hopes at the start but success now seemed as far away as ever.

"Don't give up." Kimberly slipped one arm lightly across Jaime's shoulder. "We still have the shelves to go, plus those two big boxes in the hall although I suspect they are both full of Uncle James' manuscripts – he published several historical novels in the early eighties under the pseudonym J. Z. Osbert."

"An author? How interesting." Jaime turned to face Kimberly. "There is so much I don't know about James, the history of Rykesby, and you..."

"I'm real easy." Kimberly smiled. "I'm not into subterfuge or hiding behind a mask. What you see is what you get, and if I want something I go for it."

The bone-melting intensity of Kimberly's gaze held Jaime captive and breathless. Her insides flipped in a very disturbing manner. Suddenly there was a palpable tension in the air that hadn't existed before, yet she couldn't begin to fathom what had provoked such a transformation.

Then, in the blink of an eye, Jaime was in Kimberly's arms. She didn't understand how she came to be there, or under the command of Kimberly's demanding lips, but unable to deny the power that drenched her in showers of spine tingling awareness Jaime simply surrendered to the magic.

Kimberly eventually broke the kiss but not the embrace. "Mmmm! Honey, you are so kissable. I've wanted to do that for such a long time." Her heated gaze rendered Jaime a boneless mess.

The intensity of Jaime's desire whipped her into a whirlwind of conflicting emotions. Caught up in the moment, her need defied the sense of impending danger. She initiated the next kiss although Kimberly quickly wrested control and deepened the contact. Under pressure Jaime's lips parted, allowing Kimberly to advance. The intimate invasion fulfilled Jaime in an amazingly exquisite way. She had no sense of time, or how long they stood locked in an enchanted world of make-believe, she just lived for the moment the like of which she had never imagined.

Reality returned when they came up for air. Jaime moved swiftly out of Kimberly's orbit. She crossed to the table to pour a glass of water, while she tried and failed to rationalize what had happened. Fate had seized control and charted an abrupt change of course in their relationship. A dangerous evolution over which she had no control.

It was just a kiss, for god's sake!

Jaime's stomach churned as if in protest at her cursory dismissal of the incident. The kiss had highjacked her idea of a carefully planned friendship.

How can I be around Kimberly with this hanging over us?

Kimberly moved up behind Jaime and snaked her arms loosely around Jaime's waist. Jaime stiffened momentarily, before allowing Kimberly to ease her back against her body. "Why so distant?"

"Not distant... just cautious and a little confused by the sudden turn of events."

"You have no reason to be." Kimberly dropped a light kiss on Jaime's neck.

"This is happening too fast. We hardly know the first thing about each other."

"That's what courting is all about – getting to know one another."

Wow! Courting sounds serious. How did we get there so quickly?

Jaime wriggled free and turned around to face Kimberly. "What about Rebecca?"

"What about her?"

"It is customary to put an end to the old relationship before embarking on a new one."

"That relationship finished fifteen years ago, there is no reason to dig over old ground."

"Are you sure about that?"

"Rebecca knows the score – I spoke to her last night."

Did you? I wish I'd been a fly on the wall for that conversation.

"How did she react?"

"Rebecca understands the situation."

"I sure hope so." Jaime noted that Kimberly hadn't exactly answered the question.

Does she know about me?

"Trust me, Jaime. You're important to me. I wouldn't mislead you in any way."

"Nor I you." Jaime met Kimberly's gaze, her resolve firm. "Nevertheless, I want to take things slowly."

Very slowly. Just a couple of days ago Kimberly was accusing me of fraud and tossing insults around like a handful of confetti blown on the breeze.

"It's your call. I have this overwhelming urge to kiss you, to touch you, and..." Kimberly grinned. "Just slap me down if I overstep the mark."

"Don't worry, I will." Jamie stepped free of Kimberly's arms and indicated the half empty room. "It's really late; I think we'd better call it a night."

"Okay, honey." They walked side by side to the door where Kimberly paused. "Can I come by in the morning to help you sort the rest of the stuff?"

"Yes, please." Jaime nodded. "I appreciate your help. Without you I'd still be floundering into next year. I just hope one of us finds what we are looking for."

"I'm sure we both will." Kimberly leaned in and touched lips with Jaime. "Good night, honey. Sleep tight."

"Same to you."

Jaime locked the door and returned to the library to clear away the remains of their meal. On her way back from the kitchen she lingered in the hall. The pile of stuff had grown considerably in the final hour as, with the end in sight, each of them had moved more purposefully. She picked over a few items that caught her eye before opening one of the two large boxes. Inside, as Kimberly had predicted, were a number of hardbound books, plus the accompanying manuscripts. The dark pink tape wound around each bundle of pages reminded her of the ribbon her mother had used on the box containing the letters. Jaime sighed. Frustrated that even with this discovery she wasn't any nearer to solving the mystery surrounding the will or the relationship between James and her mother. Curious to discover how James rated as an author she selected a book at random and carried it upstairs to her bedroom.

Lyndale was a romance, set in nineteen century Yorkshire, against the background of the Napoleonic wars with the hero, Julian Fanshawe, a young army officer, separated from his sweetheart, Kitty Ellis. Jaime quickly recognized a parallel between James and Kay especially when she got to the description of Kitty, a petite blonde with eyes the color of dark amethysts. She flicked on several pages, reading bits here and there, then stopped dead at the part where Julian was taken prisoner leaving Kitty pregnant, alone, and frightened of being forced to marry an elderly cousin for the sake of propriety.

Pregnant?

Suddenly Jaime couldn't breathe. No, surely not. Moral conventions in the nineteen seventies weren't that rigid. Anyway, she reasoned, just because James had portrayed Kitty as a blonde like her mother, it didn't mean the rest of this plot line had any substance in fact.

Jaime closed the book and set it aside. It was late; she'd had a stressful evening, and needed a clear head to tackle this new conundrum. She switched off the bedside lamp and snuggled down under the duvet. Sleep, however, refused to come. Her brain had decided to make something out of nothing, and now she couldn't get it out of her head.

Could there be any truth in the notion that James was her biological father?

She lay in the dark and weighed the facts – what she actually knew for certain – everything else remained just supposition. There were a few things that pointed toward a reasonable yes and just as many that returned an emphatic no, while several more sat on the fence of indecision.

I need positive answers.

Jaime ran through a mental list of likely sources of information then shook her head in despair.

Where am I going to get them?

James and her parents were dead, neither Henry nor Margaret Carr were prepared to give her any help, and it was clear Kimberly didn't have access to that level of personal detail. She sighed.

I need to find my mother's letters, or some other documentary proof of what occurred and when.

Even supposing she found the letters, James' diaries, or whatever, and discovered if there was any truth in this bizarre line of thought, what then? Would it make any difference to her, as a person, if she discovered James was her biological father ? She was an adult, already content with her lot. Her mother and father, Edward, and her austere childhood governed by a strict religious code were, to some extent, distant memories. It might, however, explain the weird sense of déjà vu, that she'd experienced – the feelings had begun the first day she stepped into the house and persisted ever since. There were several rooms around the house where she felt enveloped in a strange ambience as if the walls were trying to tell her something.

Kimberly returned just after eight. Jaime was half way down the stairs when she heard the Range Rover pull up outside, and she made it to the door just as Kimberly rang the ancient bell.

"Good morning!"

"Morning, honey!"

They spoke together and then laughed in unison.

Jaime sniffed the air. "Something smells good."

And somebody looks just as good. Kimberly's jeans and black vest showed her well toned body off to perfection.

"Fresh baked croissant." Kimberly grinned. "I thought we deserved a treat."

"Sounds perfect." Jaime stood aside. "Go through to the library. I'll just fetch some plates and preserves. Do you drink tea or coffee in the morning?"

"I'm easy, whatever you're having."

"Tea it is then." Jaime turned away and hurried down to the kitchen. She'd toyed with the idea of getting a small fridge for the library but that wouldn't solve the problem of water and dirty dishes. By the time she returned Kimberly was sitting at the table waiting.

"I brought raspberry or apricot conserve and butter." Jaime laid out everything then poured tea for them both.

Kimberly handed her the box of croissant. "Did you do any more, after I left?"

"Not really. After I tidied up the remains of our meal I poked around in the hall. You were right about those big boxes they do contain James' manuscripts plus some hardback copies of his published novels. I had a look at one of his stories."

"What was it like? I've never read any of his stuff."

"Not bad if one is into historical romance – which I'm not – I know it's almost verging on heresy to admit I've never found Georgette Heyer or Jane Austen particularly compelling. What little I read did raise some questions in my mind."

"Questions?" Kimberly quirked her brow.

"More in the nature of bizarre ideas... Not something I can put into words right now."

"Okay, I understand. If you want to talk later I'm a good listener."

"Thanks, I'll remember." Jaime poured more tea and they continued their meal in silence.

"Mmmm that was good." Kimberly pushed her plate away, licked a smear of apricot conserve off her finger, and then glanced at the half empty room. "Are you ready to get stuck in?"

"Give me a few minutes to clear away and take this tray back down then we'll make a start."

After some discussion they decided to work forward on the assumption the earliest things would be furthest from the door. Kimberly stood back and surveyed the shelves. "Please refresh my memory. I know you told me last night but… What exactly are we looking for?"

"From my point of view… Hopefully a bundle of letters plus anything that looks like a diary or journal relating to the nineteen seventies, but the correspondence from my mother is the most important as it will answer a lot of outstanding questions. And you're looking for a picture? Do you know how big it is? Is it in a frame?"

"Yes. Oil on canvas. The size is 36 by 48 inches plus the frame. So unless the canvas has been removed from the frame and rolled up it doesn't appear to be here."

"That's a shame. Still don't give up hope until we see what is here."

An hour into the search hopes were raised by a roll of something wrapped in linen but it turned out to be the plans of Rykesby. A very early and somewhat crude drawing on cloth, some sheets dated fifteen thirty and the remainder seventeen sixty five.

Kimberly spread the sheets out on the large table in the dining room weighted down to keep them flat so they could study them later. "It'll be interesting to compare the two main plans and see what features were retained."

By mid morning when they took a short break for coffee nothing more of interest had come to light, not even any boxes which the two smaller keys might fit. "Where do you suppose they are?" Jaime mused. She'd almost resigned herself to not finding the letters or the answers.

"I don't know." Kimberly shrugged. "Maybe we've been fooled into looking here and Uncle James hid everything in another place. We should be done here soon then we can consider our options."

"Have we got any options?" Jaime frowned. "I've looked everywhere I can think of."

"Those two smaller keys must be important or why put them in the secret drawer? It makes me sure that Uncle James chose another place to hide his secrets."

"The problem is where? I emptied the desk and the highboy; I even stripped the books from the shelves and moved all the lighter pieces of furniture without finding anything."

"I think I might have the germ of an idea." Kimberly grinned. "Let's finish up here first and then I'll show you."

"That's not fair. You can't dangle a possible solution just out of reach. Don't keep me in suspense."

"I'm not doing any of those things. It makes sense to finish here first – so we don't miss anything – and I have no idea if my hunch will bear fruit."

"Fair enough, I suppose." Jaime set her mug down on the tray. "Let's get back to work."

"Yes ma'am."

"Well, that answers one question, there isn't anything more to be had in here." Jaime added the final item from the shelves to the pile in the hall. "Shall we get some lunch now?"

"Excellent idea. I'm starving. Where do you want to go?"

"We don't have to go anywhere. I can't be bothered to get changed in order to eat out. Besides, I can rustle up some pasta and salad quicker than it would take us to drive anywhere."

"Really?"

"Yes, it's easy. Why don't you come and watch." Jaime turned and made for the kitchen.

"As long as you don't expect me to do anything."

"We'll see."

Jaime put the pasta on to cook and added a drop of oil from a jar of marinated artichokes to another pan to cook the chicken breast fillets then she handed Kimberly a handful of mushrooms. "Here, you can slice these while I do the artichokes and the lemon."

Jaime removed the chicken from the pan ready for cutting into chunks and added the sliced mushrooms then she picked up one of the trays. "I'll just do the salad and get some bread and cheese. Can you add a couple of those bowls and the cutlery to that tray?" She cut the chicken then added it together with the chopped artichokes and grated lemon rind to the mushrooms followed by the strained pasta, the lemon juice, and a dollop of crème fraîche. She divided the pasta between the two bowls. "Lunch is served."

They carried a tray each up to the library and set everything out on the table.

Kimberly took one forkful and then another. "This is amazing! And so quick."

"Thank you. It's one of my favorite dishes." Jaime grinned. "You saw how easy it was to make. I'm sure you could do something similar. You can vary the ingredients with sun-dried tomatoes, roasted peppers, or zucchini. All things you can keep in the store cupboard. In the absence of fresh mushrooms you could always substitute a jar of mushroom antipasto. In fact the variations are endless."

Kimberly nodded. "I'm sure you're right. I just got lazy. In the US it was easier to go out to eat or order in."

"So, changing the subject, you said you had an idea where James might have hidden things?

"Yes, I did, but now I'm having second thoughts. I can't see why he would have chosen that place."

"Maybe he did it for a specific reason that would only resonate with you?"

"True. I don't think anybody else has a clue about the underground passage, or if they do it's unlikely they would know how to get in without wrecking the entrance."

"Well, there is no way I would have known how to open the door if you hadn't shown me. Is the passage is shown on the plans?"

"That's a good point." Kimberly became more enthusiastic. "I must admit I hadn't considered the plans – Let's check and see if there is any information."

"Yes." Kimberly pointed to the later plan. "You can see the passage, and there is a recess marked a little way from the steps although I don't recall seeing it on my little adventure. Let's see if it's shown on the earlier plan." She moved around the table. "Mmmm. This one is not so clear, but there is something and some writing too but I'd need a stronger light, and probably a magnifier to distinguish what it says. I think we should just take a look see."

"Did you remember to bring a flashlight?"

"Yes, and a coat, it'll be cold down there. I'll go out to the car and fetch them."

Kimberly was back in no time carrying a bag, a heavy duty lantern, and a fleece. "Are you coming down, too?"

"No, I'm curious but I don't think I can risk it." Jaime's impatience to investigate was overridden by fear. She already felt goose bumps forming at the mere thought of descending into the unknown.

Kimberly donned the fleece. "Okay, it's your choice, although you may have to come down the steps to help me with anything heavy."

"I can probably manage that much."

Kimberly opened the panel and stepped into the opening. Half way down the stairs she looked up and grinned. "Well, here goes. I hope I can find the way." She switched on the light and shone it on the remaining steps.

"Good luck!" Jaime watched the beam of light move away until it was no longer visible. She shivered in the slight chill rising up from underground and wished she'd had the sense to fetch a sweater. The house itself had heating from an ancient oil fed furnace but it only gave sketchy background heat. The whole system was due for upgrade to a modern fuel-efficient eco-friendly set-up as part of the upcoming renovations but for now it barely coped with any drop in temperature.

"Can you hear me?" Kimberly's voice echoed from the depths.

"I hear you!" Jaime responded loudly, hoping her voice would reach down to Kimberly.

"I'm about where the recess is supposed to be but I can't see anything."

"Perhaps you need to go a bit farther."

"Wait, I think I've got something... Looks like there's a door in the wall here but it won't shift."

"Don't tell me it's locked."

"No, just warped, I think it's coming free... Got it!

"What's inside?

"Looks like two or three boxes and the painting… Well, I can't be certain that it is what I'm looking for but at least the package is about the right size."

"Thank goodness!"

"I'm bringing the first box now."

CHAPTER FOURTEEN

Jaime went half way down the steps to meet Kimberly, relieve her of the box, and carry it up to the table in the hall. They repeated the process twice more and then Kimberly carried the painting up by herself while Jaime went to fetch the keys from the desk in the library.

"This is scary." Jaime held the first key poised to slip it into the lock of the largest and heaviest of the metal boxes. "Now the moment has come I'm almost afraid to open the box."

"Same here. I've waited all my life for this moment." Kimberly examined the large package – a flat wooden crate some five feet by four and about one foot deep. "Only with this it isn't a simple matter of using a key I can't see an easy way into this one without trashing the packaging."

"Does it matter?"

"I suppose not." Kimberly shrugged. "I suppose it goes much deeper than that. Okay, let's do it together you open your box and I'll pries this apart." She reached for the bag of tools and selected a chisel.

To Jaime's surprise the key she'd chosen fitted the box she'd selected at random. She opened the lid, picked up the first item, and gave a satisfied sigh. She'd found James' diaries. The remaining key wouldn't fit the next box down in size and weight – that would be too easy. Jaime reached for the smallest box and tried again. Success! She lifted the lid and reached inside for the single item. The envelope bore her name and was marked personal in James' now familiar script. Inside was a letter and another key.

Jaime read as far as the second paragraph then the words swam before her eyes. Oh My God! So the bizarre idea she'd had last night wasn't so farfetched after all. Her breathing became erratic until she almost fainted.

"You all right, honey?"

The question penetrated the mess inside Jaime's head. She glanced up to find Kimberly watching her intently.

"Yes… no… not really. I'm—"

"Confused? Angry? Shocked?"

"You knew?"

"Not for sure."

"For how long?"

"Since last night – when you told me about the letters."

"Why didn't you say something?"

"Hold up there! I couldn't just blurt out my suspicions – and that's all they were. What if I'd been wrong?"

"You could have hinted – just to warn me what I might find."

"And bust open a hornet's nest on the strength of a hunch. No way, baby. Anyway, you could have joined the dots together yourself – you probably had more information than me."

"You think? I didn't have a clue until last night and even then…" Jaime shook her head.

"What? What happened last night?"

"It was just a story – one of James' novels… The hero was captured and held prisoner leaving heroine pregnant, alone, and frightened of being forced to marry an elderly cousin… It fitted what you told me about James but…" Jaime shrugged. "It still didn't really seem real. There were, are, so many unanswered questions."

"What does the letter say?"

"I don't know… I never got beyond the point where James admitted that he's my father. Here…" Jaime thrust the letter into Kimberly's hand. "You read it to me."

"Are you sure? It's personal."

"Yes… I'm not sure I can read it and, to be fair, you have as much riding on this as me."

"Okay." Kimberly cleared her throat and began reading.

Dear Jaime,

If you are reading this letter I must assume that you and Kimberly have come to an understanding about Rykesby. I hope she didn't make life too difficult for you. She can be very forceful where her rights are involved especially with regard to a certain painting and its place within the family. I trust you will feel able to respect her wishes in this matter.

My Dearest Daughter, I've wanted to say that all your life but circumstances, not of my making, prevented me from acknowledging you or giving you my name. I hope you will forgive me. I never intended to desert you or your mother. Knowing the situation with Edward, his religious dogma, and his desire to score points over me at any cost, I doubt she ever found the courage to tell you the truth about your conception, here in this house, or why our lives were torn apart.

I loved your mother, Kay, with my heart and soul. We were engaged to be married, the date was set but my life was not my own to command and before I could resign my commission I had to undertake one final trip to Africa as an envoy for peace. I was well known in the area and the powers that be thought I could make a difference. What a joke. The savages were not interested in peace, their tribal divisions were too ingrained. (Rather like the divisions in our own family.) On a visit to the rebel stronghold I was taken hostage by a faction in opposition to the ruling party. It was all very messy. The British government refused to negotiate, as is their wont, and I was left in limbo for months on end. By the time I got free – after the rebels overthrew the ruling party in a coup – your mother had married Edward and the rest is history. I'm glad she at least gave you the name we'd decided.

I wanted you to inherit Rykesby; it is your birthright after all. I believe the house should remain in the family, rather than being sold to a developer who will turn it into some ghastly commercial venture. As I near my end I have a vision of it being a happy family home to you, your children, and your grandchildren.

Goodbye my dear. I wish we could have met but that was always going to present too great a leap of faith for your mother and Edward.

Much love.

Your devoted father, James

P.S. The attached key will give you access to some correspondence your mother wrote to me. It might help you to understand how things were back then and separate fact from fiction. I will let you decide if you want to read or destroy the letters and the same applies to my diaries.

"Come here, honey." Kimberly wrapped Jaime in her arms. "Let it all out."

"I can't… I don't know how…" Jaime almost choked on her tears. "When I think of all the wasted years, after my mother and Edward were killed, when I could have got to know James and made his last years a happier experience."

"It's no use playing the blame game that won't change events or give you any comfort. You need to adopt a positive view of events as they are now."

"How?" Jaime pulled away from Kimberly's embrace. "When everything is rooted in the past. James, my mother, Edward, and this house. The only exception is you and that presents a whole new set of problems."

Kimberly huffed loudly. "So I'm a problem?"

"You know what I mean."

"Actually I don't. I think you need to spell out what sort of problem I represent?

Hell! No way. Jaime cursed her wayward tongue. "I… Nothing specific, it's just a turn of phrase."

"What say I help you out?" Kimberly smirked. "You fancy me big time but you're afraid of the consequences if you admit your attraction. No!" She held up her hand as Jaime tried to argue the point. "You can't deny the fact you go all breathless and weak at the knees every time I enter the room. The only thing I haven't figured out is why? Is it me? Or is it because I resemble somebody else on whom you have a fixation or crush?"

This was getting dangerous. Jaime sucked in a sharp breath. It sounded almost as if Kimberly knew about Granby – okay, there was every chance she had come across the Granby novels but she couldn't possibly know how close she was to Granby's creator. Or could she? The thought of being unmasked sent shivers cascading down Jaime's spine. She switched rapidly to defense mode.

"You're barking up the wrong tree. I don't have a crush on anybody you included. Yes, before you throw last night in my face, I know we kissed but I told you then and I'm telling you again now that's where it stops until we know each other a whole lot better." She turned away to signal an end to the conversation.

"Have it your way."

Kimberly's dismissive response left Jaime unsettled and in search of a distraction or a change of topic. She addressed Kimberly without looking around. "Did you get the picture sorted out?"

"Not yet – it's done up like the crown jewels. I may need to get some more tools to break the crate open."

"Can I help?" Jaime turned and glanced at the crate. "Maybe an extra pair of hands will solve things."

"If you're sure, I don't want to take you away from your stuff."

"No problem, mine is a big job, it'll take me days maybe weeks to sort out." Jaime had resolved to put her task aside until she was alone. She planned to marry the two groups of letters and read them through as one contiguous entity.

"If you're sure. Then yes, please, I'd welcome your help. I can't wait to see the picture – as far as I know nobody has seen it since the seventeen fifties."

"That's an awfully long time." They moved over to the large wooden crate and seeing it properly for the first time Jaime frowned. "I must say this packaging doesn't look that old – in fact it looks quite modern."

"Mmmm, you have a point. Now I'm getting worried that this may not be what I'm looking for after all."

"Don't give up yet. Let's find out what's underneath this modern stuff."

"You're right… Silly me, Uncle James probably did this to protect the contents from decay." Kimberly picked up the chisel. "If you can hold it steady, that's right, I can get into this corner and lever the join apart." After a couple of attempts the join gave a bit and Kimberly turned the crate to get at the next corner then the next. "I think it's coming." The was a loud creak and suddenly the whole side lifted out.

Kimberly laid the crate down and pulled the loose wood away followed by a plastic sheet to reveal a hand stitched leather portfolio within. "This looks more hopeful." Two flaps came together in the middle, and were tied in three places with fine strips of the same leather.

Jaime nodded agreement. The leather certainly appeared more in keeping with the age of the painting.

"Here goes!" Kimberly undid the first knot, the second, and the third, then lifted the two flaps. The painting itself nestled in the center covered in some sort of thick material.

Jaime held her breath, reacting to the heightened tension as Kimberly drew the cloth aside to uncover the painting. Her gasp of surprise at first seeing the vibrant colors echoed in the pin-dropping silence.

"Oh! That's truly amazing. It looks like a Gainsborough but…"

Kimberly smiled. "You have a good eye, that's exactly what it is – a genuine Gainsborough totally unknown to the world – I have all the provenance, but I would never part with it. The painting was commissioned as a family piece to show off the jewels. Look at the detail?"

"And now the two things are reunited. I can see why Phoebe's husband wanted a painting to record her serenity and why he was so furious when he lost his house, his wife, and her image in quick succession."

"I imagine there was probably a lot of sibling rivalry between Ralph and James before the bust up over Rykesby and the painting was just the last straw as the saying goes."

"Two hundred and sixty years is a long time to maintain a feud," Jaime mused aloud. "Whatever originally caused the disagreement must have been really serious. Did nobody ever try to mediate or get to the bottom of what went wrong?"

Kimberly's response filled the hall with harsh laughter. "You clearly know nothing about this family to ask such a question. Believe me, honey, divisions run deep and festering sores never heal, it's a fact of life."

"Are you saying that because of what happened way back in history, something in which we took no part and for which we, personally, hold no responsibility, that any friendship between us is doomed?"

"Well, not exactly." Kimberly shrugged. "I suppose there is an element of 'the sins of the fathers' but it's more a belief that the past cannot be undone."

Jaime shook her head dissatisfied at the stonewall answer. "That's a very blinkered view. As I see it my father, James, has done all he could to mend fences by making sure we work together on this and I have no desire to continue a ridiculous feud. So where does that leave us and, for that matter, who is going to judge us on our future conduct?"

"Ah, there you have me over a barrel. My mother would have cared deeply. She hated the fact that I spent a lot of time here with Uncle James – she was barely civil to him and there was an underlying tension in the air whenever she found herself in his company. Uncle James was always the perfect gentleman in every respect. Looking back, I think her attitude must have hurt him but he never let it show."

"If you don't mind me asking… What about your father? Where did he fit in?"

"Dad was American serviceman. He did something hush-hush at Fylingdales – it's a radar base left over from the cold war – up on the moor about ten miles from here. Anyway they met, married, and I came along, then dad was posted to Germany where he got killed in a freak accident. I don't remember him at all, just mom, and then for a time Uncle Edward – he was weird and very strict – after that came Uncle James who was the exact opposite."

Jaime nodded. "I agree with you about Edward. Living with him was like living in a straight jacket. You and your mother had a lucky escape – especially you – he was homophobic in the extreme. Edward held the belief deviants like us could be cured by prayer and a strict regime of cleansing the soul. I was very careful to keep a low profile. I don't think he ever guessed I'd crossed the line."

"That explains a lot about you that puzzled me from day one." Kimberly smirked. "You're like a chameleon – every time I think I've got you pegged, you change, and I have to start over."

"It's not intentional." Jaime shifted uneasily. She wasn't comfortable talking about herself on such a personal level. "How about we take a break for tea?"

"Good idea," Kimberly agreed readily. "And then, if it's okay with you, maybe I could check out the passage, just to discover where it goes?"

"Go for it, be my guest. I'm curious too," Jaime said. "Would you like cake with your tea? I've got chocolate brownies or lemon drizzle."

"You found my soft spot. Chocolate brownies, please." Kimberly grinned broadly. She picked up the lantern then dug into her bag and brought out a large magnifier. "While you get the tea ready I'll just take another look at the plans. I want to see if I can work out what it says on the early version."

Jaime carried her three boxes into the library and set them on the shelf in the secure room before she went down to the kitchen to make tea. When she returned Kimberly was still closeted in the dining room with the plans. Jaime went to see what was keeping her. "Did you find anything?"

"Yes and no." Kimberly greeted Jaime's question with a frown. "It says here on the fifteen thirty plan that the passage leads to the dower house but I've never heard mention of a Rykesby having had a dower house. There is nothing shown on the later plan other than the passage itself. I suppose I always assumed it was an escape route dating back to the English civil war but then it wouldn't be on the early plan if that were the case. Oh, well, maybe I can find out where it leads by exploration."

"I do hope so. I hate unsolved mysteries," Jaime said. "Come and have your tea now."

An hour later they stood at the entrance to the passage. "Okay, here goes, wish me luck!" Clad in her fleece and carrying the flashlight, plus a head torch, Kimberly descended into the depths.

Once Kimberly was out of sight Jaime hurried to the library to check her email – something she'd been dying to do all day. Thankfully, it being Saturday, there wasn't much and she dealt with the urgent messages in a couple of minutes then relocked the computer. Afterwards she occupied her time taking the tea things back to the kitchen before taking up position by the steps to wait for Kimberly's return.

Some minutes later the dark void was softened by an almost imperceptible light that gradually became stronger until, eventually, the powerful white beam came into view.

"What did you find?" Jaime asked as soon as Kimberly had returned to the hall and removed her fleece.

"There is another flight of steps at the other end, similar to these and a door but I couldn't open it more than a crack, something was blocking the way and I've got a pretty good idea what it is. I think the passage leads to the cellar under Aspen Cottage. There's an ancient wine rack down there – it takes up most of one wall – I guess that it's both hiding the door and preventing it from opening."

"So Aspen Cottage is the dower house?"

"No. Well, not quite. Aspen Cottage was built in the early nineteenth century so at some point after fifteen thirty and before seventeen sixty five the dower house was demolished and later on Aspen Cottage was constructed over the old cellar. It probably made perfect sense to reuse the old foundations."

"I wonder if James knew that our two houses were connected when he gave you Aspen Cottage?"

"We are only connected in the loosest sense – that wine rack is a permanent fixture and almost impossible to demolish. Yes, I imagine Uncle James knew although I can't begin to guess why he might have thought it a good idea."

"Do you get the impression that everything James did in his final years was designed to bring us together?"

"Mmmm, now you mention it…"

"Did James know about you – your sexuality?"

"Yes, I imagine he did, I never made any secret of the fact." Kimberly frowned. "Why?"

"Just curious. He couldn't have known we share the same views in that respect. I'm trying to fathom just what sort of bond he hoped we might form?"

"That I don't know, since he never confided in me, but I assume he wanted us to mend both fences and family ties."

"And... can we?" Jaime turned away unable to look at Kimberly or bear the thought that she might reject a rapprochement. They had come so far in the past few days and the prospect of any return to hostilities tied her stomach in knots.

"Only time will tell..."

Jaime sighed. Kimberly didn't sound very positive but maybe she was just being cautious. They still hadn't really got to know each other properly. She turned back to find that Kimberly had moved away to examine the painting.

"Can you give me a hand to remove all this packing? I'm not going to get this into the car as it is."

"Certainly." Jaime crossed the hall to Kimberly's side and held the wooden crate still while Kimberly lifted the leather portfolio clear.

"That's much better." Kimberly adjusted the weight between her hands then picked up her tool bag. "I should be able to manage now. I'm sure you can use the packing for the fire."

Jaime glanced at the mess of splintered wood and nodded – It would do nicely provided she could find an axe and a saw to render it manageable. "Thanks, I'll do that," she said to fresh air. Kimberly had moved away, clearly eager to carry off her prize. Jaime hurried to catch up.

As they passed by the pile of stuff in the hall Jaime grimaced. "The next job is to sort through all this and decide what to save and what to discard, but that must wait until I get back."

"You're going somewhere?" Kimberly halted abruptly and rested the picture on the floor.

"Europe, for work, I already told you."

"Ah, yes, so you did. I didn't realize that publishing involved jet setting around the globe."

"Doing business in Europe is hardly globetrotting these days." Jaime frowned.

No mistake this time, every time my work is mentioned Kimberly gets all uptight.

What is her problem?

"How long is your trip?"

"I'll be away three weeks maybe four – it depends on how quickly I can get through the schedule."

"So you're a senior executive in the organization?"

"I wouldn't say that." Jaime laughed at the thought. It's just a simple business trip. The appointments were arranged ages ago long before I knew anything about Rykesby"

"What sort of books does your company publish?"

Oh, why did I open my big mouth?

"A general fiction catalog, plus some non-fiction, and a few children's books."

"Would I have read any of them?"

"That depends..." Jaime said, choosing her words with care. "What are your tastes – fiction or non-fiction, historical or sci-fi, romance or horror?"

"I read a lot of non-fiction – mostly biographies and travel, but for fiction give me a good contemporary detective story, or better still a series, featuring a strong, capable, female character who knows how the modern world functions."

Relieved to find herself on safer ground, Jaime exhaled softly. "There is no shortage of detective stories, and series, it's a popular genre with the reading public. Have you tried the Haldane novels by Cal Bendix, or even Macy Wicker's Aldgate Files – they're very high-tech and deal with cyber crime or fraud in large-scale financial institutions?"

"No..." Kimberly shook her head. "I haven't come across either of those authors. My current favorite author to read is Corey Adams. I identified with Granby from the outset – She's my sort of woman."

Jaime swallowed hard trying to clear the lump that had formed in her throat. "Yes, that's another good series to add to the list. I'll let you know if I think of any more."

"Well I'd better be off." Kimberly picked up her painting and headed for the door. "I've got some stuff to catch up on in the morning, but I'm free in the afternoon. How about we go for a drive later and then grab a meal out?"

"That would be great, thank you." Jaime held the door open for Kimberly. "As long as we're not too late back – I have an early start on Monday."

"Got you! I'll call you late morning to confirm." Kimberly leaned in and brushed lips with Jaime. "Night honey!"

"Goodnight."

Jaime closed and locked the door then wandered back through the house clearing up the debris as she went. She carried the wood down to the coal store and left it ready to break up once she found the necessary tools.

Meanwhile James' diaries and the boxes of letters were her main concern.

She carried the two boxes of letters into the dining room. Then she cleared a space on the long table, by pushing the plans to the far end, and laid out James' letters in chronological order leaving enough space between them in which to slot her mother's replies.

There were two hundred and eighty six letters in total, including the three unopened envelopes addressed to Mrs. E. Fyre, a mammoth reading task by any standards, and not something to be rushed or contemplated in the short time available. Jaime collected the letters up, tying them in annual bundles based on the postmark, and placed them into the deed box then carried it back to the strong room to wait for a more opportune moment.

Maybe James' diaries would yield some information – she could easily carry the three or four notebooks that covered the years prior to her birth with her on the forthcoming trip. Jaime delved into the box and sorted out five diaries. She rifled through the earliest diary looking for the first mention of Kay and found one entry in October. Satisfied with her search, she set the volumes aside to add to her packing and returned the remainder to the box.

Jaime had a relaxed morning while she waited for Kimberly to call. She didn't have to pack anything, other than the diaries, her iPad, and the laptop, since she'd already set aside a bag with the clothes that she'd need for her trip and left it ready to collect from the house when she got back to London. She planned to leave the car at home and catch the underground to Heathrow for her flight to Frankfurt, then use a hire car for the duration.

Kimberly arrived a little after three o'clock and they drove out onto the moor stopping first at the tiny picturesque village of Grosmont, one of the halts on a heritage steam railway that ran from Pickering to Whitby and the original setting for Heartbeat, a famous TV show. After a brief look around they continued on to the coast and Scarborough – where the beautiful gardens and old town Victorian splendor jostled with the demands of a modern tourist resort.

After parking the car they strolled along the sandy beach toward the harbor, passing below the magnificent Grand Hotel, while Kimberly detailed the town's many points of interest, in particular several arts venues and theaters.

Kimberly caught Jaime's hand in hers and linked their fingers. "I used to come here regularly before I went overseas, there's always plenty going on. What say we catch a play or maybe a concert?"

"I'd like that. It's been quite a while since I last went to the theater."

"Okay, I'll download a program of events so we can both choose the things we like."

"Sounds good to me. We'll get together when I get back from my trip."

"Excellent! Now we need to find somewhere to eat before we head back. What do you fancy? There's a wide range of choice here. Seafood? Steak? Italian? Chinese or Indian?"

"Seafood, for me, please... I'm assuming that as you put it first it's your choice too."

"Definitely." Kimberly grinned. "I know just the place to take you, they specialize in lobster dishes but always have a good variety of other seafood on the menu if lobster isn't your thing."

CHAPTER FIFTEEN

After more than three weeks away in the hustle and bustle of Europe's capital cities Jaime was relieved to return to the peace and quiet of Rykesby. She unpacked the car and carried her personal stuff plus a few extra household items she'd brought from London into the house. Although she was trying to avoid bringing too much clutter before the renovations were complete she couldn't resist the lure of a few favorite things.

Her trip had proved a resounding success. All her research questions had been answered, she had a host of photographic background material, and the officials she'd met had given her valuable information on their protocol for dealing with hostage situations – the differences in approach from one country to another had amazed Jamie and changed her decision on where to set the proposed kidnap sequence for best effect.

With all the traveling, meetings, and research, she hadn't neglected to read James' diaries. It appeared that, by virtue of her humble origins and her chosen profession, Kay was considered an unsuitable companion for James by the those closest to him – Margaret and Henry Carr included – who took it upon themselves to make Kay's life a misery in the hope of driving a wedge between her and James. The biggest surprise, however, was that Edward – himself a teacher of modest means and with no inherited wealth – had joined the chorus of disapproval. Jaime struggled to grasp the reason behind his stance, since it was at odds with his subsequent marriage to her mother. The only conclusion she could draw for his decision was envy – he'd wanted Kay for himself – and when James fell victim to the African tribal conflict, Edward saw an opportunity to step in and win her hand. Given his infertility, he must have been over the moon when he discovered that Kay came with the unexpected bonus of a child that he could claim as his own. Like all situations, there was probably a lot more underlying the bare facts – Jaime only had James' somewhat biased viewpoint to work on but, coupled with what she already knew, it painted a picture of a group of inward looking bigots. In several entries James had also mentioned somebody called Clarissa – the only daughter of a local land owner who was wealthy in her own right – and, from his pithy comments about arranged marriages, Jaime got the impression that Clarissa was regarded as the preferred option by all but James.

As for Kay, James clearly believed in her love beyond any doubt. How wrong he was. Jaime couldn't even guess at the shock he must have felt when he returned to find both Kay and his child gone. Not only gone but aligned with one of the very people who had treated her so badly in the past. That must have been a very bitter pill for James to swallow. Unfortunately she didn't have his diary for that period.

Now she was home, Jaime began the task of setting the hall to rights and hoped for a few days without interruptions in which to finish the task. She had been in contact with Kimberly by email several times but hadn't confirmed when she would return to Whitby.

Jaime examined everything carefully, weighing the value, or otherwise, of each individual piece. Some of the items were clearly important – mainly family records, photographs, and papers relating to the property – those she returned to the strong room, placing the files on clearly labeled shelves, while other things were filtered into piles for further research or storage elsewhere in the house and a small number for total discard.

By the afternoon of the third day the hall was almost clear. Just one small group of indeterminate items plus the two boxes containing James' manuscripts remained. Jaime was loathe to discard his work, although the titles were out of print and contract for many years. She sat on the floor surrounded by all twelve of his manuscripts and pondered the viability of republishing them as eBooks? There was a definite market for Regency historical romance. Money wasn't the issue, she had the luxury of sufficient funds to finance the project, employ a team to turn the hard copy into digital, re-edit and proofread, produce new cover art and the necessary eBook formats. Jaime nodded, the idea growing apace. She wanted to do something special for James, her father, and this would be an ideal memorial, especially if she donated all the profits to his favorite charities.

Jaime fetched her laptop to list all the titles, the blurbs, and other relevant details before repacking the boxes with the manuscripts, but keeping all but one of each hardback title in a separate pile. She carried the spare hardbacks into the library and cleared a space for them on one of the lower fiction shelves. She was very proud of her father – of his artistic achievement. James deserved to have his work recognized and prominently displayed.

The doorbell rang before she finished redistributing the surplus books to other shelves. Jaime sighed, cursing the interruption, then went to see who was calling and hopefully get whoever it might be to leave promptly.

"Honey!" Kimberly pulled Jaime into a firm hug as soon as the door opened. "Why didn't you let me know you were back?"

Jaime extricated herself and sucked in a deep breath. "Because I was... I am busy." As she stepped back Kimberly pushed forward leaving Jaime with no option but to retreat into the hall.

"I'm sure you are never too busy for me." Kimberly paused and swept the area with her gaze. "Wow! Yes, I can see you've made short work of all the mess." She moved closer and prowled around the remaining items. "You should have waited for me to help you with the heavy lifting."

"There wasn't any need." Jaime flinched as Kimberly got close to the open laptop. The screen was dimmed, it being on battery, but the slightest vibration might... Before Jaime could intervene with a distraction the worst happened and the display sprang into life.

"What's this?" Kimberly bent down and examined the desktop image then she stood and turned to face Jamie. "That's the latest book in... Are you involved with the Granby novels?"

To lie or not to lie: that was the question. Faced with such a blunt request Jaime couldn't think of any viable response other than the truth.

"Yes, I am."

Kimberly huffed. "Your involvement is in what capacity?"

"As the author."

"You're Corey Adams?"

"Yes."

"And you didn't think to mention it last time we talked?"

Jaime blenched under Kimberly's frosty glare.

"There didn't seem any reason to do so at the time."

"Bitch!" Kimberly leaned closer and slapped Jaime hard across the face. "You used me. You stole my identity."

"Not stole... Invented. Granby is one hundred percent my creation – every bit of her is pure imagination. I didn't know you existed when I first conceived the character."

"Liar! You couldn't possibly have made up all that fine detail."

"Why not? It's what authors do every day."

"I'm not buying into that crap," Kimberly shook her head. "Okay, so maybe you didn't do it all by yourself... Who helped you?"

"Nobody."

This interrogation was worse than Jaime had ever imagined

"Now you're trying my patience... I've wasted untold hours looking for the person responsible. There are certain details, personal things about me, that a stranger couldn't possibly know. Who fed you the information? Give me a name?"

"There isn't anyone but me... I just put together all the attributes of my ideal woman and Granby was born."

Oh! Shit! I just told Kimberly she is my ideal woman.

Jaime wanted to crawl into a dark hole and hide – or better still die. Kimberly had a big enough ego already, now she'd given her even more ammunition. Too busy berating herself she only half tuned into the sound of Kimberly's voice.

"...You're an evil bitch! I knew from the start that you were bad. I should never have let you inveigle me into trusting you... Your deception has gone too far, and it's done immeasurable damage to my reputation. This time I'm definitely going to court... I will sue you, and your publisher, for every penny I can get."

"I'd like to see you try. You'll be laughed out of court." Jaime had heard enough to take a firm stand against Kimberly's tirade. If the stupid woman stopped to think for a moment, she'd realize that Granby only bore a superficial resemblance to her. Anybody would see that there were a number of major differences between the character and Kimberly.

"We'll soon see about that! First off, I'm going to get a high court injunction to stop all future publication and also demand a moratorium on any current books until this comes to full hearing. I have enough evidence to bury you, and your pathetic career, forever. You won't get away with making money out of parodying any other innocent people." Kimberly aimed her booted foot at the laptop and sent it skating across the polished wooden floor to crash into the far wall.

The collision caused the lid to flip shut with a loud crack. Jaime flinched, concerned for her precious machine and its contents – although everything was backed up to an external drive, and an online server… the loss of a well loved piece of hardware always hurt and it took many hours of work to *break in* a new machine.

"Do your worst!" she flung the retort at Kimberly's back as she stormed across the hall and slammed out of the house.

For several seconds Jaime remained still, stunned by the unexpected turn of events. Although she'd always feared that *coming out* as Corey Adams was likely to be a mine field – she had never imagined or even prepared herself for Kimberly's reaction, or the accusations and the violence that followed.

Kimberly had demonstrated just how volatile and unreasonable she could be. Jaime sighed – sadness washed over her – she abhorred violence. Following that unprovoked slap across the face, any hopes that they might have had a future together were now dashed on the rocks of despair. The dream of a happy ever after life with Kimberly was over.

How did I ever think I could trust her?

Jaime wiped a stray tear from her cheek. She would move on, stronger and wiser, and free of any entanglement. Having determined her future, she retrieved her battered laptop and carried it into the library.

More out of habit rather than with any real belief in miracles, Jaime plugged the power cord into its socket and she could hardly believe her eyes when the charging light glowed orange. With some trepidation she lifted the lid and the desktop sprang to life as normal. Jaime expelled a long slow breath, pressed a few keys, and successfully opened a couple of files. Inexplicably, it appeared, her faithful friend had survived the cruel treatment unscathed.

Next she called her publisher. Although Jaime viewed Kimberly's threats as a rush of hot air, she needed be proactive, to protect her own position and keep everybody else in the loop. Reassured that she had done all she could on that front, Jaime sought to put Kimberly out of her head and concentrate on the clear up operation. She must be prepared for the renovations – whenever they might happen – the actual timetable, however, depended on getting the necessary planning permission so building work could start.

****

"You did what?"

Kimberly winced at the shrill disbelief in her lawyer's voice.

"I told the evil bitch I was taking legal action. I want you to apply for an injunction to prevent her peddling any more material bearing my stolen identity – that means everything, print books, eBooks, the publishers website, high street and online stores, plus all the posters and any other stuff that constitutes the Granby circus."

Kimberly waited, fuming at the lack of response from Eva. The silence lengthened until exasperation forced her to ask. "Did you hear what I said, Eva?"

"I heard you the first time. I'm thinking. Are you sure about this?"

Kimberly snorted. "Yes, I'm sure. The bitch stole my identity and used it to make me look stupid. I want all the material wiped off the face of the earth."

"And?"

"What do you mean by *and*?"

"Have you thought this through?"

"Of course I have!"

"Okay, let's just suppose for one minute that I apply for this injunction and the publisher challenges the application – as they have a perfect right to do – what then? The proceedings will get splashed all over the media, there'll be a public outcry from readers that their favorite books are being removed from sale because some crazy woman – namely you – has identified herself in Granby. Do you really want the paparazzi camping on your doorstep? Likewise the gossip rags, they'll have a field day printing all sorts of lies and half truths about you"

"But..."

"But nothing, Kimberly. Right now the only people, other than yourself, who associate you with Granby are me and Jaime Fyre. The second we go for an injunction this will become public property. Even if we can persuade the court to grant you anonymity – and that's not by any means a done deal – there is still a chance your name will leak out. Are you prepared to accept that sort of exposure?"

"What are you saying?"

"I'm asking you to consider all the implications and the costs."

"I have."

"Okay... Answer me some questions: First of all can you be certain – one hundred percent certain – that Jaime Fyre even knew you existed, or that she gathered and then used information about you to create the character of Granby?"

"She must have done."

"No, Kim, you're not listening to me. You have to be certain – by that I mean you must have proof that she researched your background, either physically or on the internet, took photographs or secret recordings of your voice, and invaded your privacy before she published the first book."

"Good god, Eva. Of course I don't have that sort of proof. What do you expect? Do you imagine I can remember every little detail from that far back? All I know is that she must have snuck in and done it sometime in the period after my mother died and before I went to America. "

"I rest my case."

"What does that mean?"

"Well, it's quite likely that Jaime Fyre will have the sort of documentary proof I'm talking about showing how Granby was created – her notes, the early drafts of the first novel, plus the submission she sent to the publisher and the subsequent editorial process in which she probably made several changes to the character. All these things will give her the edge in any court. There is also the fact that Granby is seen as something of an icon – strong, faithful, and always working on the side of good. Can you honestly claim that those qualities have in any way damaged your reputation?"

Kimberly huffed. "I have my own documentary evidence. I have a database of facts researched from all eleven books, the similarities are there in abundance, you can't get away from the how many of them favor me."

"That may be the case but it still doesn't prove that Jaime used you as her model for Granby. What did she say when you challenged her?"

"I can't recall exactly... Some crappy excuse about just putting together all the attributes of her ideal woman and... Oh my sweet lord..."

"The penny just dropped, uh?"

"What am I to do?"

"You could try an apology."

"I don't think that's going to work this time."

"Why not?"

"You weren't there... I said some awful things and..."

"And?"

"I slapped her face."

"Not good."

"That's not all."

"What else?"

"I smashed her laptop."

"You did what?"

"I saw the damned laptop as a symbol of her treachery and I kicked it right across the hall – it smashed into the wall with an almighty thump – my guess is it will never work again."

"Oh, Kim, you are your own worst enemy... You really must learn to control your temper."

"I know... Help me, Eva, what can I do?"

"Write her a letter of apology and offer to pay for a new laptop of her choice – you can afford it whatever it costs – then keep well away from Jaime Fyre for the duration."

"The first bit is easy but... I'm not so sure I can keep away from her. You haven't seen her, Eva, she is too damned sexy for words – I want to bed her, soon."

"Now you're really playing with fire – no pun intended – be very careful, Kim, or you'll land yourself in court for harassment."

"She wouldn't... Jaime hates any sort of publicity. She's a mistress of disguise, like a chameleon, just think how clever she's been hiding behind the façade of Corey Adams all these years – believe me, I've tried everything to find a chink in her armor and failed miserably."

"Everybody has a weak spot."

"You didn't see the connection, either."

"I wasn't looking. Be fair, neither of us knew of the link between Jaime Fyre and Corey Adams until today."

"Well, I did suspect her a while back but I dismissed my suspicions on the grounds that she didn't know me well enough to create such a detailed image. It wasn't until I saw the new Granby cover on her laptop that all the dots lined up and made sense. How did she do it if she isn't using me?"

"I doubt we will ever know unless Jaime chooses to share the information with us. She's a successful author with a string of best selling crime novels to her credit, that tells me she has a good brain and knows how to use it. The fact that she's writing under a pseudonym is irrelevant."

"You think? I find it highly suspicious. What's wrong with using her real name?"

"Lots of authors write under a pseudonym – for all sorts of practical reasons – probably fifty or sixty percent choose not to use all or part of their proper name, the same goes for actors and pop stars."

"Really? I can't say I've ever thought about it before. So, her using another name is not that odd, especially given what I know about her life with Uncle Edward."

"Exactly! Look, Kim, I have to go now. Please just do as I say – and keep away from Jaime Fyre, at least for the time being."

"Yes ma'am! I hear you."

"Make sure you listen. Bye!"

"Bye, Eva, and thanks."

Kimberly dropped the phone back into its charging cradle and paced her lounge deep in thought. She hated having to climb down and apologize to Jaime, but Eva had demonstrated that there really wasn't any other option.

The identity of Corey Adams had occupied her mind for several weeks as she worked on the database and pondered how she would deal with the person responsible for her predicament – if she ever found them. Meanwhile, as she'd got closer to Jaime and begun to unravel her life, Kimberly had convinced herself that, despite her job in publishing, Jaime had nothing to do with either Granby or Corey Adams.

The subsequent unmasking of Jaime had shaken her to the core. Was it really possible that Jaime had put Granby together from her 'ideal woman' list? Kimberly grinned, if so, it was somewhat flattering that her own attributes featured so high on Jaime's list. What did that say about the chances of them forming a relationship?

Whoa!

Kimberly reined in any thoughts of the future to concentrate on the present and the apology. She began to draft the words in her head before moving to her desk and opening up the computer.

Two hours later she had several drafts but none of them pleased her. Some were too formal, others too casual, or worse still, dismissive – glossing over the events as if she didn't really care.

Why is this so difficult?

Kimberly berated herself, and her inability to find the right tone. She shut the computer down and went for a long walk across the moor to clear her head.

****

With all her current work up to date Jaime decided to devote the entire weekend to reading the correspondence between James and her mother. She set up a basket in which to store the letters as she read them, then carried the box from the strong room to her seat beside the fire.

The first bundle related to a time, just after their first meeting, when James spent a few months in Germany with his regiment. They were predominately chatty letters between friends – two people getting to know each other – rather than the intimate correspondence of lovers. By the following group the relationship had moved on a year and had become intimate. James was somewhere in

Africa, he never said exactly where or why and their letters were transmitted via the diplomatic bag rather than the postal service. However, now the language of love was woven into every syllable:

James: How I long for the day when we are reunited. I will rain kisses upon you – one for every hour of each lonely night we have spent apart.

Kay: So many kisses... I will savor each and every one of them.

James: I will forever recall the wonderful night you gave yourself to me. Even now your responses echo in my head like beautiful music.

Kay: You made me feel so very special that night.

James: My dreams of you, and of our glorious passion, must sustain me until we are once again as one.

Kay: I will be waiting...

James: I love you beyond all reason. You are my moon, my stars, my universe, my whole life.

Kay: And you mine, my love.

Jaime wiped the tears from her eyes. She couldn't imagine what it must be like to have someone love her with such passion.

The next batch spanned several short trips that James undertook to various states in the Middle East and a longer spell of duty in Northern Ireland. Following their engagement, James returned to Africa and Jaime reached the point she had dreaded, the final envelope:

My Darling,

I got your much delayed letter today. Thank you for the photograph – you are so beautiful. I miss you beyond words.

This may be the last opportunity I will have to send or receive mail for a while. I'm stuck in some godforsaken outpost, as far from civilisation as it is possible to imagine, trying to prevent the savages killing one another.

Please take care of yourself until I return.

All my love.

James

Jaime returned the letter to its envelope and added it to the pile in the basket. There were no more letters left – apart from the three unopened envelopes addressed to Mrs. E Fyre – either Kay had not responded or her letter got lost somehow. Jaime put the decision on the final three letters off for another day, she didn't know if she wanted to read of James' pain and loss when she had her own battle to fight. A battle she was losing more than winning.

The desire to see Kimberly again nagged at her incessantly and far outweighed the vow she'd made to sever all ties. Yes, Kimberly was unpredictable, volatile, and totally unreasonable in the way she viewed just about everything, but Jaime had seen beyond those faults to the woman Kimberly could be. To the woman she had lusted after since day one. The woman who bore all the physical attributes from which she had crafted Granby. Attributes that were a tangible part of Jaime's life.

Kimberly, and her thirst for payback at any cost, was the main obstacle to Jaime's desire for a possible reconciliation. Would Kimberly carry out her threat to take Jaime and her publisher to court? Previous threats had proved nothing more than hot air and bluster. Maybe... Jaime decided to wait a few days and see if anything came of the latest threat before she risked making any overture.

****

Jaime strode briskly along the well worn upland track, making for the outcrop of rocks known locally as Brides Fall. Folklore told of a tragic incident, way back in the seventeenth century, when a jilted bride fell to her death from the rocks. In fair weather, it was not only Jaime's favorite walk but her preferred way to clear her head of clutter.

The view from the summit was spectacular in all directions. Today, Jaime had carried a sketch pad and camera, intending to record the scene, as a prelude to trying her hand at a watercolor back in the studio. Jaime had never envisaged taking up painting as a hobby but James had left such an abundance of unused canvases and paints it seemed a shame not to take advantage of them.

Jaime took several photographs before she settled herself in the central grassy hollow with her back against a sun-warmed boulder to begin a sketch of the lichen covered rocks.

A faint scraping noise disturbed the silence. Jaime glanced up from her sketch pad and her heart jumped for joy at the sight of Kimberly who stood, like an iconic vision of Granby, on the far side of the plateau.

"You! I don't believe it!"

"What are you doing here?"

They spoke in unison.

Jaime recovered first. "I'm just doing a sketch of these rocks," she said defensively, pointing to her pad.

"So I see. I won't disturb you." Kimberly began to turn away.

Jaime took a deep breath. More than a week had elapsed since their last bruising encounter. Time enough for Kimberly to carry out her threat, if she intended to go through with it, and nothing had happened, so far. Maybe the time was right to build bridges?

"Stay, if you want. You're not disturbing me."

"Thanks." Kimberly stepped closer, unhitched her backpack and sat down on the grass. "Are you an artist, too?"

"Not really... No, not at all. This is my first attempt."

"Looks good."

"Thanks. Do you do any drawing or painting?"

"Not for pleasure. Occasionally I have to scribble a rough sketch in connection with my work but most of the artwork I do is computer aided design."

"Yes, it's the same with my book covers, the company employs several talented artists who create the original designs, then the finished image is uploaded to the computer to produce the print ready artwork."

Kimberly unhooked her water bottle took a long drink and then cleared her throat. "I... I wanted to see you, face to face, to say that I'm sorry about the other day. I was going to write you a note but that seemed like a cop out. No excuses, I overreacted big time, it was unforgivable and... well, apart from an abject apology, I reckon I owe you a new laptop."

"Actually you don't. The laptop survived your violence and the disgraceful display of bad temper, although I'm not sure the same can be said of our relationship."

"Whew! That's a relief – for you, I mean – I was concerned you might have lost a lot of valuable work."

"That may easily have been the case. Something you clearly didn't take into account when you kicked the machine across the hall. As it is, I was lucky. Aided by the fact I that back up my work on a regular basis."

"You're not making this easy for me."

"What do you expect?" Jaime huffed. She wasn't prepared to give Kimberly an easy ride – no way – she wanted to prove her mettle, and her ability to remain resolute in the face of threats. "We've been here before, several times, and quite frankly I've had enough. No more second, third, or even fourth chances. We're done. Finished."

"Ouch! That hurts." Kimberly clutched at her chest. "What if I can demonstrate that I've taken what you said on board?"

"How?"

"Well, I signed up for an anger management course – twelve sessions – one hour every week. I had my first appointment yesterday."

"And?"

"It's too early to say... The counselor got me talking, at length, about you, and our relationship. She's looking to discover why I get so uptight around you in particular, but not so much with other people."

"So, this is all about me?"

"Mostly, yes, I don't normally behave in such a crass manner."

Jaime found that statement difficult to take on board. What was it about her that rubbed Kimberly up the wrong way? Granted they had got off to a rocky start, with misunderstandings on both sides, plus the several weeks it had taken to unravel the mystery behind James' bequest, the missing letters, and her complicated parentage. Even now, Kimberly didn't have the full picture but she knew enough to understand the situation. Then there was her pseudonym, Corey Adams, and the problem of Kimberly's likeness to Granby. Or was it the other way around? Jaime still hadn't worked out how the attributes of her ideal woman and Kimberly were so inextricably linked.

Maybe I need to see a counselor, too.

"I don't understand."

"Neither do I." Kimberly shrugged. The more I see of you the more I want you in my life, and my bed – especially my bed. You're a very sexy woman and my desire for you knows no bounds – yet, at the same time,

I have this overwhelming urge to fight with you. Does that make any sense?"

"Not a lot. I can't see any correlation between your desire for me and your anger. For my part I admit to an initial shock at your superficial resemblance to Granby, however, I soon discovered that it's purely physical and doesn't extend to your personality – there you and she are divided by an unbridgeable chasm."

"I disagree..." Kimberly frowned. "There is a lot of me in Granby's personality, too, if you look closely. I can show you the database I compiled to prove the point. That's why I was so convinced that you'd used me as your model. How could you know all those personal things unless you'd studied me in detail? Only later did I begin to question that theory. Then I thought back to the first book and realized that Granby is portrayed there much as I am now – very butch, with graying hair and tanned skin – that look wasn't so evident before I went to America. Back then, I confess to playing down my sexuality in order to conform. All through uni, and beyond while I worked as a junior architect, I hid my true self from the world – from everyone except those closest to me like Uncle James and, Rebecca."

"We've both done that," Jaime admitted. "Unlike you, though, I never stopped hiding behind a façade of heterosexuality. You, at least, had the courage to come out eventually."

"Much good it did me. All the women I've got close to on a physical level – three in total – have lied and cheated on me. I thought you were different, once we got over the hurdle of who you were and why Uncle James made you his heir but... The discovery that you'd lied to me, albeit by omission, shook my world on its foundations."

"I didn't lie to you, I was just being myself. Nobody knows about my being Corey Adams – aside from a couple of people who only know me as Corey, but that's another story – my pseudonym is a closely guarded secret. I have it written into my contract: no public appearances, book signings, or photographs. However, when you asked me the question, I told you the truth, right away, and I've regretted doing so ever since."

"Why? I don't see the need for regret."

"It destroyed our relationship. I can't see any prospect of us ever getting back to where we were before you discovered my identity."

"You seriously think that?"

"Yes, I do. To coin a phrase: Granby is always going to be a spectre at our feast."

"Don't say that. We can get over this if we put our minds and hearts into finding a solution. I can guess how much Granby means to you, I could learn to love her, too."

"It's not so much about love..." Jaime faltered, struggling with the emotional turmoil building inside her. "It's about trust – on both sides – real, unequivocal, trust in one another. Without trust we have nothing and no foundation upon which to build a relationship." Jaime turned her head away so Kimberly wouldn't see the tears forming in her eyes.

"Come here."

Jaime struggled when Kimberly pulled her up and enfolded her in a gentle embrace. She was torn between fear and excitement in equal measure. Her head said no! Get out of here, now! Her heart offered a totally different message: a message of hope, of passion, and of love. Which feeling should she trust?

Kimberly suddenly tightened her hold and dropped a light kiss on Jaime's head. "No more tears. I can't bear it when you're sad."

"I'm confused... I know what I should do but... I am being pulled in opposite directions by my feelings for you." Jaime blinked away her tears and glanced up at Kimberly. "Yes, you heard right, I admit to having feelings for you – you, not Granby in disguise – but I can't decide if those feelings are simply lust, or if they have any real substance and the potential to become love."

"There's an easy test." Kimberly lowered her head slightly.

"No!"

"Yes..." Kimberly completed the move and sealed their lips together.

Jaime's objections dissolved in a shower of bright stars. While her body melded with Kimberly's in a way that settled her internal argument against acceptance once and for all.

Kimberly broke the kiss. "Oh, Jaime, honey... I hate to spoil this special moment, or to worry you unnecessarily, but I don't like the look of that sky." She reached for her backpack.

Jaime glanced up to see a mass of threatening black clouds on the horizon. "Okay, point taken." She was well aware how unpredictable the weather could be. It took just seconds to collect sketch pad and camera and return them to her rucksack then she slipped her arms into the straps. "I'm ready."

"Good girl..." Kimberly dropped a light kiss on Jaime's lips. "Let's go! We need to hurry."

The storm reached them before they got half way back to Rykesby. The heavy driving rain transformed the track into a slushy mess of mud and small stones in minutes, making it absolutely lethal underfoot even in hiking boots. There was no place to shelter, and no respite from the deluge. Jaime was mighty glad of Kimberly's support just to remain on her feet.

"Whew!"Jaime exclaimed when they reached the safety of Rykesby. They both shook the water off their hair and clothes then slipped out of their boots in the outer hall, before Jaime opened the inner door. "I need a hot shower and some dry clothes."

"Me too." Kimberly shivered visibly.

"I can provide the hot shower but..." Jaime assessed Kimberly for size. "...not much in the way of clothes, nothing that will fit you at any rate. We can put your stuff to dry but it'll take hours."

"Clothes aren't high on my list right now," Kimberly quipped.

"Come on!" Jaime ignored the loaded suggestion and led the way upstairs, although Kimberly probably knew the house better than her. She stopped outside the first bathroom. "You can take this one, there's shower gel on the shelf, I'll just get you some towels."

When Jaime returned with towels and a loose-fitting bath robe a few minutes later, Kimberly had already coaxed the ancient shower into life. She stood in the large old-fashioned bath tub, her back toward the door, enveloped in clouds of steam. For a split second Jaime was tempted by the sight of water cascading over Kimberly's firm, well-toned, skin. Embarrassed by her erotic thoughts and the way her body responded, Jaime dropped the towels and fled. She didn't want to go there, yet, she wasn't ready to drop her guard on the strength of a single kiss and Kimberly's vague promise of action to address certain behavioral problems. Evidence, she needed real evidence that Kimberly had changed.

Jaime took a shower in her own bathroom then redressed in comfortable velour sweat pants with a matching top before she went down to the kitchen to get some food. She was just crossing the hall with a tray when Kimberly came down the stairs. The bath robe barely fitted Kimberly. Jaime quickly averted her gaze, away from the amount of exposed leg.

Kimberly sniffed the air. "Something smells good." Then she went ahead of Jaime to open the library door.

"Homemade chicken soup, bread, cheese, and fruit."

"Perfect! Just what we need to recover from our ordeal." Kimberly revived the fire with a couple of logs from the large basket then joined Jaime at the table.

Kimberly dug into her soup. "Mmmm, this is good." She quickly finished one bowl and helped herself to more with another piece of bread. "Tell me about your trip.

Now I know who you are and what you do, I presume it was some sort of research."

"Yes, it was. The story involves a leading political figurehead who is kidnapped and held for ransom. I primarily wanted to test my theories on the ground – from the initial snatch, the frantic drive across the border from one country into another, and lastly the location of a suitable hideout. I also met with many officials to check on the approach that the different national police forces apply to kidnap."

"Sounds like a lot of work. Do you do this sort of thing for every book?"

"No, not all the stories are so complex. Probably only a third of the total have required that sort of in depth research. I don't know which titles you've read, but you can probably guess those that needed the extra mile."

"I've read them all, including Undiscovered Truths, I must say you have changed my reading habits. Before I discovered Granby I was a confirmed non-fiction reader."

"I'm curious... How did you find Granby? Did somebody recommend the series? Or did you stumble upon one of the titles by accident?"

"Neither. It was something you let slip after you fainted and I carried you in here. You muttered the name so quietly, I wasn't even sure I'd heard you right, but I typed Granby into the Google search box and got an amazing long list of entries. When I saw the images on the fanzine I went ballistic and immediately began the hunt for whoever was responsible. The rest, as they say, is history."

"I had no idea," Jaime said. "That probably explains the weird reaction I got from you every time publishing was mentioned." She took a banana and passed the fruit bowl to Kimberly.

"The funny thing is I'd discounted you. I'd convinced myself you couldn't have known all those things about me that it must have been somebody closer to home. I even suspected Rebecca for a short while, until I reasoned she didn't have the dedication to write one book let alone a series."

"And?"

"What?"

"Now that you know the truth, and you've got over the shock... How do you feel?"

"Strange."

"That doesn't tell me anything."

"It seems you know me better than I know myself."

"I don't agree. There is so much about you that is a complete mystery." Understatement of the year. Jaime cut into an apple, divided it into quarters and removed the core, then she indicated the debris on the side of her plate. "How many pips are hiding inside these segments? Nobody knows. That's my dilemma – as soon as I think I have you taped something else pops up to throw me off balance."

"You're a bit of an enigma yourself, I suppose everybody is," Kimberly agreed. "Discovering all your little foibles is going to make for a very interesting life."

"I need some stability, too," Jamie said. "For the last few weeks it's felt as though I've been stranded on a gigantic roller coaster ride. With my life punctuated by a series of incredible highs and lows but not much evenness in between – suddenly finding oneself poised on the brink of plunging into the abyss is very unnerving. I'm not sure I want to live like that."

"And if I promise you stability?"

"That would be a start... But can you deliver?"

"I can try... I will try." Kimberly stood and held out her hand. "Please, honey, I need you to show a little faith. Despite our many differences, you have become my one constant and now I can't imagine life without you by my side."

Jaime took the offered hand then let Kimberly draw her close. Wrapped in Kimberly's arms, Jaime felt safe. Their lips met gently at first then, driven on Jaime's part by the energy from another explosion of stars, the kiss deepened and became more intimate. A mutual urgency for satisfaction wove their tongues together in search of that special moment. Jaime felt a vibration flutter through Kimberly's body, like a small motor building up speed, before it settled into a natural rhythm.

Kimberly suddenly broke the kiss. "Oh, Jaime, honey... I can't wait another second. Please, let me make love to you?"

"Now?"

"Yes."

"But I'm..."

"I'll be gentle, I promise."

Jaime had run out of arguments. She submitted to being undressed. Reassured when Kimberly moved slowly, showering her with kisses and tender caresses as each item of clothing was removed. Kimberly carried Jaime to the chaise longue then knelt alongside, and kissed down her neck to the swell of her breasts, feasting on one nipple then the other, using her fingers to tease the free nipple into jewel-like hardness.

"Such sweetness..." Kimberly murmured. Then her lips began the long meandering journey down Jaime's body gently praising each inch of skin.

A feeling unbearable expectation overwhelmed Jaime. Her body sang to the tune that Kimberly's lips played on her skin. Kimberly's hands preceded her lips, with featherlight precision, the tips of her fingers gliding slowly over heated flesh. Jaime's tension built to a crescendo of need as Kimberly worked her way down to her toes, then back up until she reached the top of Jaime's thighs.

"Open for me, honey," Kimberly commanded softly as she applied gentle pressure to ease Jaime's legs apart. "Let me see how much you want me."

This was too close to her... Jaime snatched a breath, as her body tensed in fear of the unknown – nobody, other than herself, had ever touched her there. Nigela didn't really count, as that was only ever a fleetingly brief pressure through two layers of clothing.

An urgent pulse throbbed in Jaime's center begging for contact.

Then Kimberly placed her mouth over the sensitive lips and used the tip of her tongue to probe inside.

Jaime's body responded with a rush of unbelievable sensation that kept building well beyond the point where she normally cut off when masturbating. She felt suddenly weightless, out of control, and yet totally at ease with her sexuality for the first time in her life.

"Oh, honey, you are sensational. I knew you would be," Kimberly said. Then she began the slow trip back up Jaime's body paying full attention to each area as she had done on the way down and murmuring sweet nothings between the kisses.

By the time Kimberly reached her lips again Jaime had come down from her high and her breathing had returned to near normal, although she was still in something of a daze at both the speed and ease with which Kimberly had seduced her. And there was a nagging question: Jaime didn't know how she was supposed to respond.

"Let's get you dressed again before you catch cold."

"But… I didn't… You?"

"Later, honey." Kimberly placed a lingering kiss on Jaime's lips. "That was merely an aperitif, the entrée is still to come. You can have your turn when we get upstairs. We have the whole night, and many more to follow, to get to know one another. You will enjoy the experience better with more room to move about and the comfort of a proper bed."

Fourteen months later...

On a bright January afternoon with a light dusting of snow covering the ground, Jaime and Kimberly approached the newly renovated Rykesby for the first time as a married couple. They had tied the knot earlier in the day at a private ceremony in York, with Leta and Paolo as the only guests.

Jaime and Leta had become much closer after Jaime revealed her true identity and the reason for her previous deception. Leta for her part had welcomed Kimberly into the fold, and assumed the role of *'bride's mother'* with boundless enthusiasm. She'd insisted on them both following the old English custom of *something old, something new, something borrowed, something blue.* Jaime, however, drew the line at the final item, *and a silver sixpence in her shoe,* claiming the tiny coin felt like a large rock and she couldn't walk comfortably.

Henry and Margaret Carr had, predictably, reacted with horror to the prospect of a lesbian wedding in their midst. Their opposition to the union forced Jaime to take her affairs out of Henry's hands. She had opted for the York based lawyer she'd spoken to earlier rather than Eva, whom Kimberly favored, purely on the basis of her age.

"Welcome home, honey." Kimberly slipped her arm around Jaime's waist.

Jaime smiled and kissed her wonderful new wife. She was happy to be home again, having shared Aspen Cottage with Kimberly while the renovations took place and, as well as this being their wedding night, it would be the first night back in Rykesby in over a year. Her heart skipped a beat as she moved forward to unlock the door.

"Wait!" Kimberly grabbed Jaime's arm before she could enter. "This should be done in style. I need to carry you over the threshold."

"I'm too heavy."

"No, honey." Kimberly stroked Jaime's barely rounded stomach. "You and our baby are just perfect."

Lydian Press

ABOUT THE AUTHOR

Dalia Craig loves to both read and write a variety of contemporary fiction. While her particular leaning is toward lesbian romance, her writing encompasses all heat levels and diverse genre. She has a number of eBooks to her credit and is also a contributor to several print anthologies including: Where the Girls Are: Urban Lesbian Erotica, Best Lesbian Romance 2010 both from Cleis Press. Plus the Goldie 2013 nominated anthology, Sapphic Planet, edited by Beth Wylde & Kissa Starling.

She published many short stories in eBook format with loveyoudivine Alterotica, where she was also managing editor for the FemErotica line until loveyoudivine closed in June 2013.

After considering all her options, Dalia decided to set up as a publisher. Her company, Lydian Press, opened for business in August 2013 with several ex loveyoudivine authors on board. Lydian Press, is devoted to publishing quality GLBTQ literature in both eBook and print formats. Website: http://lydianpress.com

Dalia has wide and varied interests but mainly she loves to write. She is quoted as saying, "Writing is my life. It is what fulfils me as a person."

Aside from writing, and now publishing, Dalia loves to travel, fiddle with computers, listen to classical music, cook, grow her own fruit and vegetables, and befriend the wildlife that visits her garden.

You can connect with her online at: www.daliacraig.com

OTHER TITLES BY DALIA CRAIG

All For Love
A Reckless Affair
Bound by Consent
Consuming Passion
Desire And Deception
Hold Me Tight
Loving Ellie,
Seduced by a Stranger
Taming Bryana
Weathering The Storm,
For an up to date list please visit Dalia's page at:
www.lydianpress.com

Lydian Press is dedicated to bringing you the finest GLBTQ erotic literature on the web.

Visit us on the web at:

http://lydianpress.com

www.ingramcontent.com/pod-product-compliance
Lightning Source LLC
Chambersburg PA
CBHW051543030726
47592CB00001B/110